Barb

JAZZ WITH ELLA

JAZZ WITH ELLA

JAN DeGRASS

To Barbara & Jim
Thanks for your support!
(Coming out on a rainy day
to visit!)
Jan DeGrass

libros libertad

First published by:
Libros Libertad Publishing Ltd.
2091 140th Street
Surrey, BC
V4A 9V9
Ph (604) 838-8796
Fax (604) 536-6819
www.libroslibertad.ca

Library and Archives Canada Cataloguing in Publication

DeGrass, Jan, 1950-
Jazz with Ella / Jan DeGrass.

ISBN 978-1-926763-24-8

I. Title.

PS8607.E473J39 2012 C813'.6 C2012-905461-5

Author photo by Linda Sabiston

Design and layout by SpicaBookDesign

Printed and bound in Canada

★

Dedicated to the members of all of my writing groups,
past and present.
Thank you for your critique, your support and your laughter.

ACKNOWLEDGEMENTS

During the summers of 1973 and 1974 I visited Russia, then known as the Union of Soviet Socialist Republics, with a group of Canadian students who were studying Russian language and literature. I was young and daring; soon after I arrived in Leningrad (now St. Petersburg) I met a man who would become the subject of this novel. Like my character, Volodya, he desperately wanted to leave the country. I hope he got his wish.

Many of my adventures in that strange, foreign land behind the iron curtain have been recounted here based on my own notes and those of the other students. Thanks go to the teachers and students of the 1973 and 1974 Russian immersion program of University of Waterloo for asking many questions, drinking much vodka, making new friends and generally enriching our experience in the Soviet Union.

As described in the book, we were the first group of westerners to take a Volga River cruise. The visitors from a political-social club at the automobile plant in Togliatti who met with us on board the riverboat were as enchanted to meet us as we were them. Thanks go to Intourist, the state-owned travel agency, for making it happen.

The excerpt from *Vesna v Leningradye* is from a longer poem written in 1942 by poet Margarita Aliger who lived through the siege of Leningrad. I have translated the excerpt myself. I hope I have done it justice.

This book was a decade in the making and there are so many people to thank that I can't list them all. That's why I dedicated it to my writing groups, past and present. Without their support and encouragement—particularly from group leader Betty Keller and my own Sunday writing group in Gibsons—I would have given up a long time ago. *Bolshoye spasibo*, as they say in Leningrad. Thank you.

Jan DeGrass
Gibsons 2012

CONTENTS

1.

A PIECE OF THE KREMLIN

LENINGRAD, JULY 12, 1974

The evening rushed past Jennifer—dreamy, hazy, fuelled by the brandy and vodka that they had sipped at Volodya's apartment. When they arrived on foot at the busiest, fanciest restaurant in Leningrad they had to wait in line for entry.

"You must wait. It's all part of the Russian experience," Volodya told Jennifer dryly.

From the carpeted hallway they peeked around the corner and saw empty tables and a buffet that stretched the width of the huge, vaulted banquet room, effectively inhibiting the dancers who squeezed around it to continue their foxtrot. On the table was an elaborate centrepiece of fruit topped by a pineapple.

"Aaah, pineapple," she murmured, salivating as a sombre waiter waved them back. No one had taken fruit from the table centrepiece. It was not pineapple to eat, it was only for show. All part of the experience.

They entered the steamy room. She felt Volodya's hot breath tickling the nape of her neck as they were led into the throng. They sat at a long table, covered in white linen with greasy spots, amid the warring smells of smoked fish, sour grain, ripe plums. Vodka quickly appeared in front of them. They listened to a desperate band, rigid with the supposed cool of western jazzmen, stiffly strumming, unblinking, ugly, dressed in matching lime green suits of cheap fabric. The band played a jerky, almost unrecognizable *Satin Doll*, a tune arranged with military precision. Volodya winced, his fingers tapping out a better rhythm.

A short, balding man with shirt open at the collar loomed at their table. Volodya introduced Jennifer as a visitor from Canada. She did not catch the man's name. There was some connection, some voltage, between Volodya and this man. They sneered like rival dogs and bared their teeth. She could not catch their mumbled conversation. Abruptly the current was broken. Volodya leaned back in his chair, innocent, fresh-faced. The newcomer looked over his shoulder repeatedly as if someone might see him in this den of decadence.

"Dance with him," Volodya ordered her.

Surprised, she stared. The stranger's fingers were already on her wrist. He opened his mouth in a grin, revealing several black teeth and a large gap in his smile. His breath smelled like sour milk. Dance. Just a two step. One-two, one-two, and back again. Twirl. He pulled her around the dance floor, breathing heavily, then closer, tighter, until his belt buckle pressed uncomfortably in her abdomen. She pretended not to understand his language when he spoke to her. "*Krasavitsa*, beautiful woman," he said.

Just smile and twirl, she thought.

When the music ended, he returned her to the table. Volodya's eyes were on her. Thank you, they told her. The man sat with them, uninvited. There was more vodka, toasts to Soviet-Canadian friendship—this from Black-Teeth. A toast to Jennifer, the beautiful, amazing woman from Canada! This wish was from Volodya and a slobbering drunk from the next table who smiled an elastic grin. More dancing. This time with Volodya. Black-Teeth left without saying goodbye.

Then someone was suggesting a toast to the cosmonauts, another was toasting his mother, another cheered a black-eyed seductress called Masha, who was not present to hear her toast.

Someone passed a bottle of vodka up to the band. The musicians handed it around, took swigs, became more animated. The ugly bass player took four steps to the front of the stage, four steps back and the piano player flashed spasmodic smiles in between frowns of concentration. The band broke loose on a popular modern song; the crowd roared approval. Only the waiters were unsmiling, weary.

In a brief, lucid moment between drinks, Jennifer looked around her in surprise. She had been in the Soviet Union what?—eight, nine days? "It's all part of the Russian experience," she murmured. Then there were more stomach-turning toasts, the pungent sweat of bodies that shared bathrooms, the rigid motions of the jazz band. Volodya and Jennifer laughed, danced. By the time they left, bursting into the street, it was empty of people. His arm rested lightly on the back of her waist. She knew they would make love that night.

MOSCOW, JULY 3, 1974

The Aeroflot plane thumped ominously as it cut through an angry dark sky then levelled out into a bank of ragged grey mist. From her window seat Jennifer White felt a thrill as she watched a distant lightning bolt crackle between two high, purple storm clouds. She glanced at the tour group around her, squirming uneasily in their seats. Fifteen Russian language students from Canada—17 counting herself and Professor Chopyk—sandwiched in rows seven through ten. She smiled when she observed that Chopyk was wedged in beside a garlic-breathing Armenian tourist. Anything that caused discomfort to her fussy, aging professor gave her a moment of pleasure. On his other side sat a student, Lona Rabinovitch, who remained unruffled by the turbulence and continued to page through a glossy magazine, using one elegantly manicured fingernail.

The seatbelt lights flashed on and the stewardesses became grim.

"Now *there's* a pair of healthy-looking women," David Joiner, another student, had remarked when the group had changed planes in Montreal. Two stocky women with ample chests and wide hips, plumped up by years of perogies and sour cream, they were dressed in utilitarian navy blue serge uniforms.

When Maria Shevchenko had asked for a pillow, one of the Amazons had snapped in reply, "If there are no pillows above you, then there are no more pillows. Where do you think I would find more pillows?"

Maria had apologized in her quiet voice, while the others snickered. *Poor Maria, she's such a gentle soul,* thought Jennifer. Maria was an English major with a family interest in Slavic languages. She had spent her last few hours before leaving Vancouver visiting her Ukrainian grandmother in hospital. This loving ritual had no doubt scored her points at home but had not endeared her to Professor Chopyk or to Jennifer, who had waited at the gate anxiously for the young woman's last minute arrival. Two more minutes and they would have left without her.

Another lightning bolt flashed, closer this time. With a slight shudder, Jennifer turned her head away from the storm clouds. Paul Mercier, in the next seat, touched her arm reassuringly and smiled his slow, lazy smile. "We'll make it, Jen. We'd better. I've waited 15 years to see this country."

She nodded.

"Just close your eyes and think of something else," he told her.

Paul's a good buddy, she thought, *and he stuck with me through all of the Michael years.* She realized she was already thinking of Michael in the past tense and wondered if that was a sign of healing. The last time she had been on a plane she and Michael had flown to California for their first wedding anniversary. That had been just one year ago.

As instructed, she shut out the sight of the storm clouds and retreated into her thoughts. She wondered for about the fifth time why Paul had not been selected to assist Chopyk in leading this Soviet Union trip. It meant prestige and academic advancement. Paul was at least as well educated as she was with all the same qualifications: experience as a teaching assistant and going for his Ph.D. Besides, he was a man and the department favoured men in positions of authority. The graduate women often got no farther up the tenure track than lecturer. Jennifer was a loose cannon; she knew that was her reputation around the department. She was not one to toe the party line—or to sleep with the chairman to improve her grades.

Could it be, as her women's lib friend had told her, it was because she would accept less money for the job? Just the cost of the trip and a small daily stipend—that was all she was receiving. *Paul would have held out for a real salary,* she thought uncomfortably. But she had to take this trip. It was ridiculous to think she could continue as a University of Vancouver graduate student in Russian Literature without actual exposure to the Russia of today—the Soviet Union. The department had been trying to organize this language immersion tour, a first for any Canadian university, for years. It was time to damn the expense and go.

This plan had seemed pretty clear until a warm day in May when the departmental chairman, Dr. Hoefert, summoned her to a meeting at Professor Chopyk's office, and he had hinted to her on the phone that he might have some good news regarding the language tour. It turned out that she had been summoned not so much to Chopyk's office as to his adjacent waiting room. She spent three quarters of an hour glued to a sticky orange vinyl chair, feeling her hair frizzing wildly in the humidity of the overheated building, one foot bobbing in time to the tapping of the secretary's typewriter.

Occasionally, Chopyk and Hoefert had glanced through the glass panel as if to determine that she was still there. At first she mentally railed at professors who expected papers to be turned in on time but couldn't be bothered being punctual for appointments, then she realized that a war was being waged in the office. Finally, Hoefert shot out of the door and flashed past her with a sly smile before signalling the secretary to usher Jennifer in. Chopyk was fuming. He had obviously lost the battle and she could guess the subject was her.

"You are to be my second-in-command for the Soviet Union tour," Chopyk spit out.

No pleasantries. No "Won't you be seated." She brought a chair around and sat anyway.

"Hoefert's decision. Not mine," he went on, his trim, pointed beard quivering.

She kept her voice neutral. There was no sense in sharing his ill temper. "That's great…I'm honoured. But what does it involve?"

"We'll divide the group according to ability. You teach the beginners class. I'll handle the advanced…and still have time for my research, I hope." He sniffed.

"Of course," she said soothingly. Chopyk's research always took precedence over boring classroom time. He was forever droning on about the linguistic roots of Russian as found in Old Church Slavonic.

"You'll have to check with Hoefert for the honorarium details," he went on. "You'll be paid something, I suppose. Now is that all?" He took a deep breath and turned back to his books. Jennifer opened her mouth, closed it then decided to toss the fat into the fire. "You tell me," she replied. "I was called here by the chairman. And if I can be frank, Professor Chopyk, you don't seem too happy with the prospect of us working together."

With an effort Chopyk dragged his attention away from his books, pondered the statement, removed his glasses and stared at her. "I don't even know how to address you. Are you still a Mrs. or do you now go by that appalling new epithet, Ms.?

"I'm Mrs. White until the divorce," she replied, feeling a sudden flash of shame, "but I hoped you'd call me Jennifer."

"I'm an old-fashioned man, Mrs. White. No, just let me finish. I know you're going to say something nauseating about the role of career women in the twentieth century...that's not the issue…at least, not in this case."

The last living dinosaur, she thought.

"I do believe that a man should earn an honest living to support his family—I've made no bones about my views—but if young ladies choose to teach or whatever that's no concern of mine."

Jennifer swallowed her protest and asked instead, "Is it my teaching ability that's a problem?"

"Honestly speaking, Mrs. White, though you lack the rigor necessary for academic research, your teaching ability is sound. Hoefert said as much to me just today."

Chopyk fiddled with his glasses for a few seconds. He was a small man, not quite her lanky height and seemed dwarfed behind the antique oak desk. She willed herself to wait patiently.

"How shall I put it? I'm a bachelor, as I think you know, but that doesn't mean I don't believe in marriage vows." Already she had an uneasy feeling where this monologue was heading. "Since the advent of the pill," he shot her a quick look, "young women, even married women, have so much more freedom."

"Well, we're not kept chained in the kitchen," she responded pertly.

He appeared not to have heard her but went on, eyes on the ceiling. "Just, please—if you're going to share leadership of this trip—remember you are a mature woman and a professional academic."

Mature woman? She was about to turn 30. She wasn't ready for the old folks' home yet. "I would always act with professionalism, if that's what you mean...Has there been some suggestion that I haven't?"

"It pains me to mention this"—though he didn't look pained—"but word of your marriage break-up and consequent separation has circulated within the department with some vigour."

"That's my personal business," she murmured.

"Not if we're travelling together with a gaggle of adolescent students. Do you understand? You must be an example to them."

At least the interview had cleared the air on that score. After that, while trip preparations got under way, there had been an uneasy truce between them, and she found she was looking forward to the opportunity to teach as much as she was looking forward to the Soviet Union.

★

As the plane bucked and rolled, Jennifer's ears popped, and she recalled reading how dangerous it was for a plane to land during an electrical storm. Where were the emergency exits? One passenger, a sombre man who had embarked at Paris, appeared to be praying. Paul had closed his eyes though she was comforted to see that he was still smiling. David

Joiner stared out of the window, having abandoned his study of a map of the Soviet Union on which he had marked their route: Moscow, Leningrad, then Rostov and by boat up the Volga River.

Jennifer glanced again at the glacially cool Lona. "She's so calm," she commented to Paul. "I'll bet her hobby is skydiving."

Paul laughed and opened his eyes. "I hear she's going to school in New York and living in a ghetto. That's got to make you brave."

It had been hard to get a fix on Lona. Ever since the woman had called the Russian department from New York State University to register for the trip just two weeks before departure, Jennifer had been both repelled and fascinated by her, particularly the smirking glances from her vivid green eyes and an irritating habit of always being under foot. The college had balked at allowing her to participate at that late date because this study tour to the Soviet Union had been in demand—the first of its kind in Canada and somewhat of a diplomatic and academic coup aimed only at serious language students. However, there had been a last-minute cancellation and Lona had pleaded. She was Canadian by birth, she explained, and could arrange her visa herself through the New York consulate. Then she had volunteered a large sum of money—or so Chopyk had told Jennifer.

"It was for a single room supplement at the hotel," he had said, "although I believe she overpaid."

There had been no time to check her academic qualifications. It seemed to Jennifer that the other qualifying students had been rigorously screened and had vastly more knowledge than Jennifer had at their age. Like, for example, the kid they called Hank with his shock of bright red hair who had to fold his lean six-foot frame into the cramped airline seat. He was a bit too loud and adolescent for her tastes but maybe he would shape up. He caught her glance and winked. *Cheeky, too.* His real name was Winston Henry Jones, Jennifer knew from reading his application, but she suspected he didn't want the others to know that. He had already struck up a friendship with Marty Miller, an equally adolescent 20-year-old who had reported his hobbies as frisbee and pub crawls. Surprisingly, he had managed to field straight A grades in the University of Vancouver's Economics Department. Russian language had been an elective for him yet he had come very far, very fast.

Across the aisle sat the twins, Eve and Dawn. Jennifer doubted she'd keep them straight—two University of Winnipeg graduates encouraged to go on this trip by their huge Polish family, which was odd because there was usually no love lost between the Poles and the Russians.

Finally the plane broke through the cloud banks, the turbulence vanished and the sight below pushed all thoughts of adolescent students out of Jennifer's head. She was flying over the birch forests and ragged patchwork fields of the mighty Soviet Union. She gazed eagerly. An image formed easily in her imagination: two young women—her mother and her aunt—thin and desperate, still grieving the loss of their parents, tramping across this very landscape in 1945 following the path of the victorious troop convoys. How far had they walked to the Polish border? It must have been a wearying journey for the two refugees…

Suddenly a wedge of apartment blocks appeared on the horizon signalling the suburbs of modern Moscow. The plane circled once, the wing dipping to reveal wide straight highways, clusters of huts amid evergreen trees, and finally, the runways of Moscow's Sheremetyev Airport.

"Hallelujah, we're really here!" Paul exclaimed. Eve and Dawn giggled. David opened his eyes. A wave of relief flooded the passengers as the plane bumped to a halt. Applause broke out. One stewardess allowed herself a thin-lipped smile while the other busied herself in the galley.

The thunderstorm's humidity hit them the moment the cabin door opened. The summer air was moist and the black clouds still rolled overhead, but for the group from Canada, now shuffling down the steps to the tarmac, no amount of bad weather could destroy this imperial moment. For some, such as Maria, it was a return to the land her parents spoke of, though not always fondly. For others, Jennifer included, it was their first glimpse of a powerful myth. She had never understood Winston Churchill's quote about Russia—"a riddle wrapped in a mystery inside an enigma"—and suspected it was hyperbole, but as she stepped from the plane onto Soviet soil, she shivered. Churchill had met Stalin. He should know.

What was this country all about? She had first come to know it through the literature of long dead authors, Pushkin and Dostoevsky, considered dissidents in their time. Lately she had come to understand its dark underside through the secret writings of Alexander Solzhenitsyn, banned in the USSR, published in the west. Yet she had also studied its most glorious moments in the ecstatic language of its revolutionaries. Despite the ordeal of the landing, she felt eager, charged, ready to go everywhere, to see it all.

The first hurdle was the customs inspection. It was not perfunctory as they had been told it would be. It was rigorous and methodical with attention centred around Carlos Warren, one of her students, who had fifteen Bibles taken away from him, leaving him just one for his own use.

"Hmmpph," snorted Chopyk. "I warned them during orientation what not to pack—no pornography, no seditious literature, no religious articles." He threw up his hands as the strains of "Hey Jude" filtered through the waiting room. Ted Rather, an exceptionally bright physics student who was taking Scientific Russian as a credit course, had brought Beatles records as gifts for distant relatives. A customs officer was making a laborious business of opening the records and removing them to the back room where he and a group of assistants were playing each one.

"This is nothing," said David, the only one of their group, apart from Chopyk, who had previously visited the country. "They *really* examine you when you leave."

Jennifer thought he was joking although he seemed in earnest.

"Mrs. White," Chopyk said suddenly. "If you're through Customs before me, look out for our guide. Her name is Natasha and she'll be holding a sign. Looks like we'll be here some time."

Jennifer extracted her passport from the money belt she wore around her waist and examined her photo. *Why do passport photos always make you look as if you have a hangover?* Her long, wavy chestnut brown hair was her best feature, she thought critically, and it did not show to advantage in a black-and-white picture. Forget the nose, a little on the large side, and the hazel eyes, which were okay but bloodshot behind her contact lenses after the long flight… At that point the line shuffled forward, the customs officer snatched the passport from her hand and began his own examination. Then with a stern expression, he handed it back and waved her away. She grabbed her bag, which had received only a cursory glance, and walked through the swinging door. For a major airport, it was quiet but she knew that only the international flights landed here, not the busy domestic ones or the military aircraft. A diminutive middle-aged woman wearing a neat brown suit and carrying an umbrella stood at attention at the waiting room door.

"Group from Canada," she called.

"*Dobry dyen*, good afternoon," Jennifer said politely, stepping forward.

"*Doroga, doroga, doroga,* make way." A porter with a handcart suddenly wheeled across her path, almost knocking her off her feet.

Natasha's face broke into a smile as she followed the unruly man's path. Her eyes pierced Jennifer. "Welcome to Moscow. Here is one of our efficient Soviet comrades at your service."

Irony or not? Jennifer wasn't quite sure. This woman would be the group's constant companion for the whole three weeks. Jennifer suddenly found herself a little shy. What should she say to her?

"Did you have a pleasant flight?" Natasha asked in faintly accented English, one eyebrow rising and falling in interrogation.

"No, actually the last stretch was rough! We flew through a storm."

The eyebrow went up again and Natasha frowned. "Statistically, you were safe," she said. "Only safe landings have been recorded at this airport for the past 15 years."

Jennifer stifled the urge to ask about the unrecorded flights, and she and Natasha stood in silence until the others began to trickle through the gate.

★

The highway into Moscow was wide with very few cars, some antiquated buses that belched black soot and many putty-coloured military vehicles, each displaying a stencilled number. Massive concrete bus shelters lined the curb, their panels dwarfing the few pedestrians. There were no houses. On the outskirts of town a sea of apartment buildings loomed, blocks of boxy housing, surrounded by paving stones between which weeds sprouted. Above, clotheslines were strung across the many balconies. At street level, the store windows displayed no colourful signs, no advertising, and not many goods behind the glass panels. Over each storefront was written a single word describing the store's contents: Footwear, Produce, Dairy. As their bus left the suburbs and entered the city, they saw their first statue on a street corner. Almost two storeys high, it could easily be identified as Vladimir Ilyich Lenin by the pointed beard and round, smooth head.

"King Fred," giggled Len Whalen, one of the undergrads. Natasha's gaze soon silenced him.

Several of the group brought out their cameras, but Natasha called out, "No photos yet, please. Save your film for Red Square, coming up on your right." The famous square flashed past in a blur—the Kremlin walls, the mausoleum, the striped onion domes of St. Basil's Cathedral.

The bus drew up in front of the Hotel Rossiya, which had space for 6,000 guests, Natasha informed them. As they unloaded, she called out, "There are so many rooms you must memorize which door we are entering by—the East Door—or you'll get lost."

"Holy cow, look at this lobby," David said. "You could set the entire town of Plainville, Saskatchewan, in the centre and you'd still have room for a square dance."

Jennifer noticed Maria, her white dress now wrinkled from travelling, leaning back, hands on her hips, her mouth hanging open as she took in the enormity of the crystal chandelier that loomed over them. *She looks how I feel.*

At the desk they were handed their room keys in return for giving up their passports and having their names recorded on a folded card. "Take the card up to your *dezhurnaya*—there's one on every floor—and she'll help you," Natasha called out.

"To our *what*?" asked Maria.

David was heaving his giant suitcase toward the elevator despite admonitions from Natasha that the baggage would be taken care of. "Your *dezhurnaya*," he replied. "She's a kind of floor clerk, a concierge or pit bull, depending on how you look at it." He enjoyed Maria's look of horror.

Just outside the elevator on Jennifer's floor an elderly woman, the dreaded *dezhurnaya*, sat knitting. She demanded to see the card issued moments earlier, grunted her satisfaction and resumed her task. After Jennifer found her room with its adequate single bed and adjoining bathroom, she pulled out her notebook. She had considered recording her first impressions of the Soviet Union in an article for the university's newspaper. Now, with pencil poised, all she could think of to write was: "Nice room, stale smell. Maybe cabbage. Radio permanently on."

She paused to fiddle with the knob but she could effect no change in volume. Judging by the announcer's monotone, he appeared to be reading from the telephone directory. *Perhaps he's there to put us to sleep.* "Buildings huge, sidewalks huge, hotel huge." *Hmmm, she would have to find another word for huge.* "People grim." She hadn't met many yet, but the porter who had nearly run over her, their officious tour guide, and the cheerless *dezhurnaya* had certainly been grim. Hemingway could rest easy; the article did not show promise. She decided to search for Professor Chopyk's room instead so they could finish drafting their schedule of lessons and sightseeing for the next five days.

She took the elevator down one floor, intending to ask the *dezhurnaya* the location of Chopyk's room but for some reason, that floor was unguarded. It took another 20 minutes of getting lost in a maze of hallways, returning to the lobby, inquiring and returning to Chopyk's floor, only to find that he was not in his room. She rode the elevator back to her own floor, and the doors opened on a pleasant domestic scene.

The *dezhurnaya* no longer sat alone. On two straight-backed chairs sat a young man and a woman with her arms around a gangly child of about ten who pointed her toes, first right, then left, pressing her sandals into the worn carpet. The man looked up eagerly when the elevator doors opened. She caught his eye for a second, took in the freckle-faced child and petite mother who sat in the shadows, then sped on up the hall. But she could feel the young eyes boring into the back of her head.

"Attention! *devushka*, woman," shouted the *dezhurnaya.* "You have guests."

Even before Jennifer turned to face the family, it was a moment of knowing, a sense that already on this first night in Moscow profound changes would take place, and this was only the first of them. She stared. Yes, the man did look familiar in a comfortable way. The woman—his wife?—was a stranger. The child was awkward and cute at the same time. The man walked toward her, smiling, his arms outstretched in greeting. He struggled with her name in thickly accented speech.

"Do I know …?" she began and stopped.

"Mikhail Alexandrovich Abram," he said, grasping her hand. The woman tossed a mane of glossy black hair and approached smiling. "And this is my wife, Marta, and my daughter Nadya." The child stood knock-kneed, bowed slightly and touched the red Young Pioneer scarf tied around her neck.

"We are your family."

Jennifer was thunderstruck. "But I have no family here…" she finally responded. She didn't want to appear rude but she was quite sure that her mother…but then there was a lot she didn't know about her mother's background.

"Yes, you do. You are shocked," Mikhail continued. "I beg your forgiveness for our sudden arrival. May we enter?" He indicated the hotel room.

"Certainly. Go in."

They were seated, Jennifer on the bed, Mikhail sitting on her suitcase, Marta on the only decent chair. She had accommodated young Nadya on the floor where she was fascinated by a fashion magazine that Jennifer had bought in the Montreal airport.

Mikhail explained. "We are your cousins. My father is Alexander, your mother's older brother. Your mother, Lila, is my aunt, though I never met her because as you know she left Russia right after the war."

That rang true for Jennifer—she had heard of Alexander and this man had the Roman nose and brown eyes of her mother. "But I thought he was missing in action during the war? At least, that's what mom said. And how did you know I was here?"

"Your mother told us, of course."

"My mother...," Jennifer struggled to understand this concept. "But my mother doesn't talk very much. How could she tell you...?"

Marta answered, "She wrote us letters. See?" Marta pulled a blue airmail letter from her bag and Jennifer could read the familiar spidery handwriting of her parent.

"May I?" She held the crinkly sheet and saw that her mother had addressed Mikhail fondly as "my dearest Misha." The thought that her mother would address another so tenderly in the way she had once addressed her daughter gave her a niggling jealous feeling. The letter contained much talk about the weather, and then Jennifer's date of departure including a bit of her itinerary.

"Yes, I gave her my itinerary, but she never said... she never told me...and I didn't even know she was writing to you." She looked up at the man again, then to the young girl on the floor. "So you are all my cousins." They were silent while she digested this information. "I'm still in shock. Excuse me for staring."

"We have surprised you," Misha said. "I thought that Lila had told her family about us."

"No, I don't even know how she found you. I thought that when she left Russia she was alone except for Aunt Eva. The two walked out of the Soviet Union, you know, before ending up in one of those displaced persons camps in Austria. She doesn't talk about it much." The story of her mother's arrival in England, a penniless refugee, and her marriage to the stern Englishman, Jacob Huggins, was part of family lore.

"Oh, it was the GDUE agency...we found *her*," Marta said, then seeing that Jennifer looked blank, she spelled out a lengthy name for the acronym—an Israeli agency that Jennifer had never heard of. "They reunite families, if they can. It helps for those who want to leave the Soviet Union—like we do."

Jennifer suddenly realized she was the hostess. "Listen, let me order some drinks or coffee. Tell me about yourselves. Do you live here in Moscow?" She moved to the phone then realized that room service might be a foreign concept in the Soviet Union.

"No need," said Misha, pulling two tall bottles of fizzy water from his satchel. "We cannot stay very long and we have brought some drinks. May I pour?"

"Yes, please." She picked up the two cups that sat beside a metal teapot on a corner table, and Misha poured and passed the drinks to his wife and Jennifer. He took a swig from the bottle.

"We live in Tula," Marta said. "It's about 60 miles south of Moscow. You know about it?" Jennifer shook her head. "The traditional samovar town—we make the finest samovars for all of the Soviet Union there. It's also close to Tolstoy's estate, *Yasnaya Polyana*. You are a language student, correct? Surely you will be visiting the home of such a great author?"

Misha cut in, "You must come to visit us. Tula is 100 kilometers east of the village where my father and your mother were born."

"Yes, I'd like that," Jennifer replied. She had so many questions. "When my mother got to England and met my father it was the start of a whole new life. She wouldn't have known that her brother was still alive. Did he go back to the village after the war?"

"Only to find everyone gone: father and mother dead, sisters missing," Misha replied. He fell quiet for a few seconds. "He said it was the saddest moment of his life."

Misha continued to describe their family background, Marta chipping in occasionally and smiling fondly at Jennifer. Even little Nadya left her magazine and put her arms around Jennifer's neck, calling her "auntie."

I could grow quite fond of these people, Jennifer thought.

"We have applied to leave the country," Misha told her. "As you know, Jews are allowed to leave—some of them. We will go to Israel." He looked about uncomfortably. "But perhaps it's best not to speak of these things here." He nodded at the wall indicating a grating with a tilt of his head. *Of course, microphones.* They had been told that the hidden spying devices were in all the hotels that catered to foreign tourists.

"Sorry if I seem a bit dazed by all this. I guess—I just didn't know that my mother–that is, we just don't talk much. She rarely talks at all any more, as you might know?" They looked confused, so she went on, "Ever since my brother's accident, she hasn't been herself, but still..." She wasn't sure she wanted to elaborate on the painful story, and she wondered why they had not heard of it. Putting these thoughts aside, she added, "Well, how wonderful. I have family in Russia and I never knew!"

Misha smiled and raised his bottle high. "I propose a toast to family." Solemnly they toasted this thought with gassy water as if drinking fine champagne.

★

"It's like being told that you own a piece of the Kremlin," she said later that evening to Paul over dinner. They were the last two in the dining room.

"Wow, that's incredible. I would have liked to meet them," he said. "Will you see them again?"

"They returned to Tula last night, and Misha suggested that I phone or send them a telegram towards the end of our Volga cruise. We'll be flying out of Moscow so I think we can get together when the group returns here."

Paul looked thoughtful. "How did you know they were really your cousins?"

"What do you mean? Of course they are. They had a letter from my mother to show me."

"Well, here I am being the cynic again...it's just that lots of people would like to leave the country but they're not allowed. Or did you know that? Even some Jews are not allowed. But if they got the name of a possible sponsor in Canada, someone who has Russian background and might be convinced that they're legitimate family..."

"What a thought! I'm ashamed of you, Paul." But Jennifer frowned. "It's true there were some gaps in their knowledge...but Misha said how sad his father was when he arrived back in the village to find his family gone..."

"But Misha wouldn't have been born then. Anyone could invent that."

"Really, Paul! Why are you doing this?"

"Yeah, you're right. It's pretty far-fetched," he said hastily. "It's great having family here in the Soviet Union. You are so lucky, Jennifer."

"Yes, I am. Do you think I should phone my mom? Tell her that I've met with Misha—Can you believe it? She calls him Misha—like she's known him for years."

"Well, you'll be phoning your folks anyway to tell them you've arrived safely, won't you?"

"No, they aren't like that. It's not that they don't care. They just…"

"Yeah, I remember meeting your dad when I was studying in Toronto. He didn't have much to say. I get the sense your mom is really running the show?"

"No, she's browbeaten by my father."

"Is this to do with the accident, Jen?"

"Everything about my family is to do with the accident."

"You have Jewish background, don't you?"

"Yes, but I don't talk about it because I wasn't raised a Jew. My father was Church of England. Listen, I think I'll try a telegram. It's easier than the phone."

But when Jennifer enquired at the Rossiya's front desk, they directed her to the telegraph and telephone bureau next door to the hotel. This seemed like a lot of effort and she decided to wait. If her mother couldn't be bothered telling her that she had family in the Soviet Union, then she couldn't be bothered describing her joy to her mother. Withholding, it was called. It ran in the family.

2.

NATASHA EXPLODES

MOSCOW, JULY 4, 1974

On her first morning in Moscow Jennifer awakened at 6 a.m. with the wide-eyed, restless energy of the jet traveller whose body clock has been disrupted. Vague dreams still filled her head and the hotel room seemed too small to contain her. She dressed, brushed her hair vigorously and examined her tired face in the mirror. A few days on Jericho Beach in Vancouver just before the trip had given her a tan that highlighted her gleaming white teeth so that she was quite a contrast to the pasty complexions and poor dentistry of many Soviet people.

She had finally caught up with Chopyk the night before and she recalled the icy formality of their meeting as they divided the students into two groups. Between excursions, she would lead the junior students in two-hour classes in the hotel's 10th floor lounge while Chopyk would lead the experienced ones. She had suggested candidates for her junior class. He had countered immediately with his own list. She wondered if either one had been satisfied with the outcome.

In the soft morning light, she examined her list of students. She had Maria, whose command of Russian was very shaky considering she had some knowledge of Ukrainian; the twins, who didn't seem too bright; Carlos Warren of the many bibles; and the post graduate chemistry student, Linda Appleton. The only thing she knew about Linda was that she had ruddy, red cheeks like the apple in her name. She also presented an ample bosom—already a target of snickers from Hank and Marty. Unfortunately, those two buffoons would be in Jennifer's junior class, too, even though their ability to pick up languages should have put them into the senior class. Two other junior students, Len Whalen and Christine Staples, rounded out her list.

Her friend Paul would, of course, be in Chopyk's senior group since his language ability was excellent. Ted and David would be with Chopyk, along with Otto, the German student, on an exchange program from Mannheim University. To her surprise, Chopyk had put Lona on his list. The two appeared to be getting along famously. He had also taken the exchange student from Carleton University, Ingrid Schneider. *She seems interesting and is the only one besides me who's studying Soviet literature.* She felt resentful that Chopyk had only six students to manage while she had nine but chided herself—*Come on, Jen, work with him. Don't let him spoil it for you.*

After loading film into her camera, she walked the hotel halls to the sixth floor snack counter. But this morning, no listless attendant stood behind the counter as she had done the previous evening, ready to mete out the bottles of yogurt-like *kefir*, sticky cakes and tea. Perhaps she would open up soon. Jennifer took a seat at one of the metal tables and gazed out the window. If she had been on the opposite side of the building, she would have seen the Kremlin walls, but this view gave onto some obscure side streets. At the far end of one street she could see the outline of a small church, four onion domes surrounding a fifth larger one. *Practically in the shadow of the Kremlin*, she thought, *and probably unused*. Tomorrow the group would visit Novodevichy, one of the few "working" churches in Moscow. Suddenly she decided not to wait for that experience.

Within minutes Jennifer was on the street to get a closer look, camera in hand, calling out a good morning to the elderly women who were sweeping the sidewalks. The little church was unpainted. The walls were crumbling, the windows bricked up. Quietly and with reverence she entered the courtyard. *If there was ever a graveyard here, it was paved over long ago.* In one corner was the exposed edge of a heap of rubble, food containers and broken bottles. She caught a glimpse of someone—just a wisp of apron and full skirt—vanishing behind the church. She darted ahead and saw an old woman, bag in hand, who looked back like a startled deer. The woman took in the western clothing and camera in a glance then turned and ran. Jennifer snapped a photo. *She's been picking in the garbage heap,* she thought. *And they tell us there are no poor people here.*

By the time she returned to the hotel, Natasha was already holding forth at the breakfast table about the capacity for unlimited food production in the glorious Soviet Union. *What would she have said about the old woman?* The thought continued to bother Jennifer.

The day's itinerary included lessons, a visit to the Kremlin and Lenin's tomb, followed by a trip to the Lenin Museum. Evening was reserved for the ballet.

"I'm thrilled about the Kremlin," whispered Paul, "but frankly I don't want to see the Lenin Museum."

"It's early days yet," Jennifer whispered back. "Don't start an international incident." She speared a wedge of sausage that sat in a grease slick beside a rubbery poached egg. "The bus is leaving at 9. Let's eat this delightful repast and get going."

★

Yawning and groaning, the group boarded the bus under Natasha's watchful eye, then waited while Paul was dispatched to round up the twins who had already found the hotel's souvenir shop. "Just ask if they've seen two copies of Liza Minnelli wandering about," Hank called after him. The twins certainly resembled the movie star although with an extra twenty pounds of weight per twin.

They waited again while Professor Chopyk delivered a brief but pompous speech of welcome. *Aaargh! Why does he do things like that?* Jennifer thought. *It's so irritating.*

The bus took them across Red Square and parked two minutes later at one of the Kremlin gates.

"That was hardly worth the ride," grumbled Marty.

"Arriving by bus marks us as foreign visitors," said David, who was laden with camera equipment, "and we get privileged treatment on the tours." It was true. Natasha marched them behind the Kremlin walls, past the many line-ups, ignoring the passive stares of the crowds, and ushered them into each historic location. They visited the quiet, simple Church of the Assumption, examined the Tsar's Bell that had never been rung and the Tsar's Cannon that had never been fired, and they gazed across a closely guarded, cobblestoned courtyard at the imposing edifice of the Supreme Soviet.

The Kremlin's armoury museum was not a house of weapons as Jennifer had expected. Instead, it was a dazzling display of fine crafts, jewellery, ornate costumes, royal regalia and richly decorated carriages.

Hank stopped before a hammered gold ladle outlined in pearls, which had been owned by Tsar Volodya Feodorovich and was dated 1618. "Wow, dig this jewelled pooper scooper."

Marty laughed. "Hey, take a look at Lona. She's practically salivating over that medallion." The two darted over to join her in front of a glass case.

"What is it?" Hank asked her.

"An encolpion," Lona said, without tearing her eyes away from the outsized milky-blue sardonyx. "It was made in the 17th century." Carved on its surface was a depiction of a haloed St. John set within an oval gold filigree border studded with jewels.

"Bet it's worth a bundle," Hank said.

Natasha scurried over, too, just in time to catch Hank's last words. "Treasures of the Armoury are closely guarded," she announced.

"By whom? Is that your security?" Lona asked innocently. An elderly woman, face lined, kerchief on her head, sat slumped, hands in lap, in a plain wooden chair near the doorway.

"Oh, Natasha, yoo-hoo!" called Linda Appleton. The guide winced as Linda descended on her like a warship sailing into action. "Can you tell me whether photos are permitted in here because David is taking lots of them?" As they moved off to sort out David's picture-taking proclivities, Hank took the opportunity to corner Lona.

"So what's an encolpion?" he asked, not expecting an answer.

Lona turned away from the showcase reluctantly. "It's a medallion worn by bishops, of course. Don't you know anything?"

Hank couldn't think of a suitable response so he sloped off, frowning.

★

If they had visited only the Kremlin that first morning, it would have been enough stimulation for the jet-lagged travellers. Jennifer had already used up half a notebook with details of their breakfast, the church, the soldiers' uniforms and the carriage of Catherine the Great. But instead of stopping for lunch, their tour guide led them out of the Armoury, back into Red Square and up to the longest and most silent of queues that they had seen thus far—for the mandatory visit to Lenin's tomb.

"Lenin's memorial has been closed to visitors during renovations," she told the group. "You are lucky to visit on this one day that it will be open."

Natasha chose a spot in the line less than a hundred yards from the mausoleum and inserted all seventeen members of the tour group with a polite but firm command to the waiting crowd. Then she stepped back: "Leave your bags with me, and be very quiet when entering the tomb." Slowly they walked two by two in respectful silence through the mausoleum doors into the cool darkness and past the waxen figure of Lenin in his casket.

"Now *that* is a heavily guarded treasure," Hank whispered.

"You're right," Jennifer murmured. "There are more soldiers here than in the Armoury." Their path took them down one side of the waxen figure, past his feet—never closer than about two yards away—up his other side then out from the dark, cool tomb into the sunshine. It was a necessary pilgrimage, Jennifer supposed, so she refrained from telling their zealous tour guide that they would have preferred lunch over Lenin.

Finally, after a huge meal at the hotel the students were ready for a nap, not a lesson, but Jennifer forced them to practise the words and phrases they had learned that day, all the while struggling to keep her eyes open. However this was the schedule that she and Chopyk had developed at an earlier, more energetic time.

★

On the third day Professor Chopyk took Jennifer aside in the hotel's lobby. His face bore a worried frown. "I wanted to ask you about Lona," he said. "What is she up to?"

"I have no idea. What do you mean?"

It seemed that on their second day in Moscow Chopyk had caught a taxi back to the hotel after a delightful few hours at the Lenin Library. The cab driver had taken a most circuitous route, criss-crossing Gorky Street several times and haring off down one-way roads. If this had been New York, Chopyk would have supposed that the driver was out to gouge, but in this case, they had already haggled over and agreed to a fee in advance.

"Forgive me, forgive me," the beleaguered cabbie told him in accented English. "There is much funeral. Many cars. The streets are *blockada*."

Chopyk questioned him in Russian and learned that a prestigious Praesidium member was being buried that day and the lavish funeral arrangements were occupying the attentions of the military and local police.

"It will soon pass," the cabbie told him, as he turned into a side street only to find that there was no exit through the blockades that faced a main thoroughfare. "We will wait here for five minutes." So they sat together, the cabbie impatient with lost work time, Chopyk uncomfortable with the enforced companionship, until the barricades were pulled away. Just as the procession had passed and the cabbie was starting the car, Chopyk spotted Lona on the other side of the street engaged in serious conversation with two of the roughest-looking specimens of Russian manhood that he had ever seen. One of them was tall, brutish, with a great hooked nose in profile, and it was to this hulk that she was addressing most of her attention.

When the car had inched its way onto the main street, he asked the cabbie to pull over just in front of Lona and her friends. As they slowed down, he noticed the hulk pass her something, an object. She accepted this ungraciously and he could see her mouth form a pout.

"Stop here," he had called. If she was in any trouble, he should know about it. But just as he opened the car window, a whistle shrieked from the roadway and a uniformed *militsioner* waved them on. The thugs took one look at the officer and melted instantly into an alleyway, taking Lona with them.

"It was extraordinary," Chopyk told Jennifer. "I wanted to ask her about it when she returned to the hotel, but there was no opportunity. She rushed off to the bar with someone. I did not pursue the matter." Jennifer watched him squirm as he related this incident.

"In fact," he went on, "I was a little afraid to know what she was doing. I thought that she might have opened up to you? They were rough characters. How did she meet them so fast?"

"She's a pretty girl," Jennifer replied. "She'll meet lots of guys." She couldn't help smiling. Chopyk's idea of a gang of toughs was probably men who didn't wear hats. "Sorry, I have no idea what's up. But I can try and find out." Chopyk seemed satisfied now that he had done his duty, and he turned his attention to the day's itinerary.

★

On the fourth afternoon the group was taken to Moscow's much vaunted trade fair grounds. Natasha proudly marched them around the various show buildings, reeling off statistics: so many tractors produced in the preceding year, so many bushels of wheat, so many hectares of land in industry. The tour wound up at the fairground's major landmark—an impressive communications tower. Natasha launched into her set speech. Several of the group yawned.

"Excuse me, Natasha," interrupted Ted. "In Toronto, we're just now building a free-standing tower like this one—for telecommunications. It'll be the tallest in the world." He beamed proudly, removing his baseball cap and flicking one hand through his curly hair.

For a split second Natasha's face twisted in rage. Colour rushed to her cheeks and she drew up her chin.

My god, I think she's going to explode, thought Jennifer. Several of the students backed away hurriedly.

"How many metres?" Natasha snapped.

"Oh, well, I'm not sure..."

"Ah." Recovering, Natasha smiled triumphantly. "But this one has a restaurant at the top...that *revolves.*" Ted smiled and shut his mouth.

"I thought she'd lost it that time," Paul muttered to Jennifer. "Have you noticed how touchy the Soviets are when you criticize—or even make a suggestion that anything could be wrong in their country?"

"Yeah, they're pretty defensive."

"I'm too tired to take in any more," Paul continued. "Let's zap over to that ice cream stand and sit on the grass for a while." The two slipped away and were not surprised to see Lona and David following them.

"Whoo," David shuddered, sprawling beside the others to suck on a strawberry cone. "You have to have the constitution of a bear to see this country right."

"I hear we're going to visit an elementary school tomorrow," said Lona. "I think I'll pass and go to the Trediakovsky Art Gallery instead. I must see the Rublev icons." She rearranged her cream linen suit and settled gingerly on the grass.

"I'd like to meet the children," Jennifer said mildly, dusting off her faded blue jeans. She was aware that she was supposed to be supervising this unruly crowd, but she was torn. In her opinion they were over-supervised between Natasha's military command and Chopyk's academic requirements. Fortunately, this morning the professor had dashed off on his own errand, putting her in charge. Surely the students could be allowed to explore at their own pace? That's what immersion in a country was all about, wasn't it?

"There won't be any children, Mrs. White. It's summer holidays," Lona said with a smirk. Paul rolled his eyes skyward.

Jennifer felt a little sheepish. Lona was probably correct. However, it was irritating the way she always ensured that everyone knew she was correct. It was time to change the subject. "How did you happen to study Russian, David?" she said, leaning back in the grass, ignoring Lona and fixing on the young man. He had an intelligent, open face with sparkling white teeth but even at the age of 25, his hairline was just starting its slide toward the back of his head. She knew that his family was of English descent, not unlike her own history on her father's side.

"My father's in the Air Force," said David, "and I guess we've lived on a dozen different bases as I grew up—Germany, Italy and NORAD in Colorado. I picked up a little of every language but never Russian."

"So why Russian?" Lona asked.

"Well, six years ago I got chosen along with a lot of other army and air force brats to go on a teen cultural exchange to the U.S.S.R. I had no knowledge of the country before that. We were just supposed to be shining examples of North American kids. It was sure different than this tour. It had been organized by Sputnik—that's the youth tour group—and we had cocky Komsomol leaders not much older than us in charge."

"So you have more than a nodding acquaintance with Lenin?"

"And Marx. And Brezhnev. The Komsomol is seriously political, and this was before the signing of the SALT treaty so east-west tensions were high. Believe it or not, it's more relaxed now."

"But how did you learn the language?" Paul asked.

"Oh, we had a crash course before the trip. Then we stayed in a dormitory for four months and ate with the Eastern European kids, so we learned a lot that way. We didn't visit the churches back then because they tried to pretend that they didn't exist. Instead, we had to study in the dorm a lot and debate the class struggle or dialectical materialism with our team leader. Most of us didn't have a clue!"

"My god, I'm not sure I could define them now," laughed Jennifer. "But I bet we'll know by the end of this trip."

"Well, that was what sparked my interest in Russian. Learning by talking is the best way. That's why I didn't pack my Ozhegov." This was a dig at Paul who had packed many weighty tomes to peruse in his spare time. Jennifer had thought about bringing the heavy, comprehensive Russian dictionary compiled by Ozhegov—it weighed a ton—but had decided to bring a more portable one instead.

Paul ignored the jibe. "I know what you mean about trying out a lot of languages. I love language study and the rules that define it—particularly German and Russian." He was away on one of his favourite topics. Jennifer knew his history but the others looked at him with renewed interest. Only Lona glanced away as if bored.

Paul went on, "I had a Russian count teach me the language—or he said he was a count. He was a friend of my grandmother Yvonne when I lived with her in California. He was probably just another émigré who wanted to get into the movies, but I believed that he was Russian nobility. At first it was fun to speak a language with him that my grandmother couldn't understand, but later I came to love it."

"Hey, you guys, we haven't finished the tour yet," Marty called from the ragged group that still surrounded Natasha.

"We're starting our lesson for the day here on the grass," Jennifer called back. "We're discussing language structure. Come and join us." *And let Natasha stew*, she thought but did not say it aloud.

"Pianists talk about music in much the same way as Paul talks about language," she told the others. She smiled at him, knowing that he would accept her interruption. "I know that these things are interconnected: language, music and even mathematics." She thought about how the study of language had allowed her to glimpse the structured, transcendent world that set musicians and mathematicians on fire.

Ted and the twins drifted over to hear them.

"Russian is so well organized," said Paul. "If a noun is the object of a sentence, it dresses in different letters than a noun showing possession. If the noun is to be used as an instrument it changes again. Each costume fits according to laws."

"Wow, that was so poetic, Paul," laughed Ted.

"So tell me what you like about it, clever guy."

"I like the verbs," Ted answered. "You know, the two verbs for every one in English, one imperfect, one perfect. To be imperfect—to not follow through on one's action; to be perfect—to complete one's action. Just like in life. Get it?" He chuckled.

Jennifer was struck once again, as she had been already on this trip, by the fine calibre of her students. She and Paul were graduates—and ought to be good. But to hear the younger ones, "the kids" as she thought of them, make these kinds of connections was satisfying. Most of the group had gathered around by now and many voices chipped in with how and why they had first studied Russian. The exhibition ground was forgotten. A stony-faced Natasha sat on a nearby bench alone.

"What about you, Ingrid?" asked David. "You're studying literature, aren't you?" His engaging smile willed the shy woman into speech.

"Well, I love Russian literature," Ingrid replied, "but I don't read it for the happy endings." Everyone chuckled. "Dostoevsky gives me so much insight into religion and psychology. His *Brothers Karamazov* changed my life."

"Really," said Paul, intrigued. "In what way?"

"It was Alyosha struggling to do what was right," she replied, "yet allowing himself to be drawn into killing his father. And then there's that story within the book about Jesus brought before the Spanish Inquisition. You've all read it, right?"

A few nodded. After all, it was on the required reading list. Linda lit up. "Oh yes, I know what you mean. The Grand Inquisitor episode in *Brothers Karamazov* exposes religion—it questions fundamental belief. It's very powerful."

"Yeah, trust Dostoevsky," David agreed. "If he were alive today, he'd be writing scripts for Alfred Hitchcock, don't you think? Or writing a cop show like *Dragnet*. Wonder what Gogol would be doing?"

Ted replied. "Oh, he'd be writing some absurd skit for *Laugh-In with Rowan and Martin* and probably acting in it, too." There was general laughter.

"But Chekhov will always be contemporary," Paul interjected. "We'll be watching his plays into the next century, I bet you."

"You're a Chekhov fan?" said Ingrid. "Don't you think that Tolstoy is timeless, too?"

Paul nodded and Jennifer caught the shy smiles between the two.

Lona, frowning, suddenly moved in closer. "But you didn't answer the question, Ingrid. Why did it change your life? Do you mean you wanted to kill your father?"

Ingrid reddened. "Oh no…," she began.

"For chrissake…" Paul turned on Lona. "If you'd read *any* Russian literature you'd understand its effect on a sensitive person."

"Don't lose your cool!" she snapped. "I just thought it sounded like

Ingrid was going to tell a good story." She backed hurriedly away from Paul. "And I am a sensitive person.... You just don't know me." Paul snorted but Jennifer caught the hurt in Lona's eyes and realized that she was being sincere.

Ignoring Lona, Ted continued on the theme that was causing so much laughter. "What would Tolstoy be doing if he lived in this century? Emancipating the south with Martin Luther King? Writing King's speeches?"

"No, stupid, he was white," Hank chimed in. "But he might be an evangelical speaker like Billy Graham..."

Finally, the bus driver signalled that it was time for their departure, and as they got up to leave, Jennifer considered her time well spent. She had just experienced a true sense of what it means to educate and be educated by one's own pupils and she thought about the fine words they had used. It spoke of a nice sense of academic values, but was it really true?

If she were honest with herself, what had really attracted her to Russian in the first place were the parties—and not the Communist party either. The Russian immigrant families in her old neighbourhood in Toronto had really known how to enjoy a good time. And the Ukrainians, too, with their three-day wedding feasts and January Christmas celebrations. Then there were the Poles and the Croatians, also in her neighbourhood. You could go down to the Croatian community centre any evening or to the Russian café and listen to the music, folk tunes, parodies of English songs. You could enjoy the vodka toasts, the dancing until three in the morning, the spirit of camaraderie. Even the second generation children of immigrants had danced together as if the mother country mattered to each of them, deeply and personally. In the end it was the people, not the language, that had pulled her to this country.

★

The days continued in vigorous sightseeing.

"I never thought we'd see so many churches in the godless Soviet Union," said Maria, as they completed a tour of Novodevichy Monastery and climbed onto the bus for the drive to the hotel.

"Well, at least the churches have been wonderfully preserved—or the ones in the Kremlin anyway," said Ted. "That Church of the Assumption was special. And I thought Natasha did a good job of telling us the history. For once she got away from 'Lenin said this' and 'Lenin said that.'"

"Yes, she was very informative," said Carlos, a student from the Fine Arts department. "But have you ever seen so many ugly buildings? Even that Hotel Rossiya is no prize—a big box is all it is. The biggest I've ever seen. I'd rather see the Stalin-style of architecture even if the buildings do look like wedding cakes." He stopped abruptly, as if surprised he had said so much.

Maria began to describe a church in the Ukraine where her great-grandmother had been married, but she was constantly interrupted by Ted who kept pointing out other buildings along the way, each one more drab than the last.

Jennifer allowed her mind to wander on the many windowless, anonymous buildings they were seeing throughout the city. What were they? No signs were posted; no occupants came or went. *Carlos is right. Moscow is utilitarian and drab. I can't wait to get to Leningrad.* One 19th century visitor had described it as a city full of palaces. She expected much contrast between the two: Moscow and Leningrad—one with an ancient history of a fortress settled by peasants, the other built on the Gulf of Finland by Peter the Great as his magnificent window on the west.

"Leningrad," she murmured, for no particular reason, and then she recalled its older name: *Sanct Peterburg.* Saint Petersburg. Peter's city.

3.
CITY OF LIGHT

LENINGRAD, JULY 7, 1974

Vladimir Mikhailovich Surov, usually called Volodya, dressed in only a pair of baggy jeans, leaned against his apartment window, cheek flattened against the pane, in an attempt to see if his friend Gennadi was waiting for him on the street. It was early—only 06:30 hours, but in summer in the northern city of Leningrad the peaceful false dawn had spread hours earlier, making the city's yellow buildings glow in an unearthly light. The window wouldn't open. It was stuck and had been for several years. It was only one of the many maintenance problems in this four-storey walk-up building: the hall lights were defective, the toilets sometimes didn't flush, the downspout drained onto the courtyard in the fall and the water froze in the winter. The list was endless. But whatever its faults, the building was central to downtown and on the banks of one of the city's loveliest canals, the Fontanka, and Volodya had been through hell to keep his occupancy permit so he wasn't about to start complaining about a sticking window.

The old ladies were out on the canal embankment already, a veritable army of the elderly, sweeping the streets with twig brooms. Some trucks rattled by, but no Gennadi. Volodya shifted his gaze across the street to the window one floor up and three to the left. Hopefully, the blonde woman would be dressing in front of the window again today without bothering to close her curtains. He didn't know her name, probably wouldn't recognize her on the street, but he knew every inch of her that could be seen above the high windowsill: her pale shoulders and ample breasts, the delicate way she pulled on a flimsy white undergarment, then flicked her long blonde locks over her shoulder. Today there was no sign of the titillating dresser. He sighed and turned his attention to the street again.

If he pushed his face right into the window, he could just see the edge of the canal where Gennadi often waited for him to begin their sociable walk to work together. Gennadi was younger than Volodya, 22 years old to Volodya's 31, and his taste in music was abominable, Vlad thought, but still, he was a friendly, loyal fellow and Volodya really needed support this morning.

Their job was a dull one, though it required a certain amount of mechanical aptitude. The firm they worked for serviced automatic machines: the water vending machines located on every street corner and several other types that sold carbonated fruit juices. They replenished them, cleaned them, oiled them and fixed them when they broke down, which happened frequently. It was not the profession he would have chosen, nor why he had received such a comprehensive university education at the state's expense. In fact, he loathed it. But he was thankful it was not an office job. At least this way he moved around the city regularly and it was easy to take an hour here and there for a break or to practise his music. As a job it moved along like a square wheel, and this is what had sparked his current problem with his commissar, a petty, stupid man with bad teeth, who would have him disciplined for breathing. Volodya cursed a little but not too loudly.Each day, he would arrive at work more or less on time, though his punctuality was always subject to the taunts of the administrative clerk, Ivana the Terrible as they called her, she who stamped their work orders and doled out their pitiful tools. After the morning check-in with officialdom, they were on their own. Sometimes he and Gennadi went out on foot together, sometimes they caught a lift to their destination in the service vehicle. That was why he suffered this miserable job. It was in that time, away from official eyes, that Volodya could indulge his passion for jazz music by visiting a musician friend who allowed him to use his piano.

He had always been good at finding a piano when he needed one. He had been raised in Leningrad just after the war by his mother and his aunt, and the two women had denied him nothing. In a time of excruciating hardship, they made sure he had his share of toys, candy, as nutritious food as was available, and his own little bed in their tiny, grim apartment. They discerned that he was a musical child at an early age when he would drum and tap on the table top, his bed, anything that would make a percussive noise with interesting rhythms. They bought him a toy drum which he adored though it nearly drove the two women crazy. After acquiring an excellent piano teacher at school, he knew at age of five that his instrument would be the piano but this was one gift they could not give him. They could neither afford it nor fit it in their apartment. He learned to find pianos elsewhere, and for eight years he took lessons, first from the school music teacher, then from a retired concert pianist who coached him with great enthusiasm. He might have attended the conservatory if he had continued to play classical music. But from the moment he first heard Fats Waller play on a bootleg recording—a tape of a tape, a third generation from the original recording—he knew that this glorious cadence was the music of his soul. In the Soviet Union in the late 1950s, to listen to jazz music was bourgeois foolishness. Though not punishable it made him suspect as a friend of westerners. To want to play jazz music for a living was heresy.

Then one day, just across the street from the featureless building that was his workplace, quite by accident he discovered another piano. The storefront was a state-owned furniture repair shop and in the back room among the dust and heaps of broken office furniture was a piano that no one was using. It had been sent for repair years ago and never claimed. The story went that it belonged to some government department that had since been axed. A side panel had split as if it had been punched by a fist, and the instrument listed to one side until Volodya shimmed it up with a block of wood. After that it had been easy for Volodya to decline a lift in the work vehicle, claim to be getting to his destination by bus or on foot, then slip across the street to spend his time in more useful ways. The repair shop technician, who worked by himself for most of the day, loved it; he would close the heavy inner door so no one could hear and he often provided an appreciative audience of one. He had even helped Volodya find a piano tuner.

It was too bad that Ivana the Terrible had such good hearing and that one day she had been nosy enough to follow Volodya into the repair shop. She stood in the shadows quietly until he began to play then marched up to him, shoulders quivering.

"Now I see why you skulk off, you hooligan!" she stormed. "You are a lazy Russian! This is not the socialist way—to play this decadent music." Ivana often spoke in the language of the state's propaganda as it helped her on her career path. She promptly reported him to her superior who had never really liked Volodya anyway, particularly after the young man had flirted with his wife. Here was the opportunity to rid the firm of this wastrel.

Fortunately, the glacially slow bureaucratic process kicked in and before the authorities could find a more appropriate position for him, he decided that he would confess. Apologize. Make friends with Ivana. Demonstrate that he was as pure as the driven Siberian snow. Definitely no threat to anyone's wife. A genuine good guy.

This slow process of ingratiation had taken a lot out of him, and that was why he needed the support of the trusty Gennadi who was always there to keep him honest. But deep down, Volodya realized that the entire farce designed to keep his miserable job was only a stop-gap measure. Truly, he would never be free to play his music until he left the Soviet Union. Forever.

★

Jennifer loved Leningrad from the moment she stepped off the plane. After the drabness of Moscow and the subsequent rocky flight in an antiquated Ilyushin, even the airport terminal felt cheerful and bright as the sunlight filtered through three huge domes and splashed over hanging baskets of greenery.

As their bus travelled to the Hotel Astoria, she stared with interest at the elegant buildings, now crumbling, many still painted in sunshine yellow as decreed in a pre-revolutionary time, the lacy ironwork on the bridges that crossed a network of canals, and the tall linden trees that crowded the wide streets.

Their tour halted briefly at St. Isaac's Cathedral situated on the same expansive square as their hotel. Natasha ushered them through the darkness of the foyer to stare at the dimly lit, centuries-old frescoes under the church dome. She pointed. "Seven types of marble were used in the construction of this cathedral—the red and white from Italy and the grey, green and black from the Ural Mountains." The cathedral's foundation was thick and solid, its flagstones hollowed by thousands of visitors, its wall paint blackened and peeling.

"It's real dark and creepy, isn't it?" said Lona from the foyer's shadows. Her words were caught up in the acoustics and amplified. Natasha turned to glare at her.

Carlos whispered to Lona. "Most of these domed churches were designed so that wherever the congregation stood they could hear the priest…and it works both ways."

But it *was* dark and sinister, Jennifer thought—a contrast with what she had seen of the city so far. There was so much hidden, buried in those black corners. She had an urge to scratch off the flakes of dirt and paint from the frescoes. Underneath she would find vivid scenes—the church stories just as the artists had depicted them, a wall of history from the 1700s. She determined to escape the rigorously guided tour, if only for one evening, get beneath the skin of this wonderful city with its mouldering yellow buildings and share in the vigorous Russian life beneath.

Her chance came that very evening at the hotel. After an early supper of smoked sturgeon followed by pork chops, potato and cucumber, the students broke out the liquor and traded stories about other hair-raising airplane flights. Natasha had excused herself to further duties. ("Probably sharing vodka and joking about Richard Nixon with the KGB," said Hank.) Chopyk announced his desire to unpack and have an early night.

Without saying goodbye to the group, Jennifer removed her purse from under the table, sauntered through the lobby and stepped out into the vast square that fronted St. Isaac's. A rosy light in the sky signalled the sun breaking through after a brief summer rainfall. She paused at the curb and looked around quickly for any sign of black marketers. They generally loitered by the foreign hotels, ready to purchase blue jeans.

It was the end of the workday. In the Moscow streets people had stared unabashedly, but here the proletariat, heads bowed, scurried down nearby Gertsen Street, clutching shopping bags, on their way home to make dinner. Only one middle-aged woman caught sight of Jennifer's shoes and looked up to give her an overt, inquisitive glance of envy. *It's obvious that I'm a foreigner,* thought Jennifer. Her shoes, smart and expensive, and her stylish haircut gave her away.

The square was clean, empty, swept free of humanity. There were very few cars, only ugly, putty-coloured trucks, trolleybuses, and two foreign vehicles parked by the hotel. Crossing the square, she plunged down one of the narrowest streets, wanting to be lost among the endless lindens and granite statues.

As she walked, she felt confident, large. Her knowledge of the language was the key to the city and its people. Very few western tourists could speak Russian and would be too nervous to wander the streets or to read the road signs written in an unfamiliar alphabet. She was privileged.

She stopped at the Blue Bridge, paced on past the Marinsky Palace built for the Grand Duchess Marie, and caught a glimpse of what must surely be ballerinas arriving in a chauffeur- driven car at the Kirov Theatre, their graceful arms laden with costumes and carryall bags. She would attend the ballet. It would be glorious—probably *Swan Lake* or *Giselle*.

Suddenly she felt a jolt of pain, a sensation that she recognized as missing Michael. Missing him lots. Was it just missing someone to share the experience with her? Well, she would have that experience with David or Paul. That was okay. Heck, Michael didn't even like the ballet. Yet she couldn't help but remember one of the last times they had enjoyed each other's company. Was it last February, March? It seemed like a million years ago. They had walked to a movie together, through an uncharacteristic sprinkle of snow over Vancouver's Point Grey, each of them preoccupied. The sadness and distance that enveloped them had lasted all the way to the show, but once they entered, bought popcorn and seated themselves in the sticky seats, they both relaxed. It was a funny film, and he held her hand in the dark. Later, they returned to their married students' apartment talking together with more animation about the movie, about her essay, about his thesis supervisor.

"What went wrong?" she finally asked him, knowing he would understand that she wasn't talking about his recent lab experiment. Also knowing that he wouldn't be able to answer. He would only shrug. In fact, it seemed that her life was very full of loved ones who wouldn't talk to her. Still, those moments of communication: the laughter in the cinema, the caress on her hand, the discussion about her essay—they were all good. They were shared.

Jennifer continued to stride briskly, restlessly, until she had executed a broad loop which eventually brought her back to the River Moika, one of the many canals that fragmented the city into an island network.

Here, the houses hung over the water, their upper windows nearly touching the shade trees. A graceful wrought-iron bridge, the width of a footpath, led across the Moika into a neighbourhood of worn tenements. She approached it confidently.

There were three young men on the bridge, staring into the water, laughing and taking surreptitious swigs from a bottle. She was not afraid of them. If knowledge of Russian was the key to the city and its people, she was about to make use of it. As she approached, they looked up. One of them, who appeared older than the others, appraised her in a quick sweeping glance from head to foot then addressed her in English.

"You are far from home and cold, I think. I give you my jacket like a lord." He began to remove his ill-fitting, grey suit jacket.

She laughed and addressed him in Russian. "Thank you. It's nothing. Please don't."

All three men froze. The two younger men turned to face her, surprised at the foreigner who spoke their language. She waited in front of them, enjoying their confusion. *They're just kids*, thought Jennifer, *but the one holding the jacket is about my age.* He had lean features with classic Russian high cheekbones, full lips and unruly dark hair. He swung his jacket over his shoulder, came towards her, then leaned on the bridge railing and continued to stare at her through sad, blue-grey eyes.

Finally he smiled. "It gives me pleasure if you take my jacket." He was so close now she could smell the brandy on his breath. She backed away uncertainly, then relented. A wave of tenderness had come over her, a feeling akin to when she had first met her husband. The Russian stranger sensed the emotion quickly, read it on her face, and acted. He placed the jacket over her shoulders.

On the canal a small cruiser was coming towards them—an unmarked boat. The other two men turned away from the bridge and motioned to the older one. He nodded.

"Please, my name is Volodya," he said to her. "Let's walk."

The two young men snickered, but they gathered up their packages and trailed behind as she and the Russian man strolled along the embankment.

Jennifer introduced herself and they shook hands formally. He looked at her fingers. "You are married?"

"No. Yes," she stumbled. Why didn't she have a ready answer by now? "I'm separated from my husband."

He nodded, seeming to understand.

"Where is she from?" asked one of the young men behind. "Ask her where she's from."

"Quiet, Gennadi. She's from America. Are you not from America?"

"I'm from Canada."

"Aaah, Canada. Oscar Peterson. You don't know music? Then hockey, you know hockey: Phil Esposito. Don't listen to them," Volodya switched to Russian. "Gennadi is crazy about music. He wants to talk to you about American rock bands. Dmitri doesn't like music. He likes nothing but his dinner—and his vodka." The young men laughed loudly. "I like jazz music," he went on switching easily to English. "May I ask you something most wonderful?"

"Yes, you may," she said, laughing. She was prepared for the usual questions that, to date, all the Soviets had asked: Where did you learn Russian? Do you have children? Where do you work? How much do you earn? But Volodya surprised her. As they passed a stone bench, he stopped, sat down and pulled something from his pocket. The other two men came closer to see, smiling at Jennifer and suddenly shy. Volodya flipped open a wallet and pulled out a photograph.

"Look here. Do you know who that is?"

Jennifer took the photo and examined it. It had been clipped from a magazine and had obviously been folded and re-folded before finding its present home. The wide flat nose and plain features were unmistakable. "It's Ella Fitzgerald, the jazz singer."

"Yes, yes, Ella Feetzgerald." Volodya sucked in his breath dramatically. "Some day I will go to America and meet Ella Feetzgerald."

"Why her?" Jennifer asked. "Do you like her music?"

"Yes, I am jazz musician. Of course, I don't play all the time. The great Soviet state in its glory has given me another profession...."

Gennadi broke into the conversation after picking up the one word of interest—music. He looked Jennifer in the eyes and asked earnestly, "Maybe you can send me rock records when you return. Please, do you know any of these bands?" And he began to reel off names that he had memorized in English: Deep Purple, Blood Sweat and Tears, 1910 Fruitgum Company. Jennifer recognized them as pop groups and not her thing, but she promised to look into it.

Bored with this conversation, Volodya got up from his stone bench to walk again, and the little group immediately moved with him. Just as if they had not been interrupted, he began to tell her about how he made his living—though he dismissed the employment as contemptible. He had once worked for Intourist, he said proudly, spoke English and Japanese fluently, and had spent two years during the height of the cold war escorting elderly American tourists, handing out badly written pamphlets praising Lenin and explaining how communism had helped build art galleries and museums. Until, disgusted with himself (and at this point he looked around on the Leningrad street to see if anyone was listening), he refused to repeat any more propaganda, slept with an American tourist and was immediately fired. Now he had a mechanic's job; he fixed automatic soda machines. He shuddered in disgust.

"Now, tell me who are you, Zhennifer of Canada?" he asked. "Why do you learn Russian?"

"My mother is Russian, born not that far from Moscow in a country village. She's Canadian now, of course. She was a refugee who fled right after the war along with her sister, my Aunt Eva. They lived in England for a few years."

"Many such escaped the Soviet Union at that time…" Volodya looked thoughtful. "So you spoke Russian at home?"

"No, we didn't. My mother, Lila, met my father in England; he has no Russian background. He served in the British army protecting the country from Nazis and Communists so he didn't like her speaking Russian or even talking about her life before she met him."

"But he has a most brilliant daughter who speaks Russian wonderfully."

"You're a flatterer!" She smacked him with the sleeve of his own jacket draped around her shoulders. She felt entirely at ease with him.

Eventually the conversation returned to Ella Fitzgerald. "She wrote to me—when she was on tour in Europe. Really," he said, looking at her sceptical expression. "You must see, I have the letter at my home."

As they talked, they continued to walk—through parks, past bronze horses, over canals, along the Neva River, past the homes of poets. Because Leningrad is so far north, at this time of the year, July, the sky did not darken. "White nights," the Russians called it. The light faded to a royal blue dusk, then to navy blue, until the sun rose around three o'clock in the morning. They were not the only ones walking and talking; the white nights invigorated many of the city's residents and they strolled far into the evening, played sports in the parks, listened to music in the band shells, greeted one another and conserved the light in their memories for the dark days of winter.

Jennifer thought they would continue to circle all evening, but suddenly the other men took their leave in a stilted, formal fashion, with many pronouncements of farewell and earnest wishes for the remembrance of the brief friendship. There was also a ritual gift-giving with each one: a little colourful pin from Dmitri, an East German zither record from Gennady that he pulled from his satchel, along with his address written on a postcard. Jennifer dug in her pocket for two of the Canadian maple leaf pins that the department had told her to pack. They seemed trivial gifts. First Dmitri, then Gennady disappeared into one of the dark and crumbling apartment buildings. It appeared that Volodya had left his own walk home until last and she was being led there inexorably. An alarm bell sounded in her head. *He's a stranger. You're in a strange city.*

"This has been a great evening but it's past midnight and I'd better be getting back to the hotel now, thanks," she told him. "Uh…which way is that?"

"I tell you which way." Standing stock still, he smiled. "I walk you there—only if we can meet again. Tomorrow? It's a promise?"

Was there a hint of a threat? "Okay," she said, reassured by the sight of his winning smile through a set of unusually (for a Soviet) shining white teeth. "Tomorrow."

"Good, it is arranged. I meet you at your hotel door after my work is finished at 1300."

They walked back to the hotel in a satisfied silence. He refused to come inside, stayed on the steps, wishing her an awkward good night.

Though her feet ached, her spirit was energized. As she stepped off the elevator, she even smiled at the crone who guarded the entrance to her floor. As the woman handed her the door key, she nodded in the direction of the hall. Jennifer caught sight of Chopyk pacing toward her. "I've been looking for you."

Uh-oh. She couldn't help feeling like a naughty child.

"Good evening, Professor Chopyk. Can't sleep? It's the white nights. Throws the body clock out, doesn't it?" Rattling on like this probably wasn't going to stop him from delivering her a lecture about wandering off on her own. She continued the offence. "I'd like some time off tomorrow afternoon, if you don't mind. Perhaps you could lead both classes."

Chopyk drew back in surprise but accompanied her down the hall. Whatever he had been going to say was lost in her show of independence. "Well, I suppose that would be fine—if, of course, you could reciprocate. Perhaps…I want to visit the philological institute while I'm here—and should need some time for that. Then, of course, I had been meaning to talk to you about one or two of the students who could use some extra tutorial time with you later in the trip."

Jennifer had the feeling she'd been checkmated. He had not been concerned at all about her disappearance—he only wanted to ensure she did more than her part.

"Which students?"

"David needs to develop better written skills. This is a credit course for him, and right now I can't give him a passing grade. And then there's Lona. Don't know what to make of her. She wants a grade for the course, too." His voice descended to a hush. "I really don't consider her a serious student." He hesitated and Jennifer remembered that she was supposed to be finding out Lona's agenda and reporting back to Chopyk. It didn't seem very important to her.

They had reached her room, but under no circumstances was Jennifer inviting Chopyk in. "I'll deal with the students, Professor," she said abruptly. "Goodnight now."

He harrumphed by way of comment, bowed, and left her. By the time her head hit the pillow she had already forgotten how irritating he was.

She dreamed a familiar dream. She was hovering over a lake or a pond—sometimes she was in the lake—but this time she floated above it. Her fingernails had unaccountably grown extra long like those of a Chinese mandarin, and she clawed the water searching for the face that she knew would be there. The eyes that stared up at her from among the water weeds were usually familiar eyes—her little brother—and she must save him. She alone could save him. But her outsize talons snarled in the weeds and she could not scoop up the boy. Water trickled through her fingers. And when she gazed into his eyes—now she was closer, inches above the water—she saw not her brother at all, only the blue grey eyes of the attractive stranger, sinking fast.

4.

MOTHER AND DAUGHTER

Jennifer had inherited her mother's chestnut hair and hazel eyes and she would later have her father's height and posture. Her mother, Lila, wanted to name her Yevgenia which she considered the finest name in the Russian language. But her father, Jacob, countered with Jennifer. It was a modern name, he felt, and British to boot.

Lila Abram and her sister, Eva, had fled the Soviet Union at the end of the war and at last arrived in England, homesick and weary from the constant movement between refugee camps. Though Lila had wanted to be a teacher and Eva had been a seamstress, as two young women with broken English, the best jobs they could find were in the woolen mills of Leeds. Lila met Jacob Huggins at the mill's social club and considered him an excellent marriage prospect.

"Why, even the name Jacob is Jewish!" she told Eva happily.

"But he goes to the Church of England," Eva reminded her sister.

Lila was petite, fine-boned, with a Roman nose and wide brown eyes that smiled demurely at any handsome man. She was not a raving beauty but then Jacob was also not that handsome. He was a tall man with stiff military bearing who had fought with the Yorkshire Gunners. His hair was receding although he was only 27—and he had adopted the serious outlook of a much older man. As if to make up for his years in the army and time spent away from building a career, he was now working hard at the mill and had recently been promoted to foreman.

The couple married in January 1947 in a ceremony at Leeds Parish Church in Yorkshire. Lila cried about that—she had looked forward to being married under the canopy as a Jew—but Jacob told her not to be silly. He was already breaking with his own British family tradition by marrying a Jew. "Please don't make any more fuss," he told her gently.

Nine months later Jennifer Huggins was born.

Jacob was ambitious. He considered the sooty textile mills and factory houses of the industrial revolution in Leeds to be backward, not of this century and their lack of innovation plus the rigid class structure kept him from making a successful career. In 1949 he investigated emigration to Canada where commerce was booming. He would have to provide his own passage, but if he did, there was a job for him in a Toronto tool and die manufacturer. He became eager to emigrate.

Lila was six months pregnant with Jennifer's brother when the Cunard liner steamed away from Liverpool with the family on board. Douglas was born in Toronto and Lila cried again. So far away from Eva who was godmother to Jennifer! But Jacob was delighted. He loved his son from the first moment of the boy's young life in a fierce, masculine way that he had never managed for his daughter.

The family lived near Kensington Market and little by little Lila began to enjoy it more. There were many Croatians in the neighbourhood who had lived in Canada for years and had been untouched by the war. Most of them denied that they were Yugoslavian; they denounced Tito and Communism. She understood their sunny, garrulous ways and liked to shop at their butcher. Best of all, there was a Russian café. Generally it was overflowing with men, sipping coffee, playing chess, but in this new country, Canada, it was considered appropriate for women to stop in alone, buy a pastry and exchange banter with Svetlana, the clerk.

Only one thing clouded her days: Jacob had told her not to go to synagogue, not to seek out other Jews, and furthermore, not to reveal that she knew Russian or that she had lived in the Soviet Union. In short, he wanted her to deny everything from her past. "Just become a good Canadian woman, okay?" he said, practising his new accent.

At first, she had railed against this restriction, asking him in an injured but dignified voice why she couldn't honour her ancestry. He dismissed her protests with a few words: "You wouldn't understand," and he stalked off to work. These arguments were repeated. She became shrill, yelling at him that he was a tyrant. She didn't like being this way, but she couldn't make him listen except by shouting. There was fight in her, but underneath she was dreadfully afraid he would leave her alone in this new land, and reluctantly she began to acquiesce to his demands. They were, after all, recent immigrants and anti-Communist sentiment was rampant. He wasn't the one born in a Communist country; she was. They must be careful not to rock the boat.

The Huggins family prospered and Jacob wanted to move out of their working class neighbourhood. Lila put her foot down; she liked their home and wanted the contact with others from Europe. For once he listened to her, and they stayed on. In compensation, Jacob decided to rent a cottage on a lake in southern Ontario every summer for their two week vacation. It was what other Canadians did.

Lila was less excited by the visits to the lake than Jacob and the two children were. Jacob would sit on the porch reading the newspaper he had brought from the city, pausing to light a pipe or stretch his legs by walking over to the neighbour's house where the men would talk about lawnmowers and cars. Lila worked in the kitchen, served Jacob his dinner, mixed lemonade for the children, soothed mosquito bites, and walked to the general store for groceries.

The kids loved to play by the lake. At age seven, Jennifer had learned to swim just by watching the older kids next door. Little Douglas played in the sand or went with his mother to pick berries.

One day when Douglas was five years old and Jennifer was eight, Lila left them on the lake shore by themselves. She was feeling the effects of a large quantity of fresh peaches that she had consumed the night before, and she had to rush frequently to the outhouse. Jacob was learning to play golf with a neighbour, so Jennifer had promised to look after Douglas who wanted to learn to swim.

Even at such an early age Jennifer already understood her place in the family. Dad gave new playthings to Doug, only to Doug. He talked to his son more than to her, picked him up, even took him in to work one day to meet his colleagues. That left Jennifer with her stupid mother who was always complaining about stuff. Mom didn't like the new, neat foods that they served at the barbecues: corn dogs, orange pop, potato chips. She didn't like Jennifer's school teacher who taught about British explorers and British wars. She didn't even like Jennifer learning hymns like Onward Christian Soldiers, for gosh sakes. On that day that Jennifer was put in charge of her little brother, she was resentful. Let her dopey brother play with his shovel and pail on the beach. She was going to stalk a chipmunk that she had seen chattering beneath the trees. Already dressed in her bathing suit and pulling on her rubber sandals, she skipped over to the grove of birch trees and inched her way into their thickest part.

At first when she heard someone calling out her name, she thought it was the kid next door who had first shown her the chipmunk. Crouched in the trees, she suddenly realized that it was Doug who was calling. *Let him call*, she thought. *I'm having fun here.* Even when she caught the panic in his childish voice, she had stayed, resentful. Finally she emerged from the grove to see the neighbour's son flying down the slope and into the water and to see her mother racing out of the outhouse with a look of unveiled horror on her face. All of them running, running past her, ignoring her.

★

Douglas was buried in Toronto, in the small graveyard near their home. Jennifer's father became even more distant with her, and the very life went right out of Jennifer's mother. She blamed herself for not keeping watch, and oddly enough, she also blamed the lake, but not Jennifer. It was too deep, too wild. Yes, she should have been more vigilant, but they should never have gone to such a dangerous place, she told the family.

Jennifer knew the lake was not the problem. *She* had been the problem. She had let her brother drown. Though her father had said nothing to her, she knew that he would add another black mark to her name in that mysterious record book that parents keep.

Later that same year Lila got word that her sister Eva had been killed in a car accident. She could scarcely mourn—she was already in such a depression over Douglas. Bad things come in threes, Lila told Jennifer. Sure enough, her friend Svetlana's daughter contracted polio and died. Now Lila wanted to keep Jennifer home from school where she would be safe from the disease that was crippling so many children. But Jennifer and Jacob insisted that she attend school, and Jennifer stayed healthy. She loved school and earned mostly As. From her school life she drew much of the attention and encouragement she was not getting at home. Her teachers thought her a model pupil.

At home, her mother had retreated into silence and servility. Her father rarely spoke to Jennifer, directing his commands through her mother: "Have the child clean up the kitchen. Make sure she's dressed for Sunday school."

Occasionally when she brought home her report card, he relaxed. He liked having a smart daughter, Jennifer observed. Sure, it would have been better to have a smart son, but a smart daughter was also something to brag about at work. When she was at school, she was a princess. The younger kids looked up to her, she helped the popular kids with their homework, she earned parts in the school play. And best of all, at school the ugly thoughts such as the events surrounding Doug's death were repressed, shoved to the depths of her mind. Sometimes at night in her bedroom she would think of it again. How her mother's face, her eyes, had looked as she ran past, hair streaming. How Doug's white spongy flesh had looked on the beach when the neighbour kid pulled him from the water. How her father had been summoned and how he came running from up the street. How his skin had turned to ashen grey when he arrived on the beach, panting. Then a torrent of shame would surround her until she, too, was drowning.

If Jennifer could have that day over again, what would she have done? By the lofty age of 20 she had forgiven herself for her childhood transgression—or so she had thought. The full impact of what the loss of Douglas had done to her mother became apparent years later, and somehow only when Jennifer was around the others: the huge, loving Ukrainian families, the friendly Croatian vendors in the market, the Russian café owner and his family. *This is how my mother could have been,* Jennifer thought, *if only I had acted differently on that day.*

★

As a teenager she grew close to the Ukrainian kids just up the street where there was a "house full of women" as the stout father was fond of saying: eight daughters, wife and grandmother. The Ukrainian girls embraced Canadian ways: they painted their fingernails, bought movie star magazines and spoke only English at home. But on special feast days or their name days, they all worked in the kitchen, decorated the dining room with the embroidered runners and heirloom dishes of their grandmother's youth and celebrated as a family. Jenny, as they called her, was always included in these occasions, and the phrases of Ukrainian she learned were not unfamiliar—like something she had heard her mother sing a long time ago in a lullaby.

Her true best friends were her teachers. From their advice and encouragement she was propelled toward a scholarship and in 1964 was accepted at the University of Toronto. At first her father thought it a bad idea. "Get a job in industry," he suggested but later relented when her scholarship earned her a certain amount of fame in his social circles.

She pursued a general arts education taking courses in literature and theatre. One day while browsing the Russian Literature section in the library she came across a dual language book of Russian short stories—Russian on one page, the English translation on the other page. They were classics: stories by Babel, Tolstoy, Gorky. Each was dramatic, moody, complex. She was fascinated. Although her father discouraged speaking anything but English at home, Jennifer knew many of the Russian phrases that her mother had used with her in her childhood, out of earshot of her father. On an impulse, she checked the book out of the library and took it home.

"Look what I found, mom! Do you want to read it with me?"

Lila's face lit up. She remembered some of the stories from her childhood. They pored over the book together with Lila reading the Russian sentences aloud while Jennifer tried to match up the English translation with the Russian text.

"I'll teach you the alphabet," Lila told her in a whisper. "It's easy." That semester Jennifer enrolled in Russian 101 and took to the language immediately. In the phrases, the sentence structure, the very cadence of the language, she could hear her mother's voice. She had already considered majoring in languages and now her mind was made up. She also studied German, but Russian became her major discipline. Her new Russian professor was delighted. He encouraged her, nourished her. When the grammar proved difficult and she was ready to give up, he told her, "Press on. Press on regardless." It was one of his favourite phrases and she embraced the thought.

Her own neighbourhood took on a new aura, especially the Russian café. Her mother's friend Svetlana had long ago retired, but there was a friendly young man behind the counter. It had become the focal point of the émigré community—more cosmopolitan than in the 1950s. By days it was still a retreat for the same grizzled, old men to sit and nurse a coffee or prolong a chess game, but in the evenings it attracted visitors from the suburbs for poetry readings, jazz jams, coffee, sticky pastries, and if you checked under the counter, an open bottle of brandy for those in the know—the powerful Yugoslavian variety known as *rakiya*.

Jennifer visited most weekends, took her college friends with her, who thought her very bohemian and chic. Yet it was just one of her old haunts. Her friends, the Ukrainian family, still lived nearby. Tina, one of the daughters of about Jennifer's age invited her to her wedding, a three-day affair in the best tradition. They feasted, drank numerous toasts, danced everything from the polka to the twist, fell asleep, breakfasted at the in-laws' home, danced and drank again. By the end of the second day Jennifer was reeling with lack of sleep, indigestion and extravagance, yet she felt right at home among these people. She couldn't imagine her father—still austere and proper—ever participating in such a wedding. He would buy a wedding present, come to the first dinner, kiss the bride and go home satisfied that he had done the right thing. But she *could* imagine her mother at such an affair, the person long remembered from her childhood—not the shadow of her mother who existed now—and wondered why that sad, lifeless woman didn't join in with such events. Had she ever been truly carefree even before the accident?

5.

ANGEL WATCH

LENINGRAD, JULY 8, 1974

Just as they had spent that first evening on the street, Jennifer and Volodya spent the next afternoon mostly on the street, in the peculiar privacy that Soviets find in large crowds. She bought him cognac and cigarettes at Beryozka the foreign currency souvenir store. He bought her Russian language books, stories of the city, and corrected her sentences. She showed him her contact lenses and how they worked. He marvelled. Such things were unheard of in the Soviet Union, he told her, but he had seen some Japanese tourists use them. That night Jennifer returned to the hotel, Volodya to his home.

The next day as they were passing the Hotel Europe, another accommodation reserved solely for visitors from the west, he grabbed her hand, glanced around to see if they were being followed and walked into the lobby, saying in English, "I want to show you something. Go along with me to the restaurant." They strolled to the elegant restaurant portal and waited in the foyer. There was no one in sight.

"Hey, if you're pretending to be an American, you're holding your cigarette all wrong," she whispered. "Don't curl it under your hand. Just let it sit between your fingers. Like so." She surreptitiously straightened his fingers, rearranging the cigarette. He grinned at her. She felt the warmth of the smile and let her hand linger on his.

"Thank you," he said in English. "Now look over at that table under the light. I will not point. You see?" Jennifer peered. "See the centre arrangement? That is a microphone—how they listen. Only the ones with that arrangement—and some of the others there, that table and that one."

Jennifer stared but couldn't see the difference in the various tables.

"How do you know?"

"I can tell. My director at Intourist asked me to seat special people at certain tables."

It sounded like *Mad Magazine*, she thought, Spy versus Spy. "You mean like a visiting politician or nuclear scientist? You must get a lot of those," she snickered.

"Not to laugh. It is the truth."

"But they wouldn't go to that trouble for a student group like us. Would they?"

He shrugged. "Who knows? Could be they want to watch someone in your group."

"Are you saying there *is* someone?"

"How would I know? I don't work for Intourist any more. I only fix soda machines."

A waiter sauntered over to them. "Dining room closed. Return 5 o'clock, please."

"Aaaww, that's too bad, honey," Volodya drawled to Jennifer in a passable imitation of a Texan, making her giggle. They departed, laughing.

"Is that true, what you said, that some of us might be singled out?"

"Yes, of course. Certain people in a tour group are followed or investigated. Their documents are stolen or withheld just for intelligence's sake. Intelligence! Ech… It happened in one of my tour groups. An American lady set her bag down for a moment in a busy department store without knowing that she was being followed. The watcher seized the opportunity to lift her wallet because he wanted to know her personal information. When the visitor told me that her wallet had been stolen, I knew right away what had happened."

"What did you do?"

"I was uncomfortable perpetuating this hoax; it was not honest. I felt more at ease when I could answer that the wallet had been successfully found, mere hours later, due to the excellence of the great Soviet police force!"

Jennifer frowned.

"But listen," Volodya continued, "when that tourist's wallet was returned, there was a paper missing—her birth certificate. Someone had slipped up—returning it before they had a chance to examine the certificate and use the information. All this was illegal, of course. It could provoke an incident, yet it was done all the time. On the last day of her Soviet Union trip, just hours before she was due to leave for the airport, the birth certificate was returned to her by some petty man—an Intourist functionary. She received no explanation and left the country puzzled. I am no longer party to these machinations."

★

The following day when they met in the early afternoon as usual, he pulled her up a side street, then stopped. He brought his face very close to hers and she thought he would kiss her, but instead he surprised her by asking, "Do you trust me?"

"That's a big question. What do you mean?"

Seeing her confusion, he said in English, "I mean—do you believe that I would not harm you or let others harm you?"

"Oh yes, I do," Jennifer breathed. That was so much easier to answer.

"I want to take you to a special place. But it is a low place, a modest place, and I do not want that you feel afraid of me."

"No, I won't feel afraid. Let's go." They continued walking along back streets for several blocks, then he suddenly dived into a dark alley.

"Follow me. Don't let anyone see." The alley emerged into a courtyard surrounded by a crumbling old building. Peeping through one window to a room almost at ground level, she could see that it was empty, that no one except rats had occupied it in a long time. She asked nervously, "Do people really live here?"

He led her through a door strapped with bands of iron and into a maze of hallways with no signs of occupation except for some rustling in a corner, until they reached an apartment door. Volodya knocked three times, then stopped and smiled at her. Eventually they heard an answering knock then all was quiet.

"That is my friend, Ernesto," he whispered.

"That's not a Russian name."

"No, this is a very special friend from Cuba. He plays the piano."

Volodya pressed her hand under his arm, and Ernesto opened the door a crack and peered out—two bloodshot eyes set in an olive-skinned face and topped by wisps of stringy hair. "You again," he growled.

Volodya inserted his foot in the door and pushed it in while keeping up a rapid chatter in Russian with a sprinkling of Spanish words. "Please, *molodets*, good guy. I bring you a guest from a foreign country—a *compadre*. Open the door."

Ernesto appeared to consider this information and finally succumbed to Volodya's push. The door flew open and Jennifer caught sight of a room littered with newspapers, books, ashtrays, bottles and what appeared to be a pair of grimy boilermaker overalls. Despite the odour that prevailed and Ernesto's grubby fingernails that he held out to her for a handshake, she found herself liking him.

"Welcome to my home, *senorita*."

"Be careful around him," Volodya said in English, waving Ernesto away elaborately. "He was once a Communist. He actually left his home and a career in a nightclub—a *jazz* nightclub—to move to the glorious Soviet Union." He laughed and smacked the man on his balding head. "Now hc's learned better."

"Careful with your insults, you pig," Ernesto growled again but then smiled good- naturedly. "So Volodya, you've come to play, you ham-fisted, over-sexed son of a Siberian wolf."

"Someone has to show you how to play good music."

"Just showing off for your pretty girlfriend, are you? In hopes she'll take pity on you and send you to music school?"

The two continued to grin, enjoying this verbal joust. "But pardon my manners, Comrade...Miss Jennifer. Come through to the music room and we'll have refreshment."

Jennifer held her breath as to what sort of "refreshment" he would find in this littered apartment, but she followed him through a freshly painted door into what appeared to be an elegant parlour. "This is like a scene from *Anna Karenina*," she murmured. The room had no windows. The high ceiling was lit by a chandelier and covered in a profusion of plaster mouldings: cherubs, trumpeters and grapevines ran down the walls on three sides. The fourth wall was a crudely built partition. By the door stood a small, mahogany table surrounded by four carved chairs. Surprisingly, the floor and the table were remarkably free of debris. The rest of the room was entirely taken up by a baby grand piano covered in a tasselled tablecloth. Ernesto whipped this cover off like a magician. Volodya sighed when he saw the piano.

"May I?" he asked Ernesto formally.

Ernesto also dropped his pose. "Please be my guest." He pulled up a chair in front of the piano for Jennifer.

Volodya sat at the piano, gave Jennifer one glance, then turned his attention to the keys. She didn't recognize his first song though it had a swing beat—maybe from the 1940s. Then without pausing, he launched into a tune he announced as Oscar Peterson's "A Little Jazz Exercise."

"Wow!" She applauded wildly when he finished. But he didn't stop. Ernesto left for a few moments then reappeared quietly with an enormous, half-empty box of chocolates wrapped in brown paper which he offered to her. They were old, mottled with discolouration, probably kept for his infrequent visitors, but she took one and thanked him. He left again hurriedly and this time returned with a saxophone. She settled back to listen again, a Duke Ellington number that she recognized as "C Jam Blues." Ernesto stepped in for a few riffs on the sax then put the instrument down to take up a chair beside Jennifer and listen to Volodya play. Although he appeared to be studying the keys as he played, she felt him look up every so often, gauging her reaction. Was that simply a performer who loved an audience? Or something deeper, more demanding? She wasn't sure and felt a slight shiver.

"Are you cold?" Ernesto leaned over to her and offered another chocolate. "Even in summer this room is cool." Volodya ignored them and continued to play.

"No, thank you. It's a wonderful room. It was once so elegant, I think."

"It was the formal dining room for the house when the bourgeoisie lived here. You see how this wall cuts off the rest of the room? When it was whole, the dining room took up 30 square meters of floor space—all for one wealthy family."

"And was the piano here then, too?" she asked. "It looks old." Now, she noticed how the black lustre had worn down to a scuff in many places, how the legs were chipped. "You must be the one who keeps it in tune?"

"Yes, I take care of it. It's also pre-revolutionary." Here, Ernesto smiled with pride. He might dismiss the ostentatious living quarters of the wealthy, but he obviously cherished their toys. "It's why I can't leave the apartment. I won't leave without it and we can't fit it through this door." He laughed out loud and Volodya glanced up and smiled.

"So it sat here all during the revolution and the siege of Leningrad and everything?" she asked. "I'm surprised someone didn't burn it for firewood during those terrible winters."

"Someone loved this piano—dearly," Ernesto replied, then he added sheepishly, "and you know I only let those play who also love the piano. Vlad is a flashy scoundrel, but he loves to play."

"And he's *good*." All of a sudden she couldn't contain her excitement. This man, this stranger, Volodya, had just proved to be all he said he was. A lover of jazz, a wronged man. He shouldn't be here; he should be playing up a storm in the jazz bars of Montreal or New York. She turned to Ernesto, "What did you mean earlier about the new girlfriend sending him to music school?" But Ernesto had picked up his sax again and was engrossed.

When the impromptu concert was over much later that afternoon, Volodya and Jennifer shook hands with Ernesto again, and Jennifer thought they were about to leave when Ernesto produced a bottle of vodka. "Now we drink."

"Oh, no thank you. I've got to return to the hotel and my students."

Ernesto shook his head. "She won't last long in the Soviet Union with that attitude. Hotel and students over vodka and our company! Please, it would be a sign of respect to drink with us."

Volodya replied for her. "I think she doesn't want to stay in your flea-bitten apartment any longer than she has to. Let's go to the park. Come on, bring your bottle."

So the three of them went back down the dark alley, Volodya striding along in the lead, his hand on Jennifer's arm, Ernesto trotting behind, through a maze of side streets to the park by the canal where they settled on a bench—Volodya slouched, staring across the water, wrapped in a mood, Ernesto eager, Jennifer nervous.

"Now we drink," Ernesto repeated to her. He tipped the bottle high and sucked with great attentiveness while Jennifer watched an air bubble strive to escape the clear liquid. They were silent.

"Here, your turn."

She surreptitiously wiped the mouth of the bottle on her sleeve, glanced around (there were only a few pedestrians a long way off), and took a swig. Then it was Volodya's turn. Then there were toasts—to Ella Fitzgerald, to mothers, to foreign visitors, to Comrade Brezhnev, just in case someone was listening. Soon, the shadows lengthened and the canal lapped against the embankment. Her lips tingled and Volodya appeared as if at the far end of a tunnel. She felt herself caught up in some ritual, so old, as old as Russia and as desperate.

Suddenly they were noisy. She was laughing. Volodya was chattering as if wound up with a key. Ernesto was slapping his knee. She heard music coming from a long way off, some sentimental ballad—or maybe that was Volodya singing. She would have to leave, go back to the hotel, her students would be searching for her. Besides, she needed to use the washroom and the public one would be foul. She stood up. The sky and the canal seemed to meet on the same plane, rearing up like a wall around her, containing her, isolating her from the others. She teetered before the sensation abated.

"Goodbye, goodbye," she intoned. The two men were arguing about something.

Volodya jumped up. "See you tomorrow, my *hitraya zhenshchina*, my wily woman."

"Yes, tomorrow, mmmm." Her mouth would not create any more words. She kissed him, full on the lips. That would have to be her answer. She turned toward the trolley stop. All the way back to the hotel she laughed, but it was a bitter laughter.

★

The afternoon's vodka continued to war with dinner's tough roast beef. Though Jennifer's digestion was sluggish, her mind was keen, and she lingered over the meal, pondering the day's events. Soon she realized that Paul and Hank were waving her over.

"Okay what is it?" She stood between their chairs, curious.

"We're going to head to another hotel for a drink. Want to come?" Paul told her. "Hank's got the idea that we're being watched too much here and that it's cramping his style."

"Yeah, I want to check out the nightlife elsewhere."

"We could try the Hotel Europe," Jennifer suggested. "In fact, I'd really like it if we went there." The notion of them behaving like tourists sitting in a modern bar, sipping cocktails, sounded stuffy and polite after the unabashed, Russian-style park bench drinking earlier in the day, but she wanted to act on an idea she had in mind. Hopefully she wouldn't expire from alcohol poisoning before tomorrow.

"Aawwright, let's have a wild time," Hank replied. "No Natasha, no statistics—just a chance to talk about the trip so far—and maybe pick up some women."

"Oh, you mean we shouldn't invite Chopyk?" said Paul innocently.

"I'm sure I saw him on Nevskiy Prospect with a blonde," sniggered Hank.

"No, let's just get Maria and Ted," Jennifer said. "And David. And let's have Lona along."

"I'll go find her," Hank said eagerly and took off across the lobby.

Paul looked at her. "You're up to something. I know you too well." He waited. "Jennifer?"

"Oh, nothing. I just want to see where they seat us. I'll explain later."

The small group arrived at the restaurant lounge of the Hotel Europe around 9 o'clock, and they were ushered into a line-up along the wall.

"Why must we wait?" asked Lona. "There are quite a few tables free."

Finally the same waiter that Jennifer and Volodya had spoken to that morning walked them to a place near the bar. It was not one of the tables that Volodya had pointed out. No microphone. Jennifer relaxed a little but felt some disappointment. She was becoming sure that Lona was a lightning rod, and that if anyone were to be followed by the Soviets, it would be her.

Without asking them, the waiter brought a giant bottle of Stolichnaya vodka and a round of glasses.

"Some fruit juice, please," Jennifer called out. He nodded.

Paul seemed to feel that the occasion called for a pronouncement. "I propose a toast—this country sets an exhausting pace…(hear, hear, from David), there are mind-numbing statistics and paralyzing references to Lenin…(Ted broke into his Lenin impersonation then stopped abruptly remembering that he was in a public place) but I'm sure impressed," Paul went on. "To the Soviet Union." They all murmured agreement and sipped the neat vodka.

"Full of contradictions, isn't it?" said David, glancing at a woman in a white uniform who was carrying a tray between the dirty tables, shuffling in a pair of shabby shoes. "Leaders in industry, yet have you studied her shoes?" They were made of some kind of cheap vinyl, cracking and worn with overuse. Jennifer had noticed that Soviet shoes often took on the shape of the women's feet that stood in endless lines waiting for buses, waiting for groceries. "Why can't they make decent shoes?"

"Yeah, wow," added Maria, "those line-ups are something. They must wait for hours, all of them with that slack expression on their faces."

At that moment the woman in the white uniform plopped down two bottles of mineral water, snapped the caps off professionally with an opener that hung by a chain from her waist and grunted a polite *pozhalsta*, "Please take."

"We didn't order…oh what the hell," said David. Jennifer reached for the refreshing water eagerly.

Paul chimed in. "A country that puts a man in space, yet you look at the filthy exhaust those busses are pushing out. That's no rocket fuel. It coats everything, gets into your lungs."

She agreed. "At least this city seems light and bright and modern"—everyone nodded—"whereas Moscow was so drab."

"Boy, was it ugly." David shook his head. "Though I have to say everything looks a tad more cheerful after a bottle of the local brew." He helped himself to another glass.

The waiter finally showed up with some sickly sweet plum syrup. It didn't cut the vodka, but by that time they were almost past caring. The lounge filled up with British and Americans, some of them in baseball caps, a few individuals who spoke Russian with a German accent and a party of serious, silent Asians.

"I think they're North Vietnamese," David whispered.

The Asians were seated at the table with the centrepiece, Jennifer noted. So the Soviets were not above spying on their Communist cousins. It fit with the current paranoia. Suspicion of Asian aggression was running high in the country and tension marked the border with China.

"We're going to need another bottle here. I'll get it," said David suddenly.

"Do you think that's wise?" put in Lona.

"What's wise got to do with it? We're in the Soviet Union, guys!"

The conversation continued, the waiter brought a tray of snacks, the level in the vodka bottle plummeted, and Jennifer couldn't quite remember how they had acquired another guest at their table. He was a Soviet man, about 45, with curly hair, dressed in a fashionable lounge jacket. Apparently he had been listening to their conversation for some time. He shook hands all around and told them in fluent English that he was an editor of a prominent Soviet newspaper. None of them really believed him. What would an editor be doing sitting in the bar of a Soviet hotel that catered exclusively to tourists?

"I bet he's a black marketeer," whispered Ted loudly, leaning towards Maria. "He wants to buy our jeans—or get into *your* jeans." She giggled. Lona looked puzzled.

"Is this a joke?" Paul asked.

"No, he's a spy," said David.

"Yes, I am a spy," the man repeated in a hushed voice, "but I cannot talk about it here. You understand?" He arched one eyebrow and glanced at Jennifer.

"Uh, no." She was stunned—whether from surprise or vodka, she wasn't sure. He was mocking them. If he were a spy, why would he admit it? And why was he looking at her? Perhaps they should break up the party; this man was a troublemaker. She should try and sober up.

"Now, let me see," David went on, too loudly for a normal conversation. "You're here to tell us how we're talking too openly against the Soviet system. You want to warn us that we're being watched. Is that it?"

"You are brilliant. Astute." the man replied. "Please to pour another glass." Hank complied and the man continued. "Clever young people… Students, is that correct? You will be approached by many citizens while you stay in the Soviet Union. Some will try to buy goods from you." He glanced down at David's Wrangler jeans. "Some will claim to be your relatives in order to leave the country." Jennifer felt a jolt of anxiety at these words and glanced at Paul.

Lona, who had been unusually silent up to now, leaned in closer to the man, her eyes wide. "So it's true that we're watched everywhere we go…by the authorities, I mean?"

"They will follow you," the man replied. "Not all of you. Just some of you, as recommended by your tour guide. You have Intourist guides, right?" They nodded. "My advice is don't try anything with them or you will be detained in mother Russia forever." He gulped his drink. "Watch out for the watchers. We call them 'angels'." He stood up. "Oh, and you asked about the shabby shoes? We could make better ones, but the good materials are not given to the people for such decadent uses." He lowered his voice. "They go to the military industrial complex to make weapons. Anyway, Soviets know we can't make as good shoes as in the west. See?" And he pointed at his own pair of suede Hush Puppies. "Made in the U.S.A." Suddenly, he seemed nervous and moved away from the table rapidly. "Now I leave you. Goodnight. Goodnight. Goodbye."

David looked as if he was about to jump up and follow. "No, don't," shouted Jennifer. "He was a provocateur, I'm sure. He was supposed to get us into trouble."

"Are you sure? I think he was just a disgruntled Soviet guy who wanted to bum some free booze in the bar," said Paul. He swirled his drink and looked wise. "They know we love to hear that anti-Soviet conversation. It makes us think that the cold war is for a reason."

"Yeah, Jennifer. Why? What would be the point of getting us in trouble?"

"Well then, how did he hear about the shoes? I'm sure he wasn't sitting with us then..."

"He overheard us. You can hear David talking across the street sometimes," Maria replied.

Maybe she *was* overdoing it with this cloak and dagger stuff. Where had she got these ideas about espionage? From Volodya, mostly. But now this man, if he could be believed, was confirming everything that Volodya had told her.

★

The next day she resolved to ask Natasha about surveillance. After all, as a tour leader she had a right to know if someone was following them. After breakfast, Jennifer caught up to Natasha crossing the vast lobby alone on her way to the bus.

"Could you tell me, Natasha," she asked breathlessly, "if the Soviet authorities are likely to have any of us followed if we go outside of the group?" There was nothing as good as the direct approach, she thought, but the older woman turned such a withering gaze on her that Jennifer wilted, then continued rapidly. "We often hear this in the west—that visitors are watched or followed for whatever reason."

Natasha halted her brisk walk. "Absolute nonsense," she answered crisply and stared at Jennifer as if she were demented. "The people of the Soviet Union will do no such thing to tourists. Have we not welcomed you? Am I not showing you the sights of the city?"

"Yes, of course. I didn't mean to offend you," Jennifer rushed on. "You're being very helpful. It's just that I have a friend who...well, lost her wallet in this country..." She recounted the story that Volodya had told her, concluding with: "The wallet was found very quickly and returned to her but she had reason to believe that someone was following her. She thought that the person, the one who was following her, had maybe stolen it and that's why it was recovered so quickly." She regretted starting this conversation but now there was no choice but to finish it.

This time the ghost of a smile crossed Natasha's lips.

"Your friend was undoubtedly careless and the Soviet police were more efficient than in the west." She turned toward the exit once more and Jennifer was left to ponder this extraordinary statement.

★

The golden spire of Peter Paul Cathedral glittered in the setting sun like a beacon. An answering twinkle glanced off a golden column across the Neva River at the Admiralty, an architecturally stunning 18th century square of elegant buildings that the tour group had admired just that morning. Jennifer and Volodya sat on an outdoor bench at the Strelka, an arrow-shaped promontory overlooking this widest span of the river and listened to the giggles and accordion playing of a crew of roaming young people in the park behind them.

"I bet they'll be here all night?" she asked.

"Yes, the police will turn the other way—how do you say that? 'Turn the other eye' during this time of year. It's a time to have fun. You know, we're sitting on an island in the river and in the old pre-revolutionary days the gentry came out here during the white nights to take supper in many cafes and restaurants. The gypsies would play and sing for the gentlemen and ladies who would spend all night walking the streets and talking, just like we are doing."

"Hard to go to bed in this golden light," she remarked. In truth, she was exhausted and had been so by noon of that day. The student group had been marched by an energetic Natasha through the Hermitage, the vast gallery of international art housed in the Winter Palace, at a pace that even the physically fit David found challenging. Hundreds of other visitors, talking in dozens of languages, jammed the ornate corridors and wedged themselves up and down the marble staircases along with her small group. A blur of images swirled in her memory: a giant malachite vase, a Rembrandt painting, an intricate mosaic, a gilt ceiling. It was gorgeous and rich—and too much to digest. When Volodya suggested simply sitting by the river bank, she welcomed the idea.

Even after the sun slid below the horizon, the sky shimmered with silver and bronze clouds before turning a royal blue. A fresh breeze stirred ripples in the water, and Jennifer looked up, exhilarated, at the colossal sky that stretched over this delta city built by Peter the Great.

Presently she spoke. "Considering that this city has known such suffering, it's amazing that it gives me and the others in my group such an uplifted, joyous feeling. Everywhere I look there's beauty and it makes me feel lighter, burdenless."

Volodya stirred from his place on the bench, one arm over her shoulders. His face betrayed an odd mixture of pride in his home and uneasiness at the conversation. "You have no idea how much suffering," he replied. "This very spot, these buildings around us, were built by Swedish prisoners of war during Peter's time. This was a swamp and many of them died working in it, their bodies beneath us in this earth." He shuddered. "Then, of course, there was bloodshed during the Revolution... That boat—you can almost see it from here, the cruiser *Aurora*—it fired the first shots after Our Leader, Lenin, arrived in the city to rally the workers in 1917. Those years meant war and famine. There is not much recorded because the state does not want to remember those bad times."

"The city was under siege again in the Second World War, I know," added Jennifer, "and many died of hunger." She felt privileged to hear the stories of its history from a real Leningrader and not from their pedantic tour guide.

"Yes, *those* years are well documented. The destruction was visited upon us from the Nazis, not from the revolutionary forces." He fell quiet for a time. "I love this city," he went on, "but it illustrates a horrible truth. It seems that anything that rises up and is good must always be built on suffering. This city has a legacy of suffering and bloodshed but it has survived, and it's good. What was that word you used? Joyous?"

"Yes, joyous," and the thought of the untapped beauty still to be found in this extraordinary place made her swell with emotion. She leaned over to kiss him, not for the physical act of kissing, but because she wanted to seal that thought with something meaningful. He was surprised at her gesture but soon kissed her back. When they finally fell gently away from one another, a few faint stars had appeared in the sky.

★

On the fourth day in Leningrad she noticed that, suddenly, the stores were stocked with Israeli oranges. Everywhere women shopped in pairs, each carrying one handle of a shopping bag overflowing with the fruit. At the end of a long afternoon together, Jennifer and Volodya stood in a line-up at a gloomy, old-fashioned grocery store on Nevskiy Prospect until they reached the produce counter. Volodya indicated how many oranges they wanted and a weary clerk weighed them, then handed him a scrap of paper with a number scrawled on it. As instructed by Volodya, Jennifer stood in line at the cashier to pay for the fruit, then returned with the receipt. In the park beside a statue of Catherine the Great, they ate the oranges, pressing the wedges into one another's mouths and sucking the juice from them noisily. Soon, their hands and faces were sticky and they needed to wash.

"I think it's time you must come to my home," he said, packing the remaining oranges in a shopping bag and pulling her up from the park bench. "I must tell you something and it's better we walk while I say."

"Is something wrong?" she asked while falling into step with his energetic stride. They exited the park and descended beneath the busy street through the pedestrian underpass.

"Yes," he answered her finally when they were striding through the echoing depths of the empty tunnel. "My workplace—they are pigs—they hound me. Before too long, it will be recommended that I move to a new job. All because I play the piano…" He shuddered and the chill of the tunnel seemed to seep into her soul.

"I don't understand…tell me more," she said, stopping. Jennifer's obvious confusion prompted Volodya to tell her the whole story of his discovery by Ivana the Terrible and his subsequent attempt to make peace. "If I move to another job," he finished, "it may not be as easy to find time to play. Is it right to prevent citizens from playing the piano? No, of course not." Together they climbed the steps into the daylight and Jennifer shook off the sensation of having passed through some sort of vale of despair. After this minor explosion he seemed to cheer up and the two continued their walk to his home in silence.

Later, Jennifer would remember the feelings that overtook her as she stood on the sidewalk outside his apartment building. It was typical Leningrad architecture beside one of the larger waterways, the Fontanka Canal, a four-flight walk-up with the usual peeling paint, crumbling plaster and dark hallways. Built before the revolution, as Natasha would have said. It added an aura—as if by having lived through tumultuous times the buildings had earned their decay and should not be repaired.

Jennifer hesitated at the dark hell of an entrance way that was heavy with the stench of urine and filth. Through the arch she could see into the courtyard. Lights were on in almost all of the apartments. There were sounds of babies crying, dinner pots clanking, radios blaring at full volume. This was it: the chance that she had craved to dive into the vigorous Russian life. She would be entering that portal with a man whose breath was sweet with oranges and brandy, a stranger she had met only three days ago and who had so fed her hunger for experience that she would follow him.

He turned to look at her in mute appeal. "Please come," his eyes said. She entered.

The light switch was defective. The light flickered then died. They stumbled to the top of the wide, stone stairs in the dark, her hand in his, their feet crunching on broken glass. At one point he surged ahead. She heard a jingle, then a swishing sound but realized that she had no fear of him. He opened the door and ushered her in with a loud "welcome" spoken in English. His choice of language alerted everyone that a foreigner was visiting. She knew there would be others living there because in the huge cities with their severe housing shortages, everyone shared apartments—or were out in the cold. He could be living with an old grandmother or a warring couple, she thought. She had seen pictures—you have your own room, share the toilet just down the hall and share the tiny kitchen. Often, you have your own stove in the kitchen and a place on the shelf to keep your sardines and tea.

But at this apartment there was a surprise. A dark-eyed, vibrant woman greeted them at the doorway and ushered them into Volodya's own cramped bedroom. Volodya introduced her only as "Alya, my friend."

A girlfriend? Or a curious apartment mate? The thought flitted through Jennifer's mind that in the three days since their meeting, Volodya had found out a lot about her family background and her relationship with Michael but she still knew little about him.

While he went to gather wash water in a basin from the communal bathroom, Jennifer used the time to look about curiously. The room was neat, conspicuously so; it had the air of having been recently dusted and spruced up for just such a visit. A plain table and chairs stood in the centre; a long nightstand with ornately carved doors was placed along one wall, a bookcase served as a room divider to screen the single bed in the corner. The wall above the bed was covered in photographs and telegrams. She examined them quickly. What sort of things would he keep? Souvenirs from other travellers? Of course, she knew no one in the photos and moved away to stare at a print. The artist's name, Petrov-Vodkin, was scribbled in the corner; it was garish, modern and in stark contrast to another original oil painting that took her breath away. With an almost translucent light, the painting depicted two peasant girls, intent smiles on their faces, dressed in traditional Russian costume, each carrying a basket, crossing a stream bound for an evergreen forest.

"It's called 'The Mushroom Gatherers,'" Volodya said, backing in the door with a full basin of water which he placed on a table. "They are so young, so innocent," he said with an ironic grin. "That is, before they move into the city and work in the factory."

She washed her hands and face in the basin and dried them on a small towel. "It looks very old," she said.

"Yes, it was my grandmother's. She died many years ago. I think in America it would be a valuable painting. No?"

"Maybe. It depends on the artist. I don't know much about art."

"There is no artist's signature on it, unfortunately. But look here, this is what I want to show you." He cleared away the water and then with a flourish produced a clear cellophane wrapper. From it he withdrew a photo and an envelope that contained a creased piece of paper. It looked to be good quality but was worn by countless refoldings. She opened it and read the few words: "Dear Volodya, Thank you for your letter. It's good to know that I have fans in Leningrad. Keep on smilin'." The flowery signature at the bottom was written in blue ink, different than the other writing. It said simply "Ella." The photo was a black and white portrait of the jazz singer.

"Wow, is it really from her, do you think?" Secretly, Jennifer wasn't that impressed. Many movie stars and musicians responded to fan letters with signed photos and often it was their managers or fan club that wrote the letters.

"Of course it is her," he replied. "The envelope says it was mailed in Berlin. See? She was on tour with your Oscar Peterson."

"What does she mean by 'keep on smiling', I wonder?"

"In my letter I told her that her music makes me happy. It's true." He traced the outline of Ella's face with a finger. "She is negro, right? Tell me," he went on, "do you have negro persons in Canada, too?"

"Yes, we do...but we usually call them black. The word negro is... well, old-fashioned." He looked blank and she wondered what news of the civil rights movement would make headlines in the Soviet Union. It would probably be couched in the language of the state extolling how the slave masses had risen up against the capitalist oppressors or some such jargon. She realized she had not seen a single black person since her arrival in the country, although Moscow University reportedly attracted African students.

"Excuse me. I am naïve," he went on. "I must ask a very important question. Promise me not to laugh?" She nodded. "Is it only black persons who make jazz music in Canada or America? Or can white people like me make jazz?"

She tried not to grin at his earnestness. "Why would you ask that? Lots of people of all colours play jazz! You're safe there to play whatever music you want…" She could see his discomfort, so she continued more gently. "It's true, jazz has its roots among black musicians, that's for sure. Many of them grew up singing in church choirs, like Aretha Franklin, for example. She's my favourite. Do you know her?"

"No, tell me." They spent the next while with Jennifer dredging up anything from her memory that she had ever learned about jazz, gospel or blues in the west to share with Volodya. While they were engrossed in this, Alya tapped on the door and entered with a bottle of brandy, some cheese, bread and a cut-up cake that she served. She settled herself comfortably with an air of possession. When the three were seated, the woman's eyes swept up and down Jennifer appraisingly. She asked the usual questions in broken English. Where did she work? Was she married?

Jennifer responded more quickly this time on the marriage question. She had decided to answer questions with the vague, "My husband and I no longer live together," rather than a more elaborate explanation.

Volodya switched on a radio that played American swing music. "It's time for Voice of America," he told her. "Reception is good at this time of day."

"They must be broadcasting from somewhere outside of the Soviet Union?"

"Military base in Germany, I think."

"Please eat," said Alya, who was not having any of the cake herself.

Jennifer was just getting ready to ask Alya about herself when the woman swung toward Volodya in a gesture of approval. She rose, made her apologies, and left the bedroom with a significant glance at the bed. Jennifer had the uncomfortable feeling that some kind of tacit agreement had been reached between Alya and Volodya. She wanted to ask him who the woman was, what relationship did she have to Volodya, but the questions wouldn't form on her lips. Anyway, he seemed preoccupied, listening intently to the music, humming along and dancing around the room, finally spinning to a halt at his chair.

"Will we go out again now?" she asked him, knowing the answer.

"Not tonight," he replied. "Tomorrow, I take you to jazz music. Do you like dancing?"

They didn't hear the front door open but they sensed that it had—that Alya had left the apartment. They came to a pause in the conversation and gazed at one another. It was becoming late, but Jennifer felt wide awake, alive. There was such expression on his face, in his eyes, she thought. Their bodies leaned closer and closer across the table.

Finally, he broke the silence. "You are *sladki*," he said with a cheeky grin. "You know what this means, '*sladki*'?" And he lifted one of the cubes from the sugar bowl. Sweet.

And that was it. They kissed. They made love on his lumpy single bed, lying together and breathing on one another's skin with cognac brandy breath. He was hard, muscular, but he came inside her body so gently. As her back arched to meet him, she felt exquisite joy. His skin glistened in sweat; his smile melted her to the soul.

Afterwards, he sat up in the bed and looked at her lying there. Then he frowned, fumbling for words. It seemed there was a delicate question to be asked. He spoke in Russian.

Jennifer translated it literally as, "It is good for you?" and she answered, "It's very good."

"No." He frowned some more. "That's not what I mean. It was good, but is it GOOD for you?" Which is how Jennifer White was to learn something that she could never have learned in a hundred years of post-graduate Russian study: in this language there were truly no words for some of the lovelier acts or the words had become crude. If the Russian lover didn't want to use the swear words, then there was simply no language. So it took a few minutes to understand that he was asking whether or not she had climaxed.

As soon as she realized, she answered him, "You're right. It was not good for me," aware that she was teasing, challenging him.

He embraced her again. And this time, in the midnight blue dusk of the shabby room, it was breathtakingly, deliciously good for her.

6.

JAZZ WITH ELLA

LENINGRAD, JULY 12, 1974

As she slipped into the hotel dining room the next morning, breakfast was almost over and several of the students were pushing away their plates. Jennifer was conscious of the smirks. Surely no one had observed her early morning jog from the streetcar back to the hotel. She told herself not to care. *They can't know where I was last night. Anyway, it's none of their business.* At a corner table Professor Chopyk was poring over some notes. *At least he didn't miss me,* she thought, *so I won't get another lecture on my morals.* It was unlucky that Hank, who was given to ribald comment, was standing at the buffet table.

"It's omelette this morning, *Mrs.* White. Good for your physical energy." She could have sworn he winked. The use of the word *Mrs.* grated on her. She had just slept with a virtual stranger, though she was technically a married woman. But she forced herself to smile pleasantly at the red-haired man. Catching Natasha staring at her, she met the gaze headlong. Natasha turned away and rapped her knuckles on the table, calling for silence.

"Now that everyone is present," she said with a glance at Jennifer, "I will inform you of today's itinerary. At 10 a.m. exactly, you are to assemble at the bus. We go to Peter's Palace which was built by Peter the Great after he was inspired by a visit to the great French palace of Versailles in 1717. You will see his famous office, his own Monplaisir, with its view to the west, and the picture gallery with its 365 paintings. There will be time to walk in the gardens to see the golden statues and the trick water fountains that might surprise you with a shower." She smiled.

Damn, thought Jennifer. *I'm supposed to meet Volodya at 1 o'clock and it doesn't sound like we'll be back in time.* They had arranged to meet outside the hotel after his work. How could she cancel it? She could leave a note but she knew he would not want to enter the lobby to enquire. He would just wait outside, angry or disappointed. Besides, she wanted to have a serious talk today—about that woman in his apartment. Who was she? Lost in these thoughts and busy loading up her plate with food, Jennifer suddenly realized that Natasha was still speaking.

"Because Peter's palace is 28 kilometres west of Leningrad, we will spend the day there. You will not return until late this afternoon. Naturally, your teachers will want to cancel their classes." Once again she stared at Chopyk for confirmation but he was still reading his notes and he appeared to have heard not a word, so she turned to Jennifer.

"Certainly," she replied, still standing awkwardly at the buffet table holding a plate of eggs and toast. "Class will be postponed until tomorrow…." Impulsively, she added, "And I'm sorry to say that I can't join you on this excursion as much as I'd like to see Peter's Palace. I have another appointment." They stared, curious, as she settled at a table and began eating. *Oh well, just tough it out. What can they do?*

She had made sure to sit beside Paul who was lingering over his breakfast. At least he wouldn't tease her, she hoped, even if he had questions. But Paul only needed one look to see the answers written on her face.

"Enjoying the white nights?" he asked casually, holding back a smile.

"Yes, you could say that," she replied, then told him about the letter that Volodya had shown her as the least intimate incident of the past night. "It was pathetic. Ella Fitzgerald probably never even saw the letter; she maybe signed a million of them, but he hangs on to it like it's some kind of icon."

"It is an icon—to him, just from what you've told me," he replied. "It's a symbol of all he can't get here and everything he could get from the west. Ella is someone who appreciates his love of music."

"How did you get to be so smart?" she said, sighing.

★

Jennifer had met Paul Mercier during her third year of university in Toronto.

He had come on a student exchange summer session visit from the University of Vancouver with five others, mostly men. She had been drawn to him right away and they spent a glorious day strolling the campus together, talking about the Russian language and their families. He didn't seem to have much family left except his grandmother in California and Jennifer felt as if she had been cast out of her own. They sat in the campus centre's uncomfortable chairs, too hard for sleeping, just soft enough for flopping, smoked cigarettes—even though neither were smokers—and talked far into the night. At first she thought she wanted to sleep with him and made a few subtle overtures.

Jennifer had lost her virginity during the first year of college to a fraternity man who pressed his attentions on her in the back row of the movie theatre. From there, a succession of eager males had dated her but only a few had captured her interest. She didn't believe in saving it for her husband, but she wanted respect from her partner. She wanted to find the right one—someone to love when lovemaking would be a passionate, full experience.

Paul was good-looking, tall, grey-eyed, with pronounced cheekbones, and as they wandered the campus together, she found herself wondering how he would look naked, whether he would be a good lover. But when she invited him back to her shared apartment for a nightcap, he told her about his girlfriend in Vancouver, a chemistry major who sounded as exciting as two planks of wood. Jennifer backed off. In his polite, contained style, he offered her nothing but a companionship that she would soon learn to treasure. At the end of the summer they kissed on the lips, promised to write to one another and he suggested that she apply for graduate work at his university where they could be colleagues. This parting tenderness made her feel warmer than the parting kiss of her many dates. Paul was special, no doubt about it. But he wasn't the one.

The summer had scarcely faded into autumn before she met Michael. She had noticed him in the line-up at the cafeteria; he always ate at about the same time each day, moved his tray through the line efficiently, then always sat in the same spot, a table by the door. One day when the cafeteria was full, she thought *what the hell* and asked if the seat opposite him was taken. Politely, he gathered up his sprawling papers and books and indicated the seat. Then he returned to reading. She studied him. His most obvious feature was bushy black eyebrows. His thick full hair dropped to his shoulders in the current style. He was wearing a white cotton shirt with embroidery and she could see his well-proportioned body through the material.

Suddenly she felt a spasm of interest not in her consciousness, but in her thighs. Chemistry is good, she thought. He smells nice. He got up for a glass of water and she had a chance to assess the rest of him, how he moved, how he held his head, how he smiled at her on returning to the table. She smiled back and introduced herself.

"Michael White," he responded, holding out a pale hand. They shook solemnly but she could feel a shiver pass through her body. It was as if he had already placed a hand in some intimate spot, just below her breast or on her cheek. After his introduction, Michael White had little to say and he had a curious habit of speaking in a kind of shorthand: "Genetics test tomorrow morning. Big part of my grade."

"That's okay, I understand," she replied, comforting herself with the thought that since she knew where he sat, she could stop by tomorrow. But the next day he was not there. Or the next. She took to hanging around the Sciences building in hopes they would meet by chance. She would invite him somewhere this time, leave her phone number. A week passed before she saw him again at his customary seat in the cafeteria and to her horror he was sitting with another woman who giggled and preened. Though their entire interaction had been limited to a formal introduction and a 25-minute lunch break in each other's proximity, she felt betrayed. He was suddenly more attractive than ever. She waved—casually, she hoped—as she walked past with her tray then resolutely sat on the opposite side of the hall. *He looks a bit like George Harrison, the quiet Beatle,* she thought, and wondered if that was a good or bad thing.

Thus it was a huge surprise when he phoned to ask her out, especially when he told her that he had been trying to track her down through a mutual friend.

"I'd love to go out with you, thanks," she recalled saying too eagerly. His enthusiasm appeared to match hers and they spent an evening at the local pub which Michael admitted wasn't his usual style. "Bit of a work-horse," he told her in that clipped speech. "Don't do darts or downers," he said of the fashionable adolescent practice of downing a jug of beer in one go. Instead, he ordered a scotch and soda and encouraged her to order her own. She chose a screwdriver; vodka was already her favourite beverage.

It was odd when you met the right one, Jennifer thought—and there was no doubt in her mind that she had found him—you knew exactly what to say, how to respond without thinking. "If this isn't your style, let's go to the ROM tomorrow," she said. "There's an Egyptian exhibit I've been wanting to see."

"The museum. My god!"

She didn't doubt that she was on the right track. "Yes, The Royal Ontario Museum, please, then lunch at that Swiss place that everyone talks about. Okay?"

"I'd love to. Most girls—uh women—don't want to do anything like that."

Later she recalled how he fiddled with his swizzle stick, rolling it in his hand, uncurling it, biting on the end as if it were his Bic pen. Nervous habits, she thought them now. At the time, they had seemed endearing. It was all she could do not to reach over and pull him toward her, soothe his agitated hands, kiss his lips, press next to that sculpted flesh.

It was idiotic to pretend on that first date that she didn't want him. She wanted him all over her, his face between her thighs, lying on top of her hard, ready to enter. She wanted it so badly but because he was the one, she urged herself to heel and find out more about him. Her resolve lasted for about two hours and 47 minutes. As soon as he walked her back to her door, an apartment on Woodside Street, she knew she couldn't let him go without kissing him and leaning into him, one hip thrust forward to feel his level of interest in his jeans. Her leg grazed against a formidable bump.

"I want you. You want me, too?"

He nodded. She could not believe that she was the aggressor but it was right. They hardly had time to close the front door before they were both discarding clothing. "In here, quick." She led him to the bedroom and drew him onto the bed beside her.

He sucked her nipples until she wanted to scream. Their bodies fit together precisely, her high full breasts against his chin, his engorged penis between her legs. Probing with a wet finger, he located her opening, which was now pulsing in spasms. When she could stand it no longer, she demanded that he thrust into her and he obeyed. She came in a blinding rush, relaxed her body, then immediately felt aroused again.

"Go more," he whispered and pressed himself against her thighs until another orgasm wracked her body. His tongue on her sensitive spot made number three. His member was swollen and rock hard but he had still found no release. As she was feeling the fourth orgasm building, he turned her over gently, her still erect nipples grazing the bed. He came quickly, then, rubbing his penis between her legs, withdrawing and spurting onto her back until she could feel the stickiness. He sank back beside her, smiling.

"No pregnancy that way," he said briefly.

"God, pregnancy! I was really carried away. I didn't even think of it." She made a mental note to go for the pill as soon as possible; she could get it through Planned Parenthood if her doctor wouldn't give it to her. They stayed on the bed together far into the night, caressing, then dozing. About 3 a.m., Michael got up and went home.

In the days to follow she saw him twice. Once, when he stopped by her study carrel in the library to stroke her arm and explain in his clipped fashion that he had to prepare a research assignment for next week, and once more when she found herself strolling past the Sciences building again. He was at work in the lab, facing the table, and she watched him through the glass for a long while. At that moment, there was nothing more she wanted to do in the world than be with Michael for the rest of her life.

★

They were married in the spring. Her father and mother attended but her father was cool, formal. Her mother hung at his side, occasionally smiling, more often looking desperately sad. The excitement of preparation for the wedding was somewhat overshadowed by the announcement of a scholarship offered to Michael by the University of Vancouver. This was perfect as far as Jennifer was concerned; she had wanted to go there ever since Paul's visit. Her own academic progress had suffered during their courtship because she found it hard to concentrate on anything but the relationship. The long nights spent in lovemaking and the days spent yearning for a few moments together in the cafeteria had taken their toll. Slowly, the world was getting back to normal and the prognosis looked good for her to enter graduate school in Vancouver. She would study the work of Russian author Maxim Gorky and her father be damned. For a brief time, she was gloriously, unreasonably happy.

★

When the couple arrived in Vancouver, Jennifer made immediate plans to see Paul again. They arranged to meet at Paul's apartment in Kitsilano, near the beach. As she and Michael drove down Fourth Avenue in the beater car they had just bought at a used car lot and had not yet fully paid for, she fell in love with the area. It was August under a cloudless sky and her window was rolled down. Chestnut trees hung over the street. A man in a bright serape and sandals was juggling vinyl pins in front of a health food store. Another man was handing out copies of what appeared to be the local newspaper, *The Georgia Straight*. Music blared from speakers in a record shop. Crowds of tanned young people roamed the streets carrying radios and backpacks. No one seemed in a hurry and everyone smiled. "Peace, peace," one man called out to her holding up his fingers in a V as they drove by.

"Let's live here, Michael, not in the student apartments. They're so god awful concrete and gloomy."

As usual, Michael's reply was brief. "Maybe."

He'll come around as soon as he lives in Vancouver a while, she thought. Maybe he and Paul will become friends.

But that faint hope, borne briefly as they got out of the car and entered Paul's building, was quickly dashed.

"Isn't this great?" Paul said right away, hugging her and spreading his arms wide to take in the wicker chairs, battered sofa, tiny kitchen and a balcony with a glorious view of the ocean. "It reminds me of California, you know, where I grew up. I love it here." He seemed so relaxed, so laid back, as they said out in Vancouver. He shook hands warmly with Michael who returned the handshake but stared at him as if he were a lab specimen.

"It's great to see you here, finally, Jennifer. And Michael, too. Let me show you around." They examined some of Paul's nicer possessions including a collection of Russian literature and a brightly polished samovar, with Jennifer ooohing and aahing periodically.

"We're quite close to the Russian community centre here," he told them. "It's cool to visit."

"It's perfect," she cried. "Isn't it, Michael?"

Paul relaxed. "Just about. The only thing that would make my life complete here would be a girlfriend. Sue and I broke up." Immediately Michael's expression changed from one of puzzlement to repugnance. He began to bristle, Jennifer thought later. It had to be jealousy. But why? Paul had always been her good friend. Michael knew that, accepted it, or so he had said. *Men*, she thought with exasperation.

If you had to mark a moment that your marriage ended, you might think of one incident often not recognized until much later that signified the end. That moment occurred for Jennifer on the day of that visit, after the couple returned to their temporary digs at a student residence. Jennifer was elated, caught up in the colour and atmosphere of the new city of Vancouver. Michael was depressed, glowering. Suddenly, he brightened. "I'm going in to the lab to check out the new hygroscope," he announced.

"But we just got here!" she wailed. "Don't you want to help me unpack some of these things...and we've got to find an apartment."

"We did not 'just get here,'" he replied. "We've been here two days, bought a car, looked at student housing and visited your friend. Now, I'd like to go to the lab." Without waiting for her reply, he picked up the car keys and left the room.

Even though Michael's logic sounded sensible, it left Jennifer with an ill feeling that was somewhat dispelled later that night in their tiny dorm room when he made love to her tenderly, sprawled across the standard issue, single beds that they had pushed together.

But for the most part, the pattern repeated. Jennifer alone and at loose ends until the semester started; Michael buried in the lab sometimes from morning to 10 at night. She decided not to mope. She would take the formal tour of the library, learn things, meet her new colleagues and immerse herself in work. There was plenty to do and the sooner she established credibility with her professors the sooner she would be teaching an undergraduate class which would help with income.

If Michael could do it, she could do it. Working hard warranted approval. At least, it had always worked with her father.

★

Jennifer spent the time from breakfast until 1 o'clock in her Leningrad hotel room reading restlessly, first the guidebook, then a story about the Hermitage that Volodya had bought for her, then her class notes. The group had only today and part of tomorrow in Leningrad before they would fly down to Rostov-na-Donu for a cruise on the Volga River. *Only two more days*, she thought, *and one night*. Her body ached to spend the next night as she had the last one, wrapped in Volodya's arms. Since she and Michael had parted, she had not wanted any other man in this way. *I'm crazy*, she thought. *This is the very man I can't have.*

In the afternoon, she met him on the hotel steps. They kissed shyly, like newlyweds. Today, he suggested going to a memorial cemetery which seemed a strange choice of tourist attractions.

"You asked me about the history of Leningrad, remember? Well, I will show you its history." She knew he had lived in the city all of his life and he had told her briefly that his family had endured the three-year wartime siege when the area was surrounded by German troops.

They would go by taxi, which Volodya hired using the simple expedient of standing in the square until the vehicle approached, then throwing himself in front of it and smacking the hood. The car shuddered to a halt. Volodya and the driver haggled furiously in rapid Russian for a moment, then he and Jennifer climbed in.

"I thought you were crazy—jumping in front of the car!"

"It is difficult sometimes to find a taxi," he said. "One must be courageous."

She settled back in her seat. "Vlad, we have to talk," she went on in English so the taxi driver would not understand. Volodya nodded but seemed disinclined to look her in the eye. She began, "There's something I'd like to know about you. You haven't told me much about your past. Have you never married? It may not be any of my business," she went on, "but these last few days have been great…and I'm wondering…."

He only stared out the window at the passing cars.

"That woman, Alya, in your apartment. She's more than a neighbour, isn't she?"

"She's my wife," he answered glumly.

"You mean your ex-wife?"

"No," he sighed. "We are still married. We live together."

Jennifer's heart gave a sickening lurch.

"Still married! But how could you…? Oh, I should never have stayed there last night. We made love in the same house—in the next room!"

"What is the word in English? I can't remember…," he asked.

"Adulterer, you mean?"

"No," he grimaced. "Is that what you think? You Americans do not understand this. You have big homes—you even have homes for your dogs and for your cars. Here it is very difficult to find a home. One must have papers, a permit to live in certain cities." He glanced at the driver to see if he showed signs of comprehension. "Alya and I have a residency permit to live together as husband and wife in Leningrad. But our days of marriage are over. We no longer love one another. It is like a child, you know what I mean?"

"You have children, too?" Jennifer was rapidly becoming more horrified. Could she not have asked these questions in the first three days before she became involved with him?

"We have no children," he said, smiling. "Custody. That's the word I only now remember. We both have custody of this permit. Neither of us wishes to give it up. My residency permit says Leningrad. It is my home. Without this permit, I will have to live many miles outside of the city—in some suburb."

"And that's so bad? They're new apartments, aren't they?"

"Tchaa! They are built by the lazy Soviet worker. The apartments are built one year, the next year they fall down. The lifts don't work, the windows look at other apartments. To ride the bus into the city takes many hours. It is horrible."

Jennifer was surprised. This account of modern Soviet housing certainly was at odds with Natasha's description of "well-appointed flats with all the conveniences."

"I don't know what to think. Maybe you're right. I don't understand," she said.

Just then the taxi pulled up in front of a gate with the words Piskaryovskaya Cemetery written over the arch. Once again, Volodya haggled in such a rapid fire with the driver that Jennifer couldn't follow. "He will wait for us," Volodya reassured her.

The cemetery was green and lush with birch trees, but they were surrounded by dirge music which seemed to come from the skies. It took her a moment to realize that the sound originated from the many speakers mounted in the trees. She looked around for gravestones and saw none. They walked up a wide, straight path, a boulevard overshadowed on either side by vast rectangular mounds covered in grass, each the size of half a football field, dozens of them lined up next to one another in parade ground symmetry. On each of the mounds was posted a simple sign. The first one read 1941. And the next also read 1941. Then the signs read 1942, and in the distance 1943, stretching onward on each mound toward a marble memorial at the far end of the boulevard.

"My god, they're mass graves." She turned to Volodya in bewilderment. "Just this plaque, no names, no words from their families… ." They walked on in silence toward the memorial. The eerie music grew louder.

"Sit with me here on this bench," he said, taking her hand gently. "You asked to know about me and my family. So look around you. Except for my mother and aunt, most of my family are here. My father fought the fascists—just outside of the city. He wasn't a brave man. He had no choice. To serve in the army was better than dying in Leningrad."

"And your mother?"

"She survived the siege. She had no food except the ration. She didn't get skinny though. She puffed up, she told me, her legs swollen—and her face, too—with disease."

At that moment, Jennifer could feel a disease working through her own body in sympathy, a horrible nausea, her head heavy, her arms like lead, then only emptiness.

Volodya went on: "That first winter, 1941, she told me that many people froze to death on the streets. Those who survived were too weak to bury the others. So they just stepped over the dead on their way to stand in the food lines."

"But she lived?"

"Somehow she lived. When the city was liberated, my father returned and nursed her back to health. He had an army ration; it was only a little more food than the usual ration. He died two years after I was born in 1947. He had been wounded in the chest. He couldn't breathe."

"That's ghastly. So your mother had to raise you by herself?"

"Yes, she and her sister. But I don't tell you for pity. This is what I want to tell you." He stood up. "Look around here—at this memorial. All the memorials around town are built in honour of our glorious fallen comrades. So many memorials for the dead."

Jennifer had a glimmer of understanding now. She shook off the nausea.

"A few years ago I looked at how my mother was living—how damp is her apartment, how she still stands in line for food, and I decide to write to Comrade Brezhnev. I asked him how come so many things are done for the dead and so little for the living." Jennifer shifted uneasily. "Soon two special men came to my mother's door. You know what this means, special men?"

"KGB," she whispered.

"Yes, they question my mother. What is her son doing? Does he make trouble? The neighbours see these men come to the apartment. So she is in more trouble after they visit than before. The neighbours shunned her, her friends did not call."

"Did she resent you writing to Brezhnev?"

"Yes, she wanted only to forget the war years. Finally she died, still poor, still undernourished, three years ago.

"And what did they do to you?"

"At work I was called in before the commissar. I was labelled a hot-head—that was the first trouble. A note was placed on my work record." He grew quiet. Jennifer found herself trembling. Stories like these made her realize she was not the first visitor to love Russia and hate the Soviet Union.

"You know, my mother and my aunt had given me everything," Volodya continued. "Any extra food, extra potatoes they grew on their plot. Toys. Candy. Everything to make sure I would be happy and not go hungry."

"They must have been wonderful. Is your aunt still alive?"

"Yes, but she's not quite right in the head. I think the English say she has gone crackers." He grinned at this phrase.

"The English say funny things," she replied, happy to see him smile again. "I think they'd also say barmy. In Canada, we might say that she'd lost her marbles." She tried to explain what was meant by losing one's marbles to a bemused Volodya and why a child's game should apply to a senile old woman. This phrase struck them both as so hilarious that they sat on the edge of a mass grave amid the swelling funereal music and howled with laughter.

"I think it's time to leave," groaned Jennifer. "This is disrespectful of the dead."

"One must laugh. It is necessary."

★

Their taxi had waited at the gate, and they awakened the driver and climbed in.

"After you leave Leningrad, I wonder if we shall ever see each other again?" said Volodya, suddenly serious once more.

"I don't know. It's possible that I'll come back another year." She glanced at him. "Or maybe you could leave the country. . . ."

They sat in silence, each thinking about the future. After the driver deposited them on a bridge at the far end of Nevskiy Prospekt, they climbed out, paid him, and watched him drive away. Volodya spoke again. "There are only three ways I can leave the country. One, I could marry a Jew and leave for Israel. But I am already married and I have described to you why this would be difficult. Two, I could walk out. Some winters in the past the Gulf of Finland has frozen over, and I always hoped that this would happen again. I would walk over the ice to Finland and live in freedom."

Jennifer reeled at the dramatic picture this presented—Volodya, with a frozen beard like Doctor Zhivago, staggering over the ice floes, alone, friendless.

"Three, I could get help from the west." Here he looked at her longingly. "That American I told you about, the one I met in my last year working with Intourist, she has made enquiries on my behalf. She asked the US Senator Henry Jackson for his help. Do you know this man? He listened to her plea, but so far I have heard nothing."

"I don't know him. He must be one of the Americans who tries to get dissidents out of this country. I read something about it in the newspaper. But, Vlad, does this mean you've heard from this American woman recently? How?" He shook off her questions. "What can I do? Also, I don't know any big political wheels like U.S. senators."

"Talk to him. When you return, you must contact him. Please make a case for me. Others have left the country at his request." He reached for her hand. "You do understand now, don't you? Why you must help me?" He looked as if he was about to drop to his knees and plead.

"I'll do what I can," she told him reluctantly and felt his enthusiasm drain away. He dropped her hand. *But what can I possibly do?* she thought. *And what obligation do I have to do anything?* She remained silent for a moment, recovering her composure while Volodya's expression clouded. He was not finished. His face reddened.

"My path, my future is through you. I feel it. You can do this for me. You say 'do what I can.' This is not enough. Please, I have fought for so long."

She was astonished by the passion in his words. But passion described him, for sure. Volodya in bed—the hard, muscular body, the energy. Or playing the piano with gusto, challenging the music. And his passion for living—greeting a total stranger on the bridge over the Moika, leading his crew of younger guys. But his intensity today was different; it was foreign to her, frightening.

"Those years with the American woman, I waited," he went on. "Also she said, 'do what I can, do what I can'. Every year it becomes more difficult, you understand? My job becomes more low, more despicable." He looked around as if seeming to notice for the first time that they were amid a sea of people, six across, on the wide sidewalk of Leningrad's main street. He stepped into an alley, pulling her along with him. He turned her to face him, taking her wrists in a tight grip. She saw that his whole body was trembling, his voice intense and penetrating. "Please, you must help me. If there is any way you can help me, even if it is something that is not permitted—you must do it. Do you understand?"

Suddenly she did understand. This was the price for enjoying this man. It was as simple as that. You always had to pay in the end. She had found that out with Michael. Now, she was to discover it with Volodya.

"If I can think of some way, I'll do it," she responded, her eyes filling with tears. "But right now I can't think, especially while you're shaking me. Let go!"

He dropped her arms and leaned back against the nearest wall.

"*Sladki, sladki, sladki*," he murmured. "Forgive me. It is so important to me."

They were silent for a few minutes while the traffic in the main street continued to slide past their alley.

"What did you mean 'not permitted?' How could I do anything on this trip that's not permitted?"

He straightened up, hope in his eyes. "Sometimes people can be persuaded to help. Your tour guide, for example?"

Jennifer shook her head. "Not Natasha and not Chopyk either. How could they be persuaded? You mean bribery?"

"Foreign currency is valuable here. We want your American dollars." He added dryly, "We just do not admit it."

"Volodya, I have no money. I'm here as a lecturer, like a teaching assistant, the lowest of the low. I don't even get paid, just a free trip. And how would we get you out of the country? You'd have to stow away and go through all kinds of bureaucratic stuff when we arrived in Canada, and you'd run the risk of being sent right back."

His chin sagged on his chest.

"What you've asked puts me in a really difficult position."

He nodded despondently, his outburst having apparently run its course.

"Plus the fact that we're leaving Leningrad tomorrow and I don't have time to make any such arrangements. We can't let anybody know about this," Jennifer said finally, "or I'd be in as much trouble as you."

"Agreed. But if, by some chance...." His voice sank to that low, penetrating tone again. "If by chance—no, just listen to me." She had turned away again in frustration. "If you have to get a message to me quickly—if some opportunity presents itself on the Volga cruise—please tell me that you will help. Please." He apparently took her silence for assent because he went on: "There should be some words we would say in your message. Something that means I can leave the country."

Unwillingly, she was listening, humouring him. It was as if she were a child playing a spy game. "Okay. All right," she found herself agreeing. "Some slang phrase that sounds good in English but is not known in Russian.'Exit stage left'?"

"Hmmm, this phrase is unfamiliar. Something about going to hear jazz music, maybe. Jazz with... Ella. That's it. We'll go out together to hear jazz with Ella."

"Okay, I'll remember that," she answered reluctantly. "But I'll only use it if I have to—that is, if something comes up."

He brightened. "You are amazing, exceptional!" He kissed her deeply, fully, pulling her body closer into his arms. She could feel herself responding with a dangerous warmth that turned her limp.

As quickly, he drew back. "Now, enough of these matters." Before she could protest, he took an arm and hurried her down the street. "Tonight we go to the jazz restaurant to hear music!"

7.

DANCE THE BLACK TOOTHED MAN

JULY 13, 1974

It was hot and stuffy in the small bedroom, the two of them entwined on the single bed. Jennifer awakened at four in the morning—that same royal blue lighting up the sky—craving water from the bottle on Volodya's nightstand. Her head throbbed. She grasped at a thought: something about a man with black teeth. Was he following them? And what had she agreed to yesterday on that Leningrad street? She climbed out of bed, making noise deliberately with the bottle and a cup. She wanted to know now—not wait until morning. They had been at a restaurant listening to some lousy jazz musicians…there had been many toasts. That she remembered. She sat on the edge of the bed. Today she was leaving. It was imperative that they re-run that conversation in which he asked—demanded—that she help him. Or had that all been part of the dream, a colourful, sometimes nightmarish scene in a loud, smoky restaurant…? No, it had truly happened: the bad breath in her face, the belt buckle pressing into her… She gulped the water.

"Volodya, wake up! I want to know who that man was—the one I danced with. Wake up."

He rolled over to face her, his eyes already alert, shining. He reached out for the water glass. *He knows what I'm talking about.*

"Why do you ask? He didn't follow us home. I watched." He got out of bed draping a sheet about his naked body, and searched for his cigarettes. "That man is nothing—just a man, an official. You understand."

"No, I don't understand. Has he done something bad to you?"

Volodya snorted. "Tchaa, he's responsible for everything bad. Hard to explain." He took a long slow drag on the foul-smelling cigarette.

"I believe you should try your damnedest to explain!" Before he could open his mouth, she went on, "And don't stall by calling me an 'amazing woman.' I need that explanation—before I agree to anything." Her head throbbed; it was difficult to maintain this anger.

He sighed, puffed slowly, looked her in the eye. "Do you think me intelligent? Educated?"

She nodded.

"Yes, it is true. I attended the higher learning institute. Passed my tests. Fluent in languages, good at mathematics. Then why am I working at a lowly job fixing machines for a nasty man like that one last night?"

"*He's* your boss?"

"You do not understand. He is everyone's boss. He signs the papers, he records the problems. Remember, we have only one employer in the Soviet Union—the state. You cannot understand. Let me tell you about my life…when I worked for Intourist, he—or another one like him—wrote down that I did not hand out these special pamphlets about how Lenin built the art galleries and museums. That note is placed on my record. Then he wrote down that I am friendly with the American woman. That is on my record, too."

"Yes, you told me about that…"

"So I am sent to another job—in the department store. Same thing. This man writes that I do not volunteer for the special work shifts or some other nonsense. So it goes on…."

Jennifer was silent.

"And now I work in the streets with vending machines. This is how they grind us down, make us behave." He snorted again. "And Americans worry about how many political prisoners there are in labour camps."

She shifted uneasily. It was she who had told him about the current status of the dissident author Alexander Solzhenitsyn and his books that documented the hardship of such camps.

"It is not necessary to send me to a labour camp," he continued, his voice rising. "I am just a little man. Why do they need to build a labour camp for me when I can be demeaned right here in Leningrad at no expense to the state?"

"I'm sorry," she said softly. "I had to understand." The sheet had slipped to the floor and he stood before her naked, a perfect, muscular figure but a flawed human being, a petty dissident who liked jazz, neither a threat to the state nor a blessing. She was surprised to discover that she loved him.

★

Later that morning, they walked the quiet streets back to the hotel in silence. Twice her feet stumbled along the rough sidewalk; she couldn't seem to pick them up, couldn't send the right commands from her brain. *When I'm down, it's always my motor skills that disappear first.* Strange to think they were the same feet that had been so nimble on the dance floor the night before. By contrast, her brain was still flashing bizarre and colourful pictures from her dreams to her waking imagination. She imagined Volodya getting on the plane with her, Chopyk standing at the gate spluttering with indignation. She pictured Volodya sitting in a coffee bar in Vancouver or New Orleans watching a performance of black gospel singers, happy and confident. Then the image changed to the man with black teeth. He had somehow replaced Vlad; he was triumphant, grinning. But they were no more than images; in reality, she would not see this grotesque dancing partner again.

She and Volodya said their goodbyes on a street corner opposite the Hotel Astoria. She used the word for goodbye, *proschay*. Not *dosvidanie*, until we see each other again. He responded with a solemn *dosvidanie*. The interaction was anti-climactic. They kissed, and idiotically, they shook hands as if this formal gesture would somehow distance them.

"Please write," he told her. "Send me a telegram after you finish your trip on the Volga." He smiled. "Maybe there will be some reason for me to come to Moscow for your departure." A lock of hair fell across his forehead and he swept it aside self-consciously, posing, as if to give her a perfect memory.

*He still thinks I can help him, s*he thought with a sinking heart. "Okay, sure." At a loss for anything more meaningful to say, she glanced away. It was just past eight, but she caught sight of Chopyk waving at her from inside the hotel lobby like a worried father who had waited up all night for her return. She had almost forgotten why she was in the Soviet Union in the first place. "Am I in trouble?" she asked aloud. Volodya appeared not to notice.

She stepped back from him, said goodbye once more, turned to face the hotel and, like a dutiful daughter, crossed the street and entered the lobby. She didn't look back.

"There you are, Mrs. White. I hope you'll join us for breakfast today," said Chopyk with only a hint of irony. He stroked his beard and stared at her with curiosity in his eyes. "I understand from Maria that you have a class scheduled for this morning."

"Yes," replied Jennifer tersely. *Don't explain, don't apologize. Last night is none of his business.* "I want to hear the students' experiences in Leningrad. I have my own to share, too."

"But I also know that you have been cancelling classes while in Leningrad…."

"As we discussed that first night," she broke in quickly, starting across the lobby.

"Yes, agreed…but…." Chopyk followed, taking small, deliberate steps beside her. She matched his fussy gait. *What is this nonsense all about? Surely he isn't going to punish me?*

"Since I have been carrying on with classes while in Leningrad for any who care to study," he sniffed, "I think it only right that you should lead both groups, juniors and seniors, while on the Volga cruise."

So that was it. Once again, he had hit her at her most guilty moment. He wanted to lounge on the sundeck reading his academic papers and not have to deal with a pack of rowdy students.

"Certainly. I'd be happy to do that," she answered. "I know how one's research suffers when class prep is a priority," she added archly. He appeared not to notice her tone of voice. They entered the dining room in silence.

★

That morning she ended her class by presenting a poem that Volodya had written out for her: an excerpt from "Spring in Leningrad" by the Russian war poet, Margarita Aliger. Jennifer told the students the story of the Leningrad mother who had suffered during the siege and how her son, Volodya, had been moved by this poem. Despite her own sense of loss, Hank's bad mood and Ted's hangover, the students rallied and they recited it in Russian, then took a stab at translating it.

"O city without light, without water!
One hundred and twenty five grams of blockade rationed bread…
Savage rumbling of trouble
from the pitiless, dead sky.

The very stones groaned, the pavement gasped,
but the people lived, found strength,
and those who died like warriors, lie intimately in fraternal graves."

They worked at it, trying to get it right, until the bus arrived to take them to the airport.

8.

TWIN PASSIONS

JULY11, 1974 - VOLGA REGION

The public official for the village of Suzdal, Toglyatti Oblast, Volga Region, closed his office door, stamped down the stairs and mounted his bicycle. Carefully and thoughtfully he pedalled around bumps in the unpaved road. Each smooth curve of the muddy bank reminded him of Tanya's buttocks as she insinuated them sensuously against his belly. That peaked clump of grass reminded him of her breast, her left one, majestic, without peer. Along the rutted path ahead he spied a clump that reminded him of her right breast, rounded and smooth. Today, he had several intriguing questions to ponder as he cycled, but somehow they all led his thoughts back to his mistress.

His tires skidded in some wet gravel. He cursed. "I, Pyotr Vladimirovich Korpov, am a public servant. I should not have to use a broken-down bicycle like a child!" His name was on the list for a Zhiguli, a tidy little car like the Italian Fiat. His name had been on the list for nearly a year now. He and about 5,000 others. There had been an official car, of course, a state-owned car for performing his duties, but five months ago it had heaved an enormous sigh, belched quantities of steam and crawled to the side of the road to die. According to the mechanic, it could be fixed but there were no replacement parts. There were never any replacement parts. Pyotr had requisitioned them from Moscow, of course, expressed his needs in writing on the appropriate government form, only to have it officially ignored by all concerned. It was embarrassing to have to let the mechanic pursue his own shady channels for the acquisition of car parts. Of course, Pyotr knew that filling in forms was not how to get things done in the great Soviet Union, but the fact was, no one had ever taught him that all-important lesson in how to expedite matters through unofficial channels. He pondered why his father who had been a Party member, an administrative commissar, had not taught his son this valuable lesson. Some people knew how to get things done: how to bribe, how to barter, how to curry favour. Funny that the knowledge seemed to come naturally to schoolchildren. *It's not something I was ever taught in school*, he thought. Still, he couldn't really complain; things had worked out for him. Once he had achieved this valuable post serving the public, he had also acquired a lover.

For a moment, the twin passions of sex and injustice overcame him, and he leaned into the curve, pedalling furiously, a red flush rising on his face. "I deserve a car. Tanya and I deserve a car."

After a while, he slowed once more and cycled methodically. He frowned. It seemed these same, repetitive, cursed thoughts would never leave his head. Perhaps it was just as well, for in the rare moments that he was satiated with Tanya and allowed his thoughts to wander, another powerful thought almost overcame him. Fear. Raw, stuttering fear. Last summer, he had screwed a precocious, local teenager, a fine girl of sixteen. He had been fearful of discovery then, even though half the men in the village were also enjoying her favours. He shrugged. But this year he had upped the stakes considerably by making out with Tanya, the wife of Alexey Ivanovich, the police chief.

Once, in the market square, he had watched the police chief kick a dog. It was a cur, a mean, miserable thing that was harassing the weary vendors who were standing there with their pitiful cows' heads and potatoes for sale. Some of the vendors had yelled at it; one even threw a stone. But it took a swift, decisive kick from the police chief to put the dog into the dirt. It lay there whining for hours. No one dared go near it, thinking that Alexey Ivanovich would put it out of its misery. But he didn't.

Generally, the public official didn't let these thoughts gain access to his consciousness. Occasionally the fear would intrude. Only a little bit. Only enough to make him cautious, very cautious. When he allowed the fear, he always thanked the fates that he had such a magnificent vehicle as a bicycle. It was less easily traced. He could ride across the field paths instead of through town, stash the bicycle under a bush, and enter Tanya's yard on foot at night, hiding in the shadow of the rowan trees. They didn't do it at the police chief's house, although sometimes they started there, teasing and kissing. And only when they were very sure that Alexey would not be home. Then they would leave the house quietly and go into the fields.

He would have preferred his cozy bed for love-making, or even his office in the municipal building, but it was impossible. He shared his hut with his father's cousins, an old couple—dreadful gossips both—and his office was too dangerous, just down the hall from the ministry office which was associated with the police chief. Twice now he and Tanya had found the perfect spot among a field of tall grain. Today, he was cycling over to check out an old boathouse that he had spotted while fishing on the river. It was abandoned, he was sure, and away from inquisitive eyes. Of course, it didn't really matter where they went—Tanya made him feel so good, so powerful, the way she fondled and sucked. His face transformed from grimace to delight and back to grimace. If anyone had been watching him during his country cycle, they would have seen many such expressions pass over his face in the course of his 15-minute journey. But no one was watching. In the past five months, the public official had become skilled at being invisible as he pedalled about the countryside on many circuitous routes to his secret assignations.

Not for the first time, he wondered if that old fart Shukshin was onto his game. The public official had been invited to Shukshin's house for dinner and drinking next Saturday. This in itself was very odd. Shukshin rarely invited people to drink, rarely had enough drink to offer, although he was not slow to enjoy another's booze. There was definitely something very odd about the whole invitation, although there had been some intimations about Shukshin's daughter, Vera, a pleasant, curvaceous girl, usually away working in the car factory at Toglyatti. Not a bad prospect—even marriageable. It seemed she often visited home to check on her old dad, and Shukshin had specifically mentioned that Vera would be there. But shouldn't the public official be keeping track of such comings and goings? No one had told him officially that she would be coming to his district. Of course, they never did. It could mean one of two things, he guessed, clearing his head of lusty thoughts. Shukshin wanted something: not just for himself but something for Vera. Or Shukshin could be onto his secret love affair with Tanya and was going to warn him away. Yes, maybe that was it. Shukshin wasn't such a bad guy, after all. He had no love for the police chief and would surely not be inclined to see the public official's face kicked in. He would warn of danger, and then what? Pyotr Vladimirovich returned to plan A. Shukshin wanted something.

As he pedalled, he became quite sure that he would go through this same circular debate 5,000 more times before Saturday night, and that he would see 5,000 more tufts of grass that would remind him of Tanya's breasts. Such was the life of a public official.

9.
THE VOLGA BOATMEN

ROSTOV-NA-DONU, JULY 13, 1974

The Canadian student tour group were old hands at Soviet travel by the time their plane left Leningrad bound for Rostov-na-Donu in the Ukraine. The usual plump stewardesses, more relaxed on this domestic flight, handed out the usual sticky candy. The students played the now familiar game of who had the functioning seatbelts. David had no seatbelt, and he threatened to hang on to Paul's leg for the duration of the flight should they meet turbulence.

Despite the gloom of parting from Volodya, Jennifer's spirits lifted slightly. The plane was full of Ukrainians returning home—women in harem pants, swarthy men with metallic, toothy grins carrying bundles, carpets and, in one case, something alive in a cage that screeched at intervals. The passengers moved around the plane freely, paying no attention to the attendant yelling at them.

Jennifer wasn't the only one who was mourning the loss of a friend in Leningrad. Ted had ended his stay there at a party with students from the institute. He had met them on the street, and over some powerful moonshine liquor they had discoursed heavily on the problems of the cold war and had resolved to bring peace to their various countries. Unfortunately, Ted couldn't quite recall how they had proposed achieving this lofty aim. Lona had also found some friends in Moscow, it seemed, and was only now telling the group about them. Jennifer wondered if Lona would have admitted the liaison if she had not been spotted outside the hotel with a group of sharp and eager young men whom everyone suspected of being some kind of confidence tricksters. *If anyone can take care of herself, it's Lona*, thought Jennifer, and she wondered if Lona's swains had asked her to help them leave the country. Then, in an attempt to shake off the memories of Volodya—at least keep these thoughts from paralyzing her—she began to think about the next leg of the trip, the Volga River cruise and the visit to the Gorky Museum in Kazan.

When the plane finally arrived in Rostov and the door opened, a wave of heat greeted them. Though they were now technically still in the Soviet Union, in essence and atmosphere they were almost in Asia: the city perched on the Sea of Azov, gateway to the Black Sea. Natasha was waiting for them, having flown on ahead to make their cruise arrangements. As soon as they were assembled on the bus, she launched into the history of Rostov on the Don River, how it was occupied during the war, what they would find there now.

"We will go to the market place. It is very colourful," she assured them. Her face gleamed with anticipation in showing off this flourishing agricultural centre. They stopped at the market and ate fresh strawberries bought from a street vendor, ladles of creamy *kefir* and bottles of warm beer.

Chopyk purchased a loaf of heavy black bread and showed it to Maria. "Good nutrition there," he affirmed, prodding at the loaf. "Unrefined wheat—a testimony to how the Ukraine has boosted the agricultural economy of the entire country." He didn't notice Maria roll her eyes at his speech that sounded so much like Natasha's.

Hank bought a loofah, a type of vegetable gourd, from a stall that had been decorated with dozens of them, and he entertained the shoppers by miming a clumsy man taking a shower. Soon, most of the group had bought loofahs for souvenirs or were busy taking photos of the others. There was one more stop at a local history museum before the bus finally pulled up at the dock beside an opulent, freshly painted riverboat.

"Whoa, is that whole boat for us?" Hank whistled.

Maria shook her head. "No, I think we're sharing with those guys." She pointed at another tour group idling on the wharf, snapping pictures of the river. By their well-cut blazers and designer travel bags, they looked to be Americans, somewhat older than their group and mostly men.

Natasha launched into her explanation. "Please, soon you will be boarding the motor vessel you see before you, called the *Yuri Dolgoruki*. The boat is 96.5 metres long with a beam of 14 metres and it can travel 27 mph carrying a full complement of 200 guests."

"Yuri Long Arm," Jennifer translated the boat's name to the others, "the founder of Moscow."

Natasha smiled. "Correct. This riverboat has taken Soviet citizens on their vacations before, but it has never been used by westerners. You are privileged. You might be the first westerners that villagers on the Volga have ever met." Here she frowned as if talking to naughty children. "I ask that you be considerate in this matter." She paused and scanned their faces. Most of the students stared back blankly. "We will be joined by these cultural tourists from America. They arrived in Moscow only two days ago and are interested in great Soviet achievements in the arts, so you will be sure to have mutual interests."

Lona's head shot up. Jennifer caught the movement. So did David. They glanced at one another.

"If they're interested in art, why are they on the Volga?" asked Maria in a whisper.

"Beats me," said David. Natasha continued, waving in the direction of a tall, lean man standing at attention on deck. "We will also welcome our cruise director, Ivan Nikolaevich, and his staff."

"Read KGB," said Hank under his breath.

"Do you really think they'd bother to have KGB on a boat with tourists?" asked Maria.

"Of course they would. Remember what that editor said in Leningrad—about one of us being recruited before the trip was over?"

"But he was a provocateur, Mrs. White said. We don't know he was telling the truth."

Jennifer overheard some of this conversation but only nodded. It seemed to her all a riverboat needed was a captain and crew. Natasha did quite enough directing. What other function would a cruise director serve?

Their concerns evaporated after going aboard. The vessel was sleek and large for a riverboat: two decks with a promenade at the stern and what turned out to be a glassed-in dining room at the bow that could seat fifty people. Their cabins were on the lower deck, both fore and aft, and each student had a neat compartment with a bunk bed, chair, desk and sink. Jennifer noted that a speaker hung above each bed—*to wake us up in the morning with a song?* The communal washrooms were down the passage. The boat would not carry its full capacity; they learned that they and the Americans were to be the only guests on board.

"This is lovely," Maria called out to Jennifer, emerging from her cabin next door. "I'm going up on deck. I'm sure I saw some comfy chairs. I want to glide along watching the scenery."

"I'll join you," said Jennifer, after having a quick look around her cabin and stowing her bags.

Just before sunset, the *Yuri Dolgoruki* pulled away from the wharf onto the River Don and quickly left the hum of Rostov behind. Picturesque scenes melted past: a tangle of cottonwoods, small wooden boats upturned on the shore, the shouts of children playing on the banks, and birds flocking in the trees. Quite a few of the group had assembled on the deck to enjoy the peacefulness.

It's these moments that make me love Russia, thought Jennifer, her energy rising.

She surprised herself by asking suddenly, "There's a great story written by Maxim Gorky whose pen name, as we all know, means 'bitter.' Does anyone want to hear? It's called 'The Nightingale' and it's set on a river in just such a boat as this."

Paul smiled. "Sure, tell us a bedtime story, teacher." Some of the others knew the story too, but nodded assent.

Jennifer related: "Let's see if I've remembered it right. A group of first class passengers, a mother, father, daughter and an older man, are on a paddle steamer on the Volga. They are rich and accustomed to travelling the world seeing amazing sights. While sitting on the deck one evening, just like this, they hear the exquisite singing of a nightingale, a *solovey*. They're all much moved by the clear sound of the bird, especially the two women—a young girl and a married lady, perhaps more so than the father and older man who accompany them. After the song is over, each listener becomes involved in his or her own dreamy contemplation. Finally, a sailor passes them on deck and they comment to him on the joy they feel from the uplifting song. But he tells them that what they were listening to was not a nightingale at all, but a young boy aboard the boat who whistles bird imitations for money." Jennifer paused and watched the wake ripple against the shore.

"The passengers receive this shattering news in different ways: the young girl begins to weep, the married woman becomes vague and far away. The father is truly embarrassed having delivered a sentimental soliloquy on the bird. The older man ignores the matter. It's the father that sums up the story when he points out that if the sailor had not come along they would have remained convinced that they had heard a bird famed by the poets rather than a scrubby little village lad. 'To learn the truth is not so great a pleasure...when the illusion is more beautiful.'"

David smiled. "You know, I don't know when Gorky wrote that, but it's the utterly perfect story for this country in 1974. Don't you find that so much that's told to us is a beautiful illusion when the truth is really 'bitter'?"

"Yeah, I know what you mean," Paul continued. "The Soviets are like the old man—they just ignore the failures. The elevators that don't work. The trucks that break down. The harvests that don't yield what they expect. We visitors are like the father—we have to put a name to it, admire the beauty, then we point out that it's not the truth. It's no wonder they don't really like our visits."

"This is great philosophizing," Maria cut in, "but I hear the truth right now." She leaned over the railing. "I'm sure I hear a real nightingale singing." The notes were pure and true, haunting. The group was quiet for a long time, listening, delighted.

Finally Paul got up from his deck chair. "Nah, it was just a scrubby little village lad."

★

Paul Mercier returned to his cabin with the intention of diving into the definitive biography of the Sentimentalist period writer Karamzin that he had been trying to finish before the end of the trip. It had been difficult to find any study time because of their rigorous sightseeing schedule, though his conversations in Chopyk's advanced class had been informative. *That's one thing about the guy, he is a serious scholar.* He wondered if academia was truly his own calling. Did he really want to end up like Chopyk—an old lady, unloved by students and women alike? When they started out on this trip, he had found it easier to read the Sentimentalist view of nature in literature than to be out in the streets of Moscow actually viewing the real thing. But while they were in Leningrad something new had been emerging, something not found in books. He had been taking enjoyment from the scenery; it was refreshing. And he had even been moved by the rich, barbaric Russian history he saw depicted in paintings and church frescoes. For amusement, Paul had been keeping an informal list of the countless statues of Lenin they had seen to date, the endless art galleries, museums, and palaces of culture they had visited, but now he threw down these lists in disgust. Tonight he was restless and distracted by the sound of musicians tuning on the upper deck, probably in the lounge. He realized that he wanted something else, something more, something he had wanted all his life, as far back as he could remember.

Paul's early childhood in Montreal was a jumble of memories that seemed to snag on that final, definitive week prior to his eighth birthday. He remembered buying party balloons with his mom, finding a present hidden under her bed, one that he had shaken eagerly. He recalled her last words to him before setting out for downtown. "Bye bye, dear. Listen to Angie now."

He had run to the door eagerly with his babysitter, Angie, to find two policemen standing on the doorstep. They told the babysitter, in front of the small boy, that his mother had been killed instantly in a car accident on busy Sherbrooke Boulevard. He had never liked police ever since. At first, he couldn't cry, which was odd, but that came later at the funeral.

Then, his birthday party forgotten, his Aunt Olivia arrived at the house to take care of him. He remembered her phoning his estranged father to inform him at the mining camp in Shafferville, and his father's subsequent refusal to attend the funeral.

It was difficult to recall memories from before this event. Sometimes he recaptured a few glimpses: his mother as she read him bedtime stories, some opera music playing—she liked opera—the scent of her perfume, something spicy, gingery. He recalled also a few school friends, a kindly teacher, and being a good student—the report cards confirmed that. But his life hadn't really begun until his next full, rich memory—the day he went to live in La Jolla, California.

After the funeral and five days after his birthday, he and Aunt Olivia had travelled south, a long journey on a train. It was stuffy and monotonous; he had quickly filled in all his colouring books. He slept sitting up, his small head bobbing uncomfortably on Olivia's bony shoulder. Once, he awakened in the night to feel the train rushing through darkness, and the thought became confused with his mother, how she felt now, rushing through some tunnel on her way to heaven. He cried a little, awakening his aunt but she didn't shush him.

The day they arrived at Grandmother Yvonne's house, everything changed. As he stepped from the taxicab, a soothing lightness seemed to fill his body. Coming in from the San Diego train station he had already noticed his first palm tree, and now he gazed in awe at a tree with dark green, shiny leaves in his grandmother's front yard.

"Yes, those are really oranges hanging there," Olivia told him. At home, oranges had only appeared in the fruit bowl or the refrigerator. Now, the hot, steamy air filled his nostrils with scents of flowers—he didn't know what type—he supposed roses because that's what they had back home, although these smells were more like cinnamon toast. After grey Montreal, the grass was the greenest he had ever seen and as he started up the flagstone walk, his heel came down hard on something that crunched. He looked at the bottom of his shoe and there was slime on it.

"Ooooh, yuk. That's a snail," said Olivia.

He was fascinated with the tiny chips of snail shell and was still picking them off when Grandmother Yvonne, his mother's mother, rushed out to meet them. She was a tall, tanned woman with scarves of yellow, red and blue tied in her hair. Her face was wrinkled like a peanut shell, and her hair had a streak of white through it, but she didn't act like an old woman.

"Welcome! Welcome!" she bellowed. Her movements were eager as she enveloped Paul in a huge embrace and pulled him into her life.

Grandmother Yvonne's house was pink. (In Montreal, no one had pink houses.) It sprawled all on one level—a huge living room with a piano, built-in bookshelves, large paintings with little lights above them, a dining room with cabinets of silver utensils and more bookcases. At the end of a long hall was a solarium and swimming pool. Even the bedrooms were strange—their walls covered in cowboy paintings with scenes of the desert and bleached skulls. She lived alone, having been widowed and divorced, and there was plenty of room for him. He would stay there until his father came to get him. At least that was the early pretence. Paul's father did not come to get him. Nor did Paul want him to. He hardly knew the man.

Life with Grandmother Yvonne was rich. She set tasks for him—he went to school, of course, but she ran her own educational program. On the Memorial Day weekend he was set the task of learning to play two simple tunes on the piano. In June, he was assigned to research the artists whose paintings dominated Yvonne's home. During summer vacation he read an entire shelf in his deceased grandfather's collection of physics texts. Finally rebellious, he demanded to get out of the house like the other kids and learn how to surf. By the time the surfing music craze hit America, Paul could ride a wave as well as any of the other skinny teenagers who frequented the beach. He loved summer because, after a day in the sun, all the bronzed high school kids like himself met up for dates with the many young women who had names like Candy and Suzie. They hung out in packs, used a parents' car and went to Shakey's Pizza Parlour to see if they could be served beer without having to show I.D. This was great fun.

Grandmother entertained extravagantly; there were always men at the house, most of them clever. One of her gentlemen suitors was known as Count Andrey.

"I don't expect he's any more Russian than Boris Karloff—but he's so witty," Grandmother said. Andrey would tell fine stories about his own grandparents who fled their country following the revolution and how they had become the toast of Paris. He sprinkled his stories with Russian words and soon Paul began to learn them. Count Andrey brought him language books and they exchanged simple words, *please, thank you,* to one another in Russian—to the delight of Yvonne and her other guests.

These were golden days for him, his life unfolding in vivid colour, and he delighted in it, his mother forgotten for weeks at a time. Then suddenly something would remind him of her, a scent perhaps, or some little gesture in the kitchen as when Juanita, the maid, baked cookies and scooped the dough from the bowl with her hand. He was reminded of another kitchen in Montreal—the scene seemed to scroll past in black and white—when his mother had scooped and flattened a shapeless ball, then had him press tin cookie cutters into the surface to make angels, Christmas trees and bells. When these memories occurred they made him wonder how that life would have turned out had he stayed in Montreal. He would be a different person—another Paul—like an identical twin—but knowing different things than California Paul. Montreal Paul would learn to water ski instead of surf when he visited lakes in the Gatineau, he would shovel snow in winter, certainly learn French, perhaps speak it every day. When these thoughts preoccupied him, he felt disassociated from the merriment around him, as if he was not really a part of it, only an observer. Often, it was his love of reading and studying that brought him back into his California life.

Languages, physics, music, art history—as he grew to adolescence, he tasted them all. Eventually languages won. He studied Spanish at his high school enjoying its simple structure, then revived his elementary French, but knew he would probably have to return to Canada to improve it. That idea began to grow within him. He wanted to try being Montreal Paul. Maybe it wasn't too late. In Canada, he could also study Russian, he thought. By that time it was 1963—the Berlin Wall had been constructed two years earlier, and the fear of Communists had driven many Russian speakers to deny their heritage. Yvonne's home, on the other hand, had become a safe haven for Russian emigres, a place where they could speak freely, down brandy, and discourse on Russian art without being accused of being bolsheviks.

"Surely this is the time to be learning the language of our enemies—not being afraid of it," he announced to Yvonne, with the earnestness of a 17-year-old. Although he truly believed his own words, he was also restless. He wanted to get out on his own and see Canada again so he kept at this theme as a possible reason for why he must attend university there. It worked. Yvonne had put aside a trust fund for his university studies, and she turned it over to him on his eighteenth birthday. At the same time she also told him that she would leave the bulk of her estate to him on her death.

He was selected for the University of Vancouver, on the west coast of Canada, far from Montreal but not so much of a culture shock for a kid raised in California. For seven years, he lived in Vancouver and was convinced that the Russian language department was all he wanted. He was torn from his academic shell by the news that grandmother Yvonne had died suddenly of a heart attack. At age 75, she had taken a new young lover who, it was whispered at the memorial service, had exhausted her. The gossip was malicious, Paul thought, but if only half of it were true, he couldn't help but admire Yvonne's love of life and her ability to take emotional risks even into her seventies.

Why couldn't he find a woman who exhausted him? Most of the women he met were not serious students so there was no meaningful conversation. They knew how to have a good time, kind of like the old days at Shakey's Pizza, and he badly wanted to bed one of them—it didn't matter which one—but it seemed dishonest because he knew it was purely to alleviate his own carnal desires.

Now, on this warm summer evening in the heart of the Soviet Union, some latent urge was manifesting itself. Unscholarly thoughts filled his mind: ice cold beer in the university pub, a woman's browned skin in a white summer top. Sensual things, hands-on things. Music moved him. It brought back memories of Yvonne's home and the upright piano in the living room. He hadn't gained mastery of the instrument but he had gone beyond the two tunes he had learned over school break—and he liked to sing although he considered his voice to be thin. He had also seen the looks he attracted from young, beautiful women when he sat at the piano, and he liked that feeling.

Right now the music was coming from the promenade lounge, so Paul set his book aside, combed his hair and went upstairs to take a look. Pausing in the hallway, he faced the lounge's elaborately decorated glass doors and felt an attack of déjà vu. But it was not the past he remembered. He had not been here before. Instead, he knew with certainty that he would be here again. And something on this spot, in this place, would lead him to his future—he was sure of that.

Curious, he entered the room and looked around. A small band of piano, guitar and drums were playing a fairly decent cover of Paul McCartney tunes and the other students had drifted in to sit at the tables to listen. There were some new faces among them—the American cultural group. Most of these academics were older than Paul; there were a few grey hairs and bald heads among them. *At least they're not wearing berets and smoking pipes*, he thought. To his surprise, Lona was already seated at a table with two of the younger men, in an apparently intense conversation. *She works fast.* This gave him a pang. Possibly it was a woman he craved, a girlfriend, a lover. No, not Lona, but her very bravado attracted him. He enjoyed the company of the other women in the group. Jennifer was a friend and he was thankful that he did not have to play any boy/girl games with her. She could read his moods like a book and was always able to field a decent conversation. Maria was cute, but no substance. Ingrid was more his speed, and there had been a minimal attraction but nothing more had developed. He began to mentally list the other women, finding fault with each one. His woman would be here, either among this group now or soon to be here. He sat at a table, alone, pressed to the back of the room. He didn't feel like hoisting the vodka tonight. He wanted to stay alert. He considered this new thought: that his path had led him to Russia for a reason.

★

Jennifer was soothed by this leg of the trip. The *Yuri Dolgoruki* had already journeyed up the Don River and spent almost a full day on the vast reservoir that led to the Volga-Don Canal. There was a gentle evenness to the days. As some of the pressure of Volodya's demands lifted from her, other thoughts rushed in to fill the void—particularly thoughts about her cousins. She had loved them at first meeting but had she been fooled? Paul had asked how she could know they were truly her family? She couldn't answer that. Now that she had seen how imperative it was for Volodya to leave the Soviet Union, what if others were in the same boat—desperate to leave and forging fake family connections to help themselves? The betrayal would be agonizing and she determined to put it out of her head until she could visit with the cousins again. For now it was better to concentrate on her teaching.

Fuelled by their previous ten days of sightseeing, her students were eager to practise the language they had been learning.

"*Raz, dva, tree, chetiri,*" she chanted to the group during their on board sessions. They chanted back: One, two three, four. It was a trick to stir up the energy and get them warmed up and speaking Russian. She paired them up—Len with Linda, Hank with Maria, and so on, to role play simple verbal exercises: shopkeeper and customer, ballet dancer and audience, and even Natasha and student—that one had proved hilarious—though they were careful not to let the tour guide see what they were up to. They traded phrases back and forth and soon were speaking clumsily with one another.

Chopyk, visibly relaxed, relieved of his duties for the time being, had found a scholarly friend in a touring history professor from the University of Chicago, and the two men frequented the lounge or strolled the promenade deck engaged in earnest discussion.

Every morning, David led the keeners in energetic fitness exercises on the deck to the delight of Natasha who considered such exercise healthy and a sign of the beneficial effect of Communism on the students. In fact, it was not Communism but the rich, meaty diet that drove most of the participants to David's program. In the mornings two yawning waitresses served them a sumptuous breakfast: eggs, sausage in varying hues of pink and grey, dried apricots or prunes, semolina porridge and glasses of yogurt-like *kefir* to drink. For lunch, there was ample smoked fish, sliced meat, and always a side plate of tomatoes, pickles and the ever-present cucumber. Dinner involved four courses: soup, mushrooms in sour cream, sometimes caviar, with a main dish of potatoes, chopped cabbage and meat, often a rubbery chicken or short ribs. This was followed by plates of sugary cake, puddings and glasses of weak tea. For those still hungry, a small kiosk on the lower deck opened at random intervals to sell chocolates and beer.

"I can barely push away from the table," said Maria by the third day.

Ted smiled. "Wonder what the masses are eating. You can bet it's not this. From what Pavel said—the guy I met in Leningrad—most of the people are lucky to eat meat once a week. More like lentils, eggs, cabbage. Oh, and cucumber."

Mary giggled. "It must be the diet that makes Ivan Nikolaevich so sour."

Their stone-faced cruise "director" had not endeared himself to anyone. On their first day he had reprimanded an American for laughing loudly in the passageway. The man was astonished, pulled himself up to his full basketball-playing height of six feet two inches and stared the cruise director eye to eye for a full moment. He lost the contest. "But I thought we were on this trip to have some fun," he told his compatriots later. "That includes laughing, in my book."

On the same day, Ivan Nikolaevich had marched to the port deck and instructed all the passengers to get off their lounge chairs and fold them away so that the crew could swab the decks.

"You will sit on other side," he informed them in thickly accented English. As if to underline this demand, at his side stood an ugly, squat fellow with a large carbuncle on his cheek, glowering, and slapping his thigh as if he were going for his gun holster.

★

The *Yuri Dolgoruki* rose gradually through a series of canal locks and floated out onto the wide Volga River. The bland appearance of Volgograd, the first town they came to on the river, could have been a huge disappointment. Instead, it became a catalyst for discussion among the visiting Americans and Canadians. The city itself, once called Stalingrad, had been razed to the ground during a major bloody battle of the Second World War. Residents and soldiers suffered terribly. But several nations, including the United States, had helped finance its rebuilding as a modern city, and it had been designed with the usual boxy buildings beloved of Soviet architecture, all of them arrayed in uniform rows and dotted by several pleasant green parks.

It was to one of these, the park on Mamaev Hill, scene of a prolonged battle, that the combined tour group, accompanied by Natasha, arrived by bus. This time Natasha was quiet; there was no need for her to whip up enthusiasm. The spectacle of Mother Russia—a behemoth of a statue brandishing her sword and poised on the hill overlooking the city—excited the visitors.

"That's *got* to be taller than the Statue of Liberty," exclaimed one of the Americans to Jennifer as they shuffled along with crowds of Russians winding their way through a memorial park up to the statue's base. "It's really impressive."

She smiled. "It's a commemoration of a siege that no one here has forgotten; nothing could be too big or too dramatic for that." So far the Americans had not admitted that anything about the Soviet Union was bigger or better than the good old US of A. This was a first, she reflected.

"Where are you from?" the man asked her, and when she replied, he nodded. "Y'know, that's near Seattle where I'm from," he said. "I'm Bert, by the way." He extended his hand and Jennifer introduced herself. "You Canadians know all about Russia, don't you?" Although she began to protest, he continued. "See, we weren't told much before we came. I don't know if you've heard of the cold war... yes? Well, it's pretty hard to visit this country right now without everyone at home thinking we're reds. We're probably being investigated by the CIA for even coming here."

"Wow, that's frightening," Jennifer said, amused at his naïveté—an attitude she might have shared just a few short weeks ago. *Little does he know that he's probably being investigated by the KGB at the same time.*

"You know, the people in our group just want to find out more about the real Russia," Bert went on. "We don't want to believe everything we read in the papers about the 'evil commies.' You think that way too, don'tcha?" Jennifer nodded agreement.

"This is all real swell," he continued, marvelling at the faces of warriors etched in marble around him. The slowly moving line of visitors advanced up the hill towards the statue and then indoors into a tomb-like memorial chamber at the top of the hill. Once inside, an illuminated path spiralled downward around the chamber, and they gazed at the names of the fallen soldiers and citizens inscribed on every available inch of the walls. Jennifer noticed that Bert had tears in his eyes.

"It's very moving," he told her. "All these people..." He shook his head. "It makes you think about the ugliness of war. We can't let it happen again." Then he straightened proudly and wiped his eyes. "They'll be calling me a peacenik back in the US."

Her own eyes had watered several times during the march up the hill but she had taken care not to let anyone see. Why? At least this man was being honest in his emotion. Perhaps it was because the statue raised conflicting thoughts for her. Mother Russia was not a peaceful image. She was a proud woman waving her sword but as a symbol, she was a threat to her enemies, an avenger, rather than a defender. Yet this avenging angel had stirred thoughts of peace in one of this country's so-called enemies, an American.

"No, we can't let it happen again," she told Bert. "Let's remember this when we go home." She let the tears fall this time and felt the sense of release. The two smiled and shook hands.

★

On day four, Marty and Hank went out on deck to fling a frisbee back and forth, ostensibly for their own amusement but actually to capture the interest of Lona who was reading in a deckchair.

"Whoa…sonofabitch," Hank yelled as the frisbee nearly shot over the railing and he strained to catch it. He grinned at his lucky save. "Hey Lona, that makes 100 points for me. Sure you don't wanna be on my team?"

"Yeah, Lona. Hank would really like to play with you." Marty sniggered.

Lona looked up from her book and scowled. "Grow up, boys. You couldn't handle me." She shook her blonde curls and glared at Hank. "And you can just watch your language while you're around a lady."

Just then they caught sight of Ivan Nikolaevich advancing along the deck accompanied by his ugly companion and an anxious crewman.

"Whoa, look out. Here comes Mutt and Jeff, "said Marty. "Bet you the sweaty one can't speak English. Toss him the frisbee."

"Are you kidding? He'd probably examine it for microdots."

"Yoohoo, Ivan Nikolaevich," Lona called in greeting. She switched to Russian with no trace of an American accent. "Fine weather, isn't it? The boys"—she gestured to Hank and Marty and used a diminutive that implied they were ten-year-olds—"were playing an American game. Do you have frisbee in the Soviet Union?"

The stern cruise director imparted a thin-lipped smile but only bowed in answer. He addressed them in English. "Please, Miss Lona, Meester gentlemen, this deck fixtures will be painted today. You will please to sit on other side." The ugly companion snorted a little and scratched his nose.

"Certainly," Lona replied. Ivan Nikolaevich looked as if he was about to say more then turned abruptly and strode away followed by his sidekick. Lona looked up at the handsome crewman who grinned back.

"May I help you fold the chairs?" She jumped up gracefully and, without another glance at Hank or Marty, darted off after the sailor to the far end of the deck.

Marty glanced at his friend. "You poor bastard. Sweetie pie Lona doesn't even want to look at you!"

Hank used several savage phrases until Marty slapped him jokingly on the head.

"No, really, what's she doing on this trip anyway?" Hank asked. "She's not a student. You know, some other good students got turned down for this trip, but she managed to get on the list at the last moment.

"Maybe she's a spy—Canada's Mata Hari," Marty replied. "Trained by the RCMP."

"To do what? Flaunt her boobs in the KGB's face? No, I think she's up to some shifty operation…and I want to find out." Hank's voice trailed off. "Look, she's left her books. I'm going to have a look at them. Wanna come?"

Marty was about to agree until he noticed Natasha on the deck, partly obscured by a lifeboat. She appeared to be eavesdropping on their conversation. "Not me. I'll be in the lounge with a warm beer," he replied. "Hey, don't wear yourself out—remember we're meeting with some workers from a car factory later for a good chug-a-lug and dance later on."

The books were disappointing. Just classroom notes. Hank carried them downstairs and stopped at Lona's cabin. (He had already noted its location and how far it was from his own.) He tried the door. Locked. He continued along the passage until he came to a crew station. It was little more than a cubbyhole, but in this room the staff changed their uniforms, stored cleaning supplies, heated their own tea and guarded a pegboard of room keys. Some of the Canadian women kept their room keys in their purses, but most of the students had adopted the European habit of dropping the key off with staff on their way out.

Hank recognized one of the prettier waitresses, Galya, lounging in the doorway examining her eyelashes in a small mirror. She smiled flirtatiously at him.

"*Zdrastvo*, Galya. You're looking good today. Could I ask you to do me a small favour?" Here his Russian failed him. He couldn't think of the words for "unlock the door." Galya, mistaking his hesitation for shyness, offered him a chocolate from a large box covered in brown paper.

"Oh, hey, thanks. I have some books for Miss Lona Rabinovitch. You know, in cabin 2B. She's busy with Ivan Nikolaevich at the moment, helping him, so she asked me to put these books in her cabin."

Galya started a little at the power of the director's name.

"Could you just—? The key…?" He pointed.

"It is forbidden to let others into cabins."

He grinned. Still looking doubtful, she took Lona's key from its hook, and led the way to the cabin. She stepped back for him to enter. Hank could see that she was going to stay close at hand.

"Wow, this cabin is so much bigger than mine." Indeed, its situation at the bow of the boat allowed it to curve into an L-shape, giving its user a little more privacy while in bed. He strode to the desk, searching it quickly for anything unusual. Galya, still at the door, coughed delicately.

"Yes, I'm coming. It's just that it's such a great cabin. Look how the berth slots in so snugly into that space." And there it was, poking out from under the pillow—a slim, black notebook. Of course, she wouldn't leave something like that out in plain sight. In two steps he was over to the bed to snatch up the book. He riffled through it quickly: names, addresses, doodles flashed past.

"I think this is very bad," Galya exclaimed.

"No problem. I was looking for this. Honestly! Lona borrowed it from me yesterday. So, ssshh…no need to say anything about it."

Over the waitress's protestations, he tucked the black book into his pocket, exited rapidly and didn't even wait while Galya locked the door.

★

That same afternoon, Professor Chopyk spent twenty minutes examining his face in the cabin mirror. It calmed him to stand in front of his reflection, smoothing his forehead wrinkles and rearranging the trim bristles of his moustache into neat, serried rows. Once, when he had been due for a Russian department evaluation involving an interview with Chairman Hoefert, he had arrived early at his department head's office. The door was open and there was no one about so he had wedged himself into a seat in the crowded study, his legs straddling boxes of books and papers, to await Hoefert's return. A file lay open on the desk and without too much twisting of his neck he could see that it was his own confidential personnel file. Leaning out from the chair at an acute angle, he could even read the text upside down and he quickly did so without any attack of conscience. The chairman had written a number of congratulatory things, Chopyk was gratified to see. He could read that he was a stellar professor, thorough and devoted to his publishing schedule. True. It was a bit lacklustre on the subject of his teaching abilities, but certainly adequate. But there, at the bottom of the report, was what Chopyk considered to be a damning bit of character assassination. Neatly penned in the director's handwriting were the words: "Chopyk's flaw is vanity." The subsequent interview was more tense than usual.

Ever since that day Chopyk had pondered this revelation, especially when he glanced at his trim appearance in a mirror. Later, he realized that Hoefert was not talking about superficial vanity, though he was deemed a snappy dresser; instead, Hoefert had locked onto a deeper quality: Chopyk's self-absorption. He took magnificent pleasure in his successes, however small. He took a positive delight in outsmarting Professor Hoefert, preferably in front of colleagues at the Learned Societies conference. But it was only friendly rivalry, Chopyk told himself. Where was the harm? It was the word "flaw" that niggled. He didn't like to admit to flaws; didn't think he had any. But there were moments—like today with Lona Rabinovitch—that he would consider his vanity to be a genuine weakness. She was playing him, flattering him—no doubt about it. And he had fallen for it.

She had come up to him in the dining room after lunch, when the others had drifted away, to ask his clarification on a small question of verb tense. Somehow, within minutes, she had managed to turn the conversation to their departure from the Soviet Union, and she complained that she was running out of room in her luggage. Before he knew it he had gallantly agreed to pack some of her "valuable gifts and souvenirs" in his own luggage. She was quite appealing, gazing up at him softly with those large green eyes—he couldn't refuse. She was hypnotic. Dammit.

That had been his perfect time to confront her with a question of his own about the crude strangers that she had consorted with on the Moscow street, but, wrapped in the glow of her flattery, he had forfeited the opportunity. He had an uncomfortable feeling that he would pay for this lapse.

10.

PAUL'S RELEASE

VOLGA RIVER, JULY 16, 1974

At first, it appeared that Marty's prediction of a good chug-a-lug and dance was dead wrong. The 25 workers from a local car factory's social club came on board looking nervous and formal. They had been bussed from the off-limits industrial town of Toglyatti, across the narrow neck of a bend in the Volga, to the point where the riverboat was moored.

Natasha rushed to make a characteristic announcement over the intercom: "Attention, attention. Group from Canada—your guests are in the lounge. Meet your guests NOW." This announcement was repeated until the students began streaming into the halls.

The leader of the factory group, who introduced himself as Slava, wore slicked-back hair and a shiny, rumpled gabardine suit. He nodded briefly at Ivan Nikolaevich who launched into a formal speech of welcome.

Slava responded with, "This is an honour to be invited aboard to meet westerners. I'm certain our comrades will make a favourable impression on the group from Canada."

Several of the students missed the introduction. "Why didn't they let us know what time to expect the meeting?" said David, still tucking in his shirt as he hurried down the passage.

"And whether it was supposed to be formal attire," said Maria, as she swung open the lounge doors. "Oh god, the room is full and Lona's already got a fan club. She's dressed to the nines."

"So, what do we do now? Mingle?"

"Join a group of happy workers and listen while they quote Lenin, apparently." Maria could overhear one table at which two eager men were speaking with a Texan in a curious mixture of Russian and stilted English.

"What's happening?" asked David, pulling up a chair and offering one to Maria.

"Ah don't know," the man drawled. "I was just sittin' here in the lounge with a beer when these two guys started telling me about their factory." He shook his head. "I think I'll leave y'all to it. *Dosvidanya*."

Paul was already seated at a table with two of the women guests. He was feeling an unusual sense of power. Even before Natasha's commanding announcement, he had watched the bus arrive at the wharf and disgorge the group of mostly men, some women, chosen for the day as ambassadors. He had seen them chattering nervously then falling silent as they approached the gangplank. He had noticed two of the women especially and had made a point of sitting with them as soon as they entered the lounge. They introduced themselves as Nadezhda Ivanovna, a political commissar, and Vera Fyodorovna, a factory worker. Nadezhda was tall, plump and ungainly, maybe forty years old, he guessed. Her eyes roamed the room as she reeled off statistics: the depth of the Volga River at this point, how many centimetres of rainfall in June, the population of Toglyatti, how their car factory had fulfilled the Plan. Paul learned that the city had been named after the leader of the "Italian comrades" who had arrived en masse after the war to teach the Soviets how to make the Fiat. Now dubbed the Zhiguli, the little cars were popular and could only be acquired after placing one's name on a waiting list.

"And do you work on the assembly lines, Vera?" he asked the other woman who sat quietly nodding. She was dark-haired and shapely, and Paul could have sworn that once—as Nadezhda was droning on about the Five Year Plan—the young woman had winked at him.

"Yes, I was born to a farmer but now I am happy to work for the socialist state at the factory," she replied blandly. As she spoke, her face took on the detached look of what he had come to think of as a protective screen, the Soviet public face that masked the thoughts within.

She reached for the open bottle of soda on the table and offered it around politely. "But please, I want to hear about your country," she went on before Nadezhda could wind up again. "Where is your home? What do you study?"

Paul leaned forward to tell her. Nadezhda excused herself reluctantly in order to pay her respects to the student "leader," Natasha. Soon he was telling Vera the most extraordinary things about himself, about his family, about California. Her face came alive. In turn, she described her own childhood on her father's market vegetable farm—not a collective farm but one of many such small, private enterprises that flourished far away from Moscow. None of the others approached their table. It was as if they were alone in the room.

Professor Chopyk entered late (he had been napping, having forgotten about the visit) and he surveyed the room until his glance fell on the esteemed political commissar. Nadezhda Ivanovna had given up trying to capture Natasha's interest and advanced determinedly toward him. He shrank into a space between a table and the bar counter and he knew, even as his back hit the wall, that he was doomed to stay there for the duration of the party. The woman shook hands heartily and took up a rigid soldier's posture in front of him, her formidable bosom aimed at his throat. After this introductory assault, he was greatly surprised that she proved to be an interesting companion. She was university educated as an engineer, he found out, and when she learned of his interest in literature she spoke of a number of favourite modern Soviet writers unfamiliar to him. *Probably Party hacks*, he thought, *but it's good to hear the people's true perspective.* For the first twenty minutes he enjoyed the conversation immensely, even advancing in his imagination so far as to picture Nadezhda Ivanovna's ample bottom bouncing solemnly on the berth of his cabin—until he passed some humorous comment and the political commissar responded by braying like a donkey. All fantasies of intimacy, feeble at the best of times for Chopyk, melted away at her guffaw, but as he cast about for Natasha to rescue him, he noticed her disappearing out the door with Ivan Nikolaevich who wore his usual worried scowl. Some further protocol issues to be debated, no doubt. He groaned inwardly and attempted to slide around the bar and past the commissar while she was still talking. Mistaking his intention, Nadezhda stepped in front of him and called for a bottle of mineral water and a glass before resuming her discussion.

At Jennifer's table the second mild beer had brought about a breakthrough of sorts. Slava had stopped talking about Lenin's Path and had started on stamp collecting.

"I have some Canadian stamps if you'd like them," Jennifer said eagerly, happy to disrupt the numbing discussion of vehicle production statistics. She pulled them from her purse—one depicting Queen

Elizabeth and the other a Rocky Mountain bighorn sheep. The two laughing women that accompanied Slava looked on with interest.

"Let me give you something in return." A dignified Slava reciprocated with two artistically decorated stamps from his album, which he had brought along for this purpose. Lona, who was seated at the next table, apparently took her cue from Jennifer because she also rummaged in her purse for a gift, pulled out an American nickel, and began explaining the significance of the buffalo to a group of enraptured young men.

By the time the party broke up, some two hours later, the students and visitors had warmed to each other. Jennifer had learned something about their lives: their brothers and sisters, their schools, their music and their anxiety that they would somehow discredit themselves in front of their superiors on the day's visit—this last concern added in a whisper. She glanced around. But their commissar was still engrossed in conversation with Chopyk and both Ivan Nikolaevich and Natasha had disappeared—presumably leaving the group in good hands. *What a relief,* Jennifer thought. Finally, Nadezdha brayed her goodbyes to Chopyk, while Lona exchanged addresses with at least four of the panting youths.

Just before he left the dining room, Slava turned to Jennifer. "Stay with us, *Zhennifer*, please. You can have a good life here. Stay with us." She was stunned by the request and could only smile and shake her head. *Good god, were any of the others asked to stay?*

As she walked the trio down to the wharf and waved them goodbye, she did not notice that Paul had also walked his new friend, Vera, to the bus and was now standing behind a copse of rowan trees on the footpath. And if she had not been so wrapped up in her own thoughts, she would have overheard Vera explain to Nadezhda that she would not take the bus back with the others, but instead walk to her father's farm, only one kilometre down the road.

"On your way, then, Vera Fyodorovna," the political commissar called out to her. "Get there before dark."

"See you later, Nadezhda Ivanova," she called out happily as she ran toward the rowan trees.

★

Not too far away, at an old boathouse on the same river, the public official, Pyotr Vladimirovich, and his mistress Tanya, the police chief's wife, were locked in a sweaty ball. He had discovered the boathouse one day while bicycling about the countryside, seeing faces in stones and hearing gasps of pleasure in the trees. At least he supposed it to be a boathouse, although it was hard to imagine who would own a private boat large enough for these premises. It was too small to have serviced the old river barge traffic, though the thing did look like it was pre-revolutionary. *It's dangerous*, he thought but he liked that idea. There were holes in the rough-planked floor, mouldering corners and the whole thing teetered on two tarred, weathered posts that stood in the river. As a public official he should have the rat-infested thing condemned and removed. As Tanya's lover he had greeted it gleefully.

The location was perfect. It was away from prying eyes on a narrow overgrown stretch of footpath. Anyone passing by might hear them but not see them. They'd be too worried about hooligans to come barging in. Nonetheless, they had to be careful. When he met Tanya that night before dusk at a prearranged spot—a lone birch tree on a little rise of land—he told her that he had a big surprise for her but she had to remain quiet, not only on her journey there, but—and he didn't know how to convey the matter delicately to her—she had to stay quiet through the moments of her greatest ecstasy. Sounds, he knew, carried loudly over the river. Tanya had agreed to this restriction while on the walk. In fact, she had nibbled his ear and swore to speak only into its fleshy pink folds, filling his head with such thoughts that he wanted to pull her to the ground out there in the open.

When they reached the rickety building, she looked dubious, but he had already foreseen this problem and had fixed it up with some comforts. He had cleared away the rotting planks and debris, then stretched a clean blanket on the narrow strip of floor that surrounded the boat berth. On the blanket he placed an orange, procured at some expense from old lady Ullanova's Moscow market contact. Tanya exclaimed and giggled at these attempts at ambience; they appeared to satisfy her somewhat, though she cast nervous glances at the dank, smelly corners.

She arranged the skirt of her summer dress up around her waist, and snatching the orange with both hands, dug her nails into the peel. Finally, she settled on the blanket, leaning back on her elbows. Her honey-brown eyes, slightly slanted like those of a Tatar, smiled at him and she slowly spread her olive legs, lay back and curved an arm high over her head, causing one breast to pop out of the dress. That was the good thing about Tanya, she knew exactly what a man wanted. Without removing all his clothes, he entered her immediately, hungrily. At the moment of his orgasm, he sucked in his breath and drew in the bitterness of aromatic citrus. Easing his gasp out quietly, he listened for sounds on the river, but heard only the sound of her full lips sucking juice from the fruit. He rested patiently while Tanya consumed the entire orange down to the white parchment skin. She smiled. He could feel himself rising. This time he would give her so much pleasure she would never again be satisfied by her husband. When it was Tanya's turn to climax, she gasped and moaned embarrassingly. The whole countryside could hear her.

"Devil take it," Pyotr exclaimed and slapped her breasts, feeling the urge to growl like a bear. How did she do this to him?

★

Ten minutes later, Paul and Vera were strolling the same path the public official and the police chief's wife had covered earlier, engaged in much the same furtive endeavour to keep their intimacies away from the eyes of the world. They spoke of her family's farm, the cow, her comrades at the autoworks (no sweetheart, as yet), and his professors. They told stories of her father (her mother had died two years earlier), her relatives in Rostov, his Grandmother Yvonne, the poetry of Pushkin, how he had first handled a hockey stick, when she first went to Young Pioneers, what they ate for dinner.... There seemed no end of topics.

As they walked slowly, he was aware that his skin had begun to tingle as if he'd been scrubbed with a new towel. His right arm particularly, a few inches from Vera's shoulder, felt hot. Every nuance of her face, how she moved her hands, how she stepped lightly along the grassy bank, paused, bent to pick a willow branch from the path—all became etched in his awareness, almost painfully. She filled his entire attention, yet somehow he was also stunningly aware of the sky, how still it was, how the dusk was imperceptibly moving across its arch. Just yesterday he would have categorized this sensation as merely the product of reading Karamzin and the sentimentalist writers. A man's humours expressed in nature. Today, he knew it was a true sensation, not one to read about in books.

When Paul heard the animal sounds of panting, laboured breathing and cries emanating from an old boathouse, then that too seemed not unusual. It only echoed the quickening of his own pulse; he expected to hear the very earth groan in the heat of passion. But when Vera heard the sounds, she turned a bright red and stood stock still in the path. *She's more modest than I am*, he thought, and he loved her at that moment.

"I know you have to go home now," he told her then added quickly, "How can I see you again?" He waited expectantly. She said nothing. "My boat doesn't leave until tomorrow. Maybe I could stay here—at this boathouse—and meet you in the morning." She appeared to be thinking deeply. He wondered if he had said something indecent to offend her, implying that they would meet and in the boathouse, too….

"Your boat leaves at first light," she answered quietly. "All the boats do. You go then to Maiden's Island. There, the passengers will swim in the river. It is very pretty. You will moor at Zhiguli for the night. Then the following morning you pass our workplace at Toglyatti."

She gazed up at him with questioning eyes. They stood still, facing one another. He placed his hands on her shoulders, not in a heavy proprietorial way, but lightly, as if they were about to dance. She, a half head shorter, rested her hands on his waist. There still remained a foot of space between them.

Finally she said, "You could stay. We can take you back to the boat the day after tomorrow when it reaches Toglyatti."

Paul could hardly believe it meant what he hoped. His former moment of purity forgotten, he now wanted only to hear it from her lips.

"You could spend the night here—on my father's farm—with me."

He drew her close, tight to his chest, for answer. They clung to each other on the path for minutes, maybe hours, until a muffled laugh from the boathouse intruded.

"Over here. Out of sight." Paul pulled Vera behind a bank of berry bushes from where they could watch the entrance to the boathouse.

"Akh! The public official from my father's district," she whispered. The little man was still straightening his shirt. "And he's with … *Bozhe moy*! He's with the police chief's wife, Tanya. They were making the sounds that we heard!" She stared at Paul in disbelief.

The liaisons of the locals were not of much interest to Paul; he was aware only of how good it felt to touch, crouched there behind the bushes among the tall grasses. But Vera was now animated. They watched Pyotr Vladimirovich mount his bike, drop a last wet kiss on Tanya's lips, and pedal off. As soon as Tanya strolled in the other direction, Paul and Vera emerged from the bushes.

"We must go in and see." Vera dragged him to the rickety building.

"We don't need to," he demurred.

"You think I am a spy, but it is good to have this information. It is good to know about our government officials. It can help us."

"And I thought you would be a good communist," said Paul.

She stopped in the path and stared at him. "But I *am* being a good communist. I am."

She darted away into the boathouse and Paul followed to find her casting about widely at this love nest as if she would find something incriminating that she could take away.

★

The home of Fyodor Shukshin was set half a mile down a winding dirt path that branched off the main regional road. It was a dark, old, wooden house with some remnants of the original gingerbread still clinging to the eaves, though it had long needed paint and repair. At the gate stood a cement well covered with a sloping roof and this had been kept in trim condition. The front yard was a small patch of dirt with signs of thorough grazing by chickens now gone to roost. Although the light was waning, Paul could see that the surrounding fields were covered in growth: beet greens and carrot tops showed on one side, bright green potato plants on the other. They entered the house through a groaning, battered door and Vera greeted her father.

Vera's sudden return to the farm even with a stranger in tow bothered Fyodor Shukshin not one bit. Apparently she was in the habit of dropping in at home at any opportunity in her work schedule.

"So it's you," he snorted. "Come from across the Volga."

"Some day I'll go much farther away than Toglyatti," she said, smiling at her father fondly, then turning to Paul. "Meanwhile, I like to visit here."

Her father returned the smile a bit cynically. "Of course, when you can get fresh vegetables here—and sell them for a profit—why wouldn't you like to visit your old father?"

She grinned, searched through the cupboards and served pickles in a bowl accompanied by slices of heavy black bread. At first Vera's father appeared delighted to meet the foreigner. He escorted Paul into the kitchen, sat him at the plain wooden table, and brought out an unlabelled bottle of clear liquid and two glasses. "*Na dne*, to the bottom," he shouted, tossing back the fiery substance and watching while Paul did the same. "To Vera's comrade! What's your name again, lad?"

To Russians, the word "Paul" in English sounded much like the Russian word for sex, *pol*. He wanted to divest himself of this name ever since he had noticed Russian speakers smothering a giggle when he was introduced.

Vera cut in quickly. "It's Pavel in Russian, Papa. He speaks good Russian, don't you think? He learned it from a bourgeois—a Count."

"You don't mind that Vera brought me here?" Paul asked.

"Of course not. Welcome, Pavel," the older man repeated, but a nervous flicker appeared in his eyes and he addressed Vera next. "He comes from the riverboat excursion of foreigners, you say?"

Vera repeated the whole story of the meeting, including the part about sitting with the political commissar (which was some kind of honour or some kind of punishment, Paul wasn't sure which) and receiving permission to visit her father's farm for her time off the following day. She went to some length to describe the passenger lounge, the drinks, the snacks, the western clothing, and the unsmiling cruise director. She excluded the part about the liaison in the boathouse. Paul was surprised that she had noticed so much. His memory of the day involved only her.

"Welcome, Pavel," Fyodor repeated to Paul, then added, "Won't you be missed?" And in an aside in a loud whisper to Vera, "It is forbidden to have visitors without permits. Keep him out of sight."

"My friend Ted knew I was leaving the boat," Paul said quickly. "They won't miss me." It was a lie but justified, he felt.

The evening passed quickly in conversation. Fyodor, mellowed by alcohol, relaxed once more and shuffled outside to tend to the chickens. Vera arranged a makeshift bed for Paul on a narrow window seat by the stove.

"I sleep up there," she said demurely, pointing at a steep staircase that led to a dark upper floor. "Papa sleeps there," and she pointed at a bed in the corner. "I'll get you some water for washing."

"Do you want me to come up there and tuck you in?" he asked grinning.

She looked uncertain. "What is this 'tuck you in?'"

He had used the Russian word for cover or hide. It was easily misunderstood. "Oh, I didn't mean…I just meant that I would…say goodnight to you," he finished lamely. She returned his look for a full moment, it seemed, standing there in the shadowy living room, the naked kitchen bulb etching her face in profile, one of her bone-white hands still entwined in the handle of an empty glass pitcher which she hugged to her chest. Her eyes were soft, vulnerable, when she said to him, "You may do as you wish—anything that you wish." She leaned forward and touched his arm, and in that one slight caress he felt her desire and something more, the fulfilment of his own longing.

As Paul lay on his narrow cot that night, waiting to hear the snores of the elder Shukshin, his thoughts about this present adventure mingled with knowledge of forthcoming loss. He wanted to be with Vera—she felt the same way. He knew that. But after tomorrow his group would leave the area. Just two days after they returned to Moscow they would be flying back to Canada. To what? A career as a perpetual academic? One thing Grandmother Yvonne had always taught him was to seize all opportunities, live life to its fullest. He missed her presence. He would have wanted the two women to meet. Yvonne would likely chew Vera up and spit her out. No, maybe not. He didn't know Vera that well but he suspected she might possess a core of steel. She certainly stood up to that boring political commissar—and to her father.

The unfamiliar scents of the barnyard through the open window, the damp hand laundry on the line, the musty hearth assailed him and made him nostalgic for a home. The La Jolla house had always been his grandmother's place—the art, the furniture, the constant company; they reflected her feminine, changeable personality, not his. This place felt old, centred, solid—it was probably a farm even before the revolution and would ever be so. He liked it. He yawned. It was surprisingly comfortable here on the window seat. Should he go up to her now? Sneak past Papa asleep around the corner. No, he would wait a little, close his eyes for a moment. Soon he was watching while Grandmother Yvonne led a chorus of Russian folk singers at the Moscow Palace of Culture. *Oh, she's still alive*, he thought. *That's good*. He searched for Vera in the audience but couldn't see her. He felt loss. Then he realized that the morning light was streaking across the kitchen floor. Shukshin was already pulling on rubber boots and was out the door to do chores, while Vera was approaching Paul with only a hint of pique.

"Did you sleep well?" she asked stiffly.

"Yes," he replied, rising groggily through the dream. "And I'm even better now that you're here." He reached out to draw her close to him and she snuggled on to the bench.

She relaxed a little, then asked, "You didn't come up to me to 'tuck in'?"

"I wanted to. Guess I fell asleep right away." He remembered his conflict, thought about telling her of his fears, then changed his mind.

She watched these emotions pass across his face. Her eyes widened. "No matter. It's my rest day today," she said, "and I want to spend it with you. Promise you'll stay tomorrow night as well!"

He embraced her. "Yes, of course I'll stay. I'll stay for as long as you want."

11.

CONFRONTATION

VOLGA RIVER, JULY 17, 1974

"She's madder than a hornet, and she's calling for your blood," teased Marty. He ducked out of Hank's way. It was lunch time on the morning after Hank had found Lona's mysterious black book. "I guess she tortured your waitress friend until she confessed."

"I'll go find her," Hank muttered. "I don't want Chopyk or Jennifer to find out. Don't say anything, okay?"

He didn't have far to look. They smacked into one another at the door to the dining room.

"You…creep," Lona growled at Hank, her usual Cheshire cat smile missing. "Now, give me back my book!"

He couldn't resist one last stand. "Uh…whatcha talking about?" She was about to raise her voice again, when he hustled her down the hall, one hand firmly on her back, until they were out of earshot of the passengers.

"Okay, so I took it. It was a stupid thing to do, but I wanted to know why you're on this trip—and don't give me that line about being a student."

Lona drew herself up to her full height and bristled like an alley cat prepared to do battle. She thrust out her hand imperiously. "It's none of your business, you thief. I want my book back right now!"

Hank knew when he was licked. "I just …heck, I'd still like to know. I'll get it for you." He walked her to his cabin, and she waited at the door, tapping her toe, until he placed the worn black book in her hand. "Come on, Lona. I just wanted to get to know you. Maybe we could still be friends."

In fact, the book had been a big disappointment—besides a list of Russian names and addresses there were only a few other notes on icons and such religious items. One comment, "Ask Professor Henry Smith about oil painting," was interesting especially since it had received a check mark with a big "Yes!" written beside it. Smith was one of the American riverboat passengers—a faculty member whose specialty was art history.

Her scorn seemed to waver for a moment, and she asked, "Did you look inside?" He nodded. She kicked the door shut behind her and glanced at the intercom speaker, noticed that it was hanging by a wire. "Then I'll tell you." He sat down heavily. She spoke more softly than before.

"I can't be friends with a thief…"

"Yeah, yeah, but I'm sorry."

"…you can't know how worried I was. This book is very important to my family." She took a deep breath. "You know that I'm Jewish." He nodded again. "You saw that there were names and addresses—those are Jews living here in the Soviet Union. They're survivors of the prison camps, people who have already seen so much misery in their lives. My parents and my grandmother want me to visit them…" She fell silent.

"That's it? Just visits?"

"Yeah, visits…and to give them encouragement, send them love and hope that they'll some day leave for Israel."

"Send them love,'" he repeated. "So why does that have to be a big secret?"

"Okay, send them money, too," she whispered. "That's the illegal part—I was supposed to report how much money I brought into the country and I lied. I brought lots. So please don't say anything."

"Oh, I see," replied Hank but he didn't. The story was thin. Also Lona had forgotten that, one day in Moscow when he had bumped into her on the street, she had introduced him to a man whose name he had noticed in the book. He remembered because the man's name was Krov which meant blood in English. He had been the kind of particularly ugly, bull-headed, Russian type that Hank would have avoided on a dark night. The man was a thug and no more Jewish than Santa Claus. Besides, he was too young to have been in the war.

"Yes, well, I'm sorry once again I interfered. We'd better get going." Hank was suddenly very nervous. Her story was uncharacteristic of her. There was no doubt that she had been meeting with some of these names in the book—several people had sighted her around town with strangers—but what was she doing with them? And, if they were doing something legal why didn't they meet in their homes? Why always on the street?

But while he was ushering her out of the room, she turned to him, looked up at him with an expression that was suddenly all smiles and friendship. "Before we go, can I ask you to do one thing?" she cooed.

"Sure, what?"

"The people I've visited have been so kind...they've given me all sorts of gifts to take back to America. They're proud and want to give something in return for the money. You know, family heirlooms—things they want my family to have."

"Go on." Hank could sense a trap, but he was so happy to see her face relax once more that he realized he would do anything she asked.

"I don't have room in my luggage for everything. Could you possibly fit a few of these things in yours? Oh, I won't hassle you..." She caught sight of his shocked stare. "It's just a few items—a figurine and piece of fabric—that I'm having to carry around in a satchel now because I have no room. Please?" This last was accompanied by the most melting eyes he had ever seen.

He mumbled agreement and she reached up to brush a light kiss on his cheek, then darted away down the hall. *Wow, what a woman*! Every instinct told him to stay away and he was generally a guy who listened to his gut. As he walked back to the dining room, he pondered the problem and was so intent that he nearly walked into Jennifer who seemed to be wrapped in her own thoughts.

"Mrs. White..." he began.

She looked up. "Yes?"

"Oh, nothing...some day we'll talk about this trip together."

That was strange, thought Jennifer as she headed for a table with Chopyk and Natasha who was waving at her.

"I have a message for you...from Leningrad," Natasha said before Jennifer was seated.

"For me? But how?"

"Telegrams—they are forwarded to me on the boat—hotel arrangements and so on. Also emergencies for the guests." She sniffed. "This message was *not* an emergency but headquarters kindly forwarded it." She took a crumpled bit of poor quality paper from her purse. Apparently, this was a typical Soviet telegram. The words were glued on crudely like a ransom note. It began with a number code, then read, "Thank you. You give me hope." It was signed Volodya. Chopyk sat like stone watching this interaction.

Jennifer was stunned—as much by the very public message already scrutinized by Natasha—and who else?—but also by the date. It had arrived two days ago while they were in Volgograd.

"Why didn't I get this earlier?" she asked. The tour guide and the teacher were silent and glanced at one another.

Chopyk cleared his throat. "May I speak with you frankly, Mrs. White?"

"Please do," she replied tartly.

"This man, this Volodya, you met in Leningrad. He's not a good man." He caught her horrified stare. "Oh, he's not a criminal; Natasha has checked. You know—or maybe not—that every workplace keeps records of its employees. He's lost many jobs and he's just a—now don't go flying off the handle—he's probably looking for a wife from the west so he can leave the Soviet Union. Naturally, he could apply to the authorities for an exit visa in the appropriate fashion." He glanced at Natasha, "But some people choose other, weaker ways."

"Stop right there!" Jennifer could feel a surge of embarrassment and anger rush to her face. "Professor Chopyk, with greatest respect, you are not my father—and Natasha is not my boss. If a telegram comes for me in the future it should be passed on to me immediately. No background checks of my correspondents are necessary."

Natasha turned her head away from this wanton display of western individualism. Chopyk sighed. "I'm sorry you feel that way, Mrs. White. All I was going to suggest was that you inform him that you're already married—and he might stop his attentions."

Truly angry now, and with a sense that she was burning her career bridge behind her, Jennifer stood, snatching the telegram. "I'll conduct my own life, Professor Chopyk, and that will not interfere with my teaching job." (She resisted the urge to add, "better than you accomplish yours.") "This is nothing to do with you." She pushed the chair aside and stomped away from the table.

"Wait, I ...." Chopyk seemed genuinely concerned at her anger. "There's something else." Despite herself, she turned back toward him.

"I'm sorry, Jennifer," he continued more softly, "but we *had* to check. We weren't sure that the telegram was for you... ."

"What do you mean by that?"

"Look, it doesn't have your name on it." She had the sensation of the floor moving away from her and decided to run for the door while her dignity was still intact.

Back in her cabin tears overwhelmed her. *You give me hope.* She missed Volodya more than ever. She sat on the bed and smoothed the crumpled paper, studying it, trying to understand what Chopyk had meant. True, it was not addressed to her but had been sent in care of Natasha Kuchkov as tour guide. A number followed—presumably that represented the bureaucratic Intourist agency's official designation for the tour. If it had not been intended for her, then who? Did he really send it? Volodya was a very common name—and there was no last name. So how did Natasha know whom to check? And how did Natasha know the telegram was meant for her?

Her class that afternoon was conducted in a pall of discomfort. Most of the students had overheard the dispute in the dining room without knowing exactly what had transpired. She thought of having Paul lead the class instead of her but she couldn't find him anywhere. The mood stayed with her through the formal dinner that evening, well into the hour of entertainment—several of the students had learned Russian poems or ditties and were amusing the Americans by reciting the translations—and it lasted on into the evening.

As she lay awake, she began to have doubts about her behaviour. Maybe Chopyk was only being a good guy, after all—meddlesome but showing genuine concern. Maybe Volodya *was* a dead loss. After some agonizing, she realized that Volodya must know Natasha. Of course. He must have known her when he had worked for Intourist. She had even said she was from Leningrad. They would have been colleagues. That would explain a lot. So maybe Natasha had known about Volodya and her all along. Could he have wanted Natasha to see the telegram—maybe to let her know that he was attempting to leave the country? Could it be that Natasha was helping? As Jennifer rolled on to her back in the cabin berth she felt the increased pressure from Volodya as if it were some live thing pressing on her chest. What a day! Even the strange comment from Hank in the hallway that morning. It all fit into the stew. She fervently hoped that sleep would give her some respite from her muddled thoughts.

12.

DAWN OF A NEW DAY

JULY 18, 1974

With a shiver, Paul Mercier slipped into the chilly waters of the wide Volga River. He gasped as the water leached through his clothes. He was fully dressed in brown polyester bell-bottom pants and blue print shirt, his shoes, watch and wallet tied in plastic inside a makeshift backpack. It was barely light on the cool July morning.

He drew a deep calming breath and took in the earthy smells of the rich alluvial soil and the musty odour of the small creatures that lived among the weeds. He began swimming and when the current pulled him away from the tree-lined shore he stroked powerfully to stay in control. He smiled. It was not so bad. He'd been in stronger currents in the surf off Malibu when he was a teenager.

In mid-river he broke his rhythm, pulled up and trod water to see if he was still on target. God, had he picked the right riverboat? Yes, he could see it now, the *Yuri Dolgoruki*. He savoured the relief briefly, allowing his body to float in the wide, smooth gloss of this legendary river. Then, concerned that early morning traffic might mistake him for a floating branch, he launched into a strong breast stroke toward the stern of the boat.

Within five minutes, he had gained the rungs and climbed aboard. He was not sure if he had been spotted in the water—there had to be sailors already on early shift. But even if the flinty cruise director or his ugly sidekick were up so early, Paul was not worried about seeing them. He knew how to handle them.

He hauled the plastic package off his back, checked that its contents were dry. Then, shaking himself like a wet dog, he broke into laughter. Jennifer would be astonished at what he was about to undertake. She would be the first person he would tell—maybe the only one. He sloshed his way to his cabin, leaving a trail of puddles.

★

When Jennifer had awakened at first light that morning, she had a sense that some mental dam had burst, rushing her back to reality. She stretched in bed, sighed and glanced around her small cabin. Her peasant blouse and jeans lay draped over an open suitcase. Six days into the Volga cruise and she hadn't yet managed to put all of her clothes away in the closet. Her make-up case lay open, its contents scattered into the washbasin. She remembered that she had thrown her wedding ring into the bottom of the case before she left Canada. Why, she wasn't sure. She would have to check that it hadn't disappeared down the drain.

Her reaction at lunch had been fierce, overkill, she realized. It was all mixed up with Chopyk's paternalism which reminded her of her father's interference. He hadn't wanted her to marry Michael, she knew that. Both parents had thought him too studious, too lax, too hairy—too something. It seemed there were many reasons best known or invented only by parents. *They didn't need to worry—it didn't last anyway.* For the sake of her career in the Russian Language Department she would seek out Chopyk today and apologize. Also, she would tactfully investigate her intriguing theory of Natasha as an ally.

Jumping out of bed, she pulled on her jeans under her nightgown and ran up onto the deck, barefoot, to refresh herself on another cool, clear morning on the Volga River. So early, there was no hint of the heat to come. On either side, lush green stands of birch and cottonwood overhung the water. Their boat was somewhere north of Maiden's Island where they had stopped for a swim yesterday and they were less than two days south of their destination, Kazan. One day in Ulyanovsk, one in Kazan, two in Moscow, then they would fly back to Vancouver. Just five days and she would be thousands of miles from Volodya. The thought gave her a sharp pain.

As Jennifer approached the bow of the boat, she could hear someone grunting. David, she thought, doing his ridiculous calisthenics. She did not want to admire his biceps this morning. She wanted to be alone with her thoughts.

★

David Joiner was always out on deck early, stripped down in the fresh air and performing his 5BX exercises, the rigorous program designed by the Canadian Air Force. It was a pity to be doing them so early, he thought, when there was no one on deck to admire his prowess with the combination push-ups and hand claps. He particularly liked it when women appreciated his tight, firm figure. Sadly there were only two women among the American cultural tourists that he had met who seemed promising in a summer affair fashion—and they were both older than he was.

Lying flat on his back, David stretched and flexed. When he began to do sit-ups, he sighted along the trees at shore line, watching them rise and fall as he moved. But on one of the sit-ups, he glanced out to the river and saw an object in the water, moving intently toward the boat. Soon, the object resolved into a face, head held high above the current and body doing some kind of a breast stroke underneath. He abandoned his sit-ups and stared until he was sure that it was the face of a man.

He didn't know what to make of this. The river was wide at this point and looked swift. A man would have to be desperate to attempt such a swim. But David had recently read *The Spy Who Came in from the Cold*, so he knew all about desperate men. One of ours, returning to his cover from some secret assignation? What would he find of importance in the Volga region countryside? Or one of theirs? Again, that made no sense. Why would one of their agents want to get on board a tour boat with a group of Russian language academics and a gaggle of culture-seeking tourists? And why in blazes would he swim? Surely the Kremlin could afford small boats.

David started to do some deep knee bends but didn't finish. As the figure swam more into focus he could see clearly that the swimmer was Paul. He pulled on his track suit top and zipped it up. It was time for a quick rinse in the communal shower room, then some explanations.

★

Professor Walter Chopyk had also been up since first light but was oblivious to any activity on deck or in the river. He chose to spend these quiet morning hours seated at the tiny desk in his cabin, text books arranged neatly, writing in his journal. The notes would form the basis of his report to Department Chairman Hoefert, so it was important to convey just the right tone. For example, he would make much of the fact that this particular tour of western students had been allowed in to the philological library at the State Institute in Leningrad—a great honour usually requiring a permit from the Ministry of Education. He, Professor Chopyk, was actually allowed right into the stacks, to be surrounded by a rich storehouse of scholarly literature. So much for Professor Hoefert and his boast that *he* had been allowed into the stacks at the Lenin Library. This was a feather in Chopyk's cap. Of course, he would not include in the notes that he had bribed the lowly assistant librarian (American dollars), the attendant (bottle of brandy) and even the security guard (flattery and a Cadbury's bar) to allow him the brief two hours in the library's inner sanctum. And that those two hours were ones in which the chief librarian was on her extended lunch hour or he would have stood no chance at all.

He set his pen down for a moment to relish the memory once more. The porthole was open a crack and a fresh morning breeze played across his face. Other wonderful events had crowded in since his time in the library: touring the art treasures of the Hermitage, attending the Kirov ballet, seeing the monumental statue of Mother Russia at the former Stalingrad, and cruising a stretch of the Volga where no other westerners had been allowed. Russia—no, the Soviet Union—was full of such grand experiences, though none could compare with those two hours spent among the ancient tomes of his linguistic mentors. The journal was filling up.

He supposed he would have to write something about the progress of the students—they would receive a grade, after all—and something about the leadership qualities of his second in command, Jennifer White. Chopyk frowned. It was difficult to write about Jennifer. On the one hand, she had done a miraculous job in bringing some of the younger students up to scratch with their Russian. Their verbal abilities had improved greatly during the trip. Of course, total immersion always did that. But they seemed to have more facility with the language, more interest in it. Their written skills had improved, too, if he could believe the mini-essays that Jennifer was assigning them. Even Linda Appleton, whose grammar was superb but who couldn't string together a simple sentence, had improved. Last night she had actually delivered a brief oral report in Russian on the subject of architecture. The speech had tickled that old buzzard, Ivan Nikolaevich, their Soviet "host". Even the rambunctious Hank—a student whom Chopyk thought would be nothing but trouble—had settled down under Mrs. White's teaching. She had also worked with Carlos, bringing him out of his shell to find that he had a good verbal grasp of Russian.

Then there was the other side of the coin. Even setting aside that outburst at lunch yesterday as not typical of her behaviour, Jennifer was disorganized and a trifle too friendly with the students. Of course, she was much closer to their age group than he was—she was a true apostle of the hippy era, while Chopyk had grown up during the Depression. She was—he stretched for the word, knowing that he would have to find the right one for this report—she was instinctual, a natural teacher. But in this academic context he would have to use the word "undisciplined." That was only fair.

It was that business in Leningrad that had really bothered him. He was quite certain Mrs. White had not slept in her own bed at the hotel for two, three, maybe not even one of those white nights. She had met a man—that much was the subject of gossip at the breakfast table—but he had not known who until Natasha had gone digging into the man's past record. Mrs. White had all but disappeared during their stay, showing up for lunch occasionally and for a fast shuffle through the Hermitage. She had only assembled her class once, on the last day, when she had spoken to them about the siege of Leningrad and taught them that maudlin poem. She had not introduced this Soviet man to anyone; that did not bode well. Couldn't she see that he was some Soviet *nogoodnik* who wanted to marry a foreigner for his own selfish reasons?

"Maybe I *am* being old-fashioned," he muttered to the porthole. He found that, though not married himself, he frequently felt compelled to deliver advice on the state of the decaying institution. How easily these modern career women flouted the rules! Even if Mrs. White was currently separated from her husband, she was still a married woman. He felt irritated. He didn't want to be modern; he wanted to be right.

"How is she going to explain this Leningrad dalliance to her so-called husband?" he muttered again and quickly shut the porthole in case someone overheard him.

Chopyk closed his journal and secreted it away in his briefcase. He rose from the desk, pushed the chair in neatly, examined his beard in the mirror for signs of misbehaving whiskers and was just putting on his jacket when there was a peremptory rap. From the height and firmness of the knock, he guessed its author. As he opened the door, he looked up expectantly into the six-foot tall, gaunt Ivan Nikolaevich whose square, jutting face was set firmly in a scowl.

"Doktor Professor Chopyk," he announced firmly in Russian. "Please to step outside." Chopyk had to remind himself not to be alarmed. For unspecified reasons, the man liked to do his talking in the hall. It gave credence to the theory that there were listening devices in each cabin. "Do you have anything to report to me on the matter of the missing student?" Ivan demanded.

Confound it, Chopyk thought, *it's that lecture again.* Whenever a student went off alone—even for an hour—Ivan Nikolaevich would be at his door complaining about the dangers of going about independently. He always used the Russian word for independently, *sam-o-stoy-yat-yel-no,* sounding out each syllable as if it were a dirty word.

"I know nothing about a missing student," Chopyk answered honestly. "They are adults, after all, Ivan Nikolaevich, full of energy, curiosity…"

"Hmmm. So." The cruise director snapped his arms to his sides and stiffened slightly as if preparing for the parade ground. "Breakfast is delayed," he boomed. "We are waiting for a shipment from Moscow. Please inform your other charges." Then he turned on his heel and left.

"I was just on my way," Chopyk murmured to the empty hall.

★

Jennifer padded softly to the stern end passenger deck and looked out over the wide river. Through the railing she caught sight of a figure swimming toward the boat. Soon, the head was lost to her sight. Intrigued, she crossed to the other side to lie on her stomach so that she could hang over the edge of the deck and see more.

There was a splash, and as she watched, the swimmer pulled himself up onto some rungs and scrambled onto the lower deck slopping water over the planks. He was fully dressed, his shirt slicked to his body, and he slung aside a dripping bundle.

She recognized Paul right away. *That silly twit. Is he trying to get me in trouble?*

Paul splashed his way to the hatch used by the crew. She resisted calling out to him but sprang up and entered the passenger staircase, ready to run downstairs and head him off before he reached his cabin. But rounding the corner on the stairs she smacked into Lona who was—even at this early hour—immaculately dressed in a pale blue silk blouse and white shorts.

"Good morning, Mrs. White," Lona said eagerly with the ever-present smirk that so irritated Jennifer. "You're up early."

How does she look so damn good at 6 o'clock in the morning? Self-consciously, Jennifer pulled her nightgown around her. She couldn't remember if she had combed her hair. She called a hurried good morning but even as she raced past she couldn't help thinking, *Lona and David and now Paul. Doesn't anyone sleep in?* She wondered how many others might have witnessed Paul's arrival. Natasha? Hopefully not that ugly fellow with the carbuncle who, no doubt, rose at dawn to shoot rabbits for target practise.

Jennifer knocked on Paul's door and it creaked open; Paul, now shirtless, wore a guilty expression and was still buttoning a pair of dry pants.

"So, what's the scoop? You competing for the Soviet Union in long distance swimming?" she asked, sliding in the doorway and pushing the door shut. Then she remembered the microphones. "Or shouldn't we talk about it here?" She pointed at the speaker over the berth.

"No, that's okay. I stuffed it with a sock on the second day of the cruise. Personally, I think it's just an intercom and not a bug at all, despite what David says." He turned back to wringing out the river water from his dripping shirt and pants. "So you saw me?"

Jennifer nodded. "Come on. Explain. Sooner or later I would have heard about it—from Chopyk or Natasha."

"We're friends—aren't we? I was going to tell you." He gave a big sigh. "In fact, you are the only person I want to tell. Do you remember when we met that workers' club from Toglyatti?

"How could I forget? You were very taken with that gorgeous woman. What was her name? Vera?"

"You noticed that? I didn't think anybody saw us when we…when I met her." Paul continued, rolling his shirt in a towel.

"When you what?" She was laughing now. His face reddened.

"When I left with her."

Suddenly Jennifer turned cold. "Paul, we met that group two days ago. You've been with her ever since!"

He nodded. "And you didn't even notice I was gone, did you?" He pulled on a t-shirt.

Guilt swept over Jennifer. *Why hadn't she noticed?* She was supposed to be looking out for the students. The buck stopped at Professor Chopyk, but she was closer to the students, more in touch with their needs—or so she had thought. The answer came back quickly. Because she was too preoccupied with her own love life, that's why. "But you could have been followed...the authorities...." she spluttered. "Dammit, even Soviet people can't just go where they wish. Saratov and Toglyatti are closed areas to most Russians—much less to westerners."

Paul continued to nod.

"How did you get back here?"

"I swam, remember?" It was his turn to laugh at her. "No, I hitched a ride on a farm truck. Vera arranged it. It wasn't so far. The Volga twists and turns a lot here and the boat did a big loop. Really, we aren't that far from Toglyatti or her father's farm as the crow flies." He pulled a sweater over his T-shirt. "I had a bad moment early this morning when I thought I wouldn't be here early enough. I knew the ship usually steamed off at first light. But it's not leaving early today."

"A good thing!"

"There was another bad moment," he went on, "when I discovered that I had arrived on the wrong side of the river." He stopped attending to his wardrobe and studied her. "I appreciate your concern, Jennifer, but I'm a big boy now." He moved toward the door.

"Wait a minute." Jennifer stopped him and looked into his cool blue-grey eyes, so much like Volodya, she thought, same high cheekbones, same mane of dark hair. "So you're not seeing her again?"

He didn't reply.

"We'll be in Kazan soon. Then you'll be too far away to swim back to see her."

He was silent.

Jennifer sensed that her words would make no difference but she continued. "You're still thinking about her. She won't be allowed to leave the Soviet Union, even for visits, unless she's a model Communist. You know that?" A part of her brain registered the fact that he was packing.

Paul switched off the cabin light, tucked his bag neatly into the corner and turned to her. "I know that," he said quietly. "That's why I've decided to stay here."

★

David skipped his shower in favour of following up on the sunrise swimmer. He pounded quickly down the stairs and was in time to see Jennifer disappearing into Paul's cabin. *Paul? A spy?* For sure, the trail of puddles up the corridor ended at Paul's door. Unabashedly, David leaned toward the door and listened. He could hear the murmur of voices—once or twice growing louder. "I have to try and talk you out of this," Jennifer was saying.

Note to self, David thought. *No need for bugs hidden in the intercom. The commies can hear us through the cabin doors.* Finally he decided that eavesdropping was stupid, knocked on the door and walked in. As he entered, Jennifer appeared dumbstruck. Paul looked as if he had just made an embarrassing noise.

Slowly she turned to David. "What are you doing here?"

"Well, I saw…a man swimming to the boat." David glanced at the wet garments hanging over Paul's sink.

"David, Lona, me—is there anyone who doesn't know about this?" asked Jennifer.

"Well, you can bet Chopyk won't notice a thing," Paul answered. They all laughed, even David, though he wasn't sure why.

"Please tell me I can talk you out of this," Jennifer went on. "It's a hasty decision."

"But the right one." Paul appeared to be listening but continued to pack a knapsack.

"No. It's hasty. You don't know what she's like really…."

"She's a dream!"

"And what will you live on?"

"She'll get transferred back to her father's farm—to help him. It shouldn't be too difficult to arrange. We'll live there." Paul rolled a sweater into his pack and glanced up at Jennifer with a shy smile. David fidgeted from one foot to the other. They seemed to have forgotten his presence.

Jennifer groaned. "Are you crazy?"

"Never felt saner."

"You don't know how horrible farm life will be here. Shortages of food. Rough living…"

"Since when are you an expert on Soviet farm life?"

"I know as much as you know…Oh come on! You're not cut out to be a farmer."

David seized the lack of response to ask, wide-eyed, "What's going on?" They ignored him.

"Seriously, Jen, I've never felt clearer about anything in my life. I'm staying with Vera."

"Wow! Is that the woman you met at the Workers' Club visit?" David had come up to speed. "She's gorgeous. Congratulations, you lucky sod." Then he thought. "But you mean you'll get her out of the country?"

"No. I'm staying here with her," Paul replied firmly.

Jennifer discovered that, for some reason, her heart was not really in this dispute, but she tried again. "Think of my job," she continued. "I'll be in trouble for losing one of my students!"

"Jennifer, excuse me for noticing," David pointed out, "but you're already in deepest doo- doo with Chopyk for your affair with Volodya. Or did I mishear that dispute in the dining room yesterday?"

Jennifer stared as if she had just now noticed him. "Will everyone stop interfering with my life and 'affair,' as you call it?"

"That's it!" retorted Paul. "That's exactly how I feel. This is more than an 'affair,' a vacation fling with a local chick. I love Vera. Nothing like this has ever happened to me before. And you should talk, Jennifer." He levelled a fierce stare at her. "After chasing around Leningrad with your hunk of burning man. If you felt the same way about Volodya, you'd understand."

There was silence in the cabin while Jennifer struggled with this revelation. *He's right. He loves the woman. He's going to be with her. Would I do the same for Vlad? No. Yes. Yes, I would.* Finally, she asked, "When will you go?"

"Later today when we put in at Ulyanovsk. Vera will come pick me up there. She's got something planned."

"Paul, please don't tell anyone else. There's no reason they should be involved or blamed."

"Okay, except Ted and Maria—I'll probably tell them when I say goodbye."

"And Lona probably knows there's something going on," said David, "'cause she was up on deck this morning, too."

"It doesn't have to be a big cloak and dagger issue," Paul said. "I'll just announce to the authorities—maybe Ivan Nikolaevich or Natasha—that I want to defect to the Soviet Union. It happens. They'll be delighted." He rattled on, calmed by the acquiescence. "At first, they'll think I'm a spy. I'll have to prove I'm not. Then I figure we can get on with living."

Jennifer felt a fresh wave of anger. "How naïve are you? Of course they'll think you're a spy, a plant. You'll be interrogated, maybe sent away. You don't get it. All this first class treatment we've been getting is for visitors, not for citizens. Listen"—he was waving her away—"in Leningrad I met a Cuban, a musician, who opted to move here. You think they gave him an award? Put him in an orchestra? No. He's now living in a condemned slum with a 10-rouble-a- week job sweeping floors. That's what will happen to you."

Paul sat down on the bunk with a sudden thump, his knapsack at his feet. "No, they wouldn't do that—they wouldn't break us up. And they wouldn't mistreat me. I'm still a Canadian citizen."

"Like I said, how naïve are you? You could see the inside of a Soviet jail for a long time while they're deciding what to do with you."

Paul fidgeted nervously, the bravado gone from his face.

Jennifer went on, "Think about Vera. She'll come under scrutiny, too...her family, her whole life will become uncomfortable."

David cleared his throat. "I hate to say this, bucko, but she's right. I remember when I was here in '68 one of the Italian exchange students—a real Romeo—fell for Masha, a mathematics student. Whoo, she was hot stuff, but none of us poor adolescents could get near her. Only her Romeo. Anyway, he opted to stay in the country and that's the last we saw of him."

Paul's face had turned grey. "What do you mean?"

"He just quietly disappeared. When we asked the teachers about him, some of them actually pretended they didn't know who we were talking about. My professor—he was a good guy—gave me a straight answer, or as close to a straight answer as you'll get here. He said that Romeo was being re-settled. That was his word, 're-settled'. He didn't look too happy when he said it."

"So what does it mean?"

"Who knows?"

Paul and Jennifer locked stares. "You still want to do this, don't you?" she asked him.

"Yes," he nodded. A minute passed.

Finally David spoke. "So Paul, if you're really going to leave, can I have your leather jacket?"

★

Breakfast was chaotic. At first, Ivan Nikolaevich announced to the diners that their departure would be delayed while they awaited the delivery of food supplies. Almost immediately following his speech, the riverboat moved away from the dock and waiters appeared with an adequate spread of hard-boiled eggs, bread and sausages for the buffet table. Ivan Nikolaevich appeared untroubled by this contradiction, and after fourteen days in the Soviet Union, the guests also treated it as normal. Jennifer, Paul and David helped themselves to the breakfast and sat together, saying little, distracted by their thoughts. There was no doubt in Jennifer's mind that Paul would do what he wanted. Apart from anything else, she realized how much she would miss him—and not just for his jacket, like David.

The jacket. Huh. It's very distinctive, thought Jennifer. She visualized the maroon and white leather college jacket with the appliqued letters "UV" for University of Vancouver on the sleeves. Her thoughts were already leaping ahead to the day that she and the others would have to cover up the fact that Paul had left the group. *If someone else were to wear that jacket—someone, for instance, like that American, Frank, there—with the same haircut and height, he could be mistaken for Paul from the back.* David glanced up at that moment, caught Jennifer's look and also stared at the young man from Tennessee. Thoughts swirled, cascaded, in Jennifer's consciousness: the jacket, the view of the haircut, something she had to remember, something she had promised in a dream. What was it?

"You know," David spoke, his mouth full of toast, "that pretty boy from Tennessee is a real nice guy. I think he's got his eye on you, Jennifer."

She silenced him with a glare and went on with her breakfast.

13.

ULYANOVSK, LAND OF LENIN

JULY 18, 1974

"They've got to be joking. Have you seen this itinerary?" Hank waited beside the bus that would take the group on the day's sightseeing.

The boat had steamed into Ulyanovsk, a small port city, exactly at noon. After the hastiest of lunches served in the dining room, all the passengers were asked to assemble in the parking lot promptly, ready to board the tour bus. Snatching their cameras and travel bags, they had been ushered off the boat so rapidly several of the students thought it was a fire drill.

"Is this rush-rush anything to do with you?" Jennifer asked Paul as they filed off the boat.

"Couldn't be. I haven't told any of the authorities yet."

"Have you got cold feet?"

"No...yes, I do," he replied with a frown. "It was what David said about being sent away. I couldn't stand to be apart from Vera."

"Young love. It's a grand thing," Jennifer blurted out, then wished she hadn't. Paul appeared more agitated than before.

Despite Natasha's insistence on haste, when they got to the bus, the driver was conspicuously absent, leaving the door locked, enough reason to send the tour guide into a fit of expletives. Handing Hank the day's itinerary, she darted off in search of the driver. Chopyk followed her, full of self-importance. The two, it seemed, had come to some kind of liaison.

The wharf was an austere square of concrete. An attempt had been made at ambience along one unkempt, grassy strip that surrounded a lone linden tree. At the other end of the strip stood an ugly statue of a stern Bolshevik who, the plaque noted, had been party leader in the region during the revolution. The man's concrete form appeared to be overstuffed as if to pad his importance, and his chiselled eyes gazed skyward. Paul lounged against the statue, Ted and Maria at his side, the three of them wrapped in intense conversation. Paul's bulging backpack rested against the stone.

Just as Jennifer was about to go over to him, Hank tugged at her sleeve saying, "Jen, uh, Mrs. White, you've got to look at this. Listen to this itinerary. 'First, we go to the family home of Vladimir Ilyich Ulyanov, now better known as Lenin,'" he read aloud from the guide. "'We see the humble abode where our great leader passed his childhood years in preparation for the workers' struggle.'" Some of the students snickered. "'Then we go to Lenin's school to be shown his very classroom and his desk which is kept as a special shrine'—it really says shrine! Presumably we see where he parked his chewing gum and where he kissed little Krupskaya, too." Everyone was laughing and Hank basked in the attention.

Jennifer glared at him. "Show some respect. Remember where we are. This city is Ulyanovsk—named after the Ulyanov family. What were you expecting? Disneyland?"

"Yeah, think of it like a visit to Graceland," David said, "only instead of seeing Elvis, we see Lenin."

"Oh, I get it," said one of the twins. "It's like a Lenin theme park. I hope there's rides and cotton candy."

"Please stop laughing or we'll have a diplomatic incident. The Soviets take their leader very seriously."

Hank waved the schedule. "But Jen, you haven't seen the rest of it yet. After this sojourn with the family's life, we get a 15-minute break. Oh yeah, after which—now get this—we go to the Lenin Museum!"

Jennifer smiled despite herself. "That does seem like too much. I'll ask Natasha if we can pass up the afternoon visit to the museum in favour of some free time for everyone. But please, act interested in seeing the Lenin home. It's a very big deal to the Soviets."

As she moved away to search for Natasha, Paul took her arm. "Don't talk to her about that right now. It might put her in a bad mood. Truth is, I don't know what to do, who to talk to about my leaving."

"I don't know how to help you." Jennifer felt genuine concern.

"What if I was interrogated?" Paul went on. "I couldn't take it. I thought Natasha would be savvy about defecting but what if she has to report this to her boss?"

A shaft of light broke through the overcast sky and the lonely linden tree was thrown into sharp relief, each branch outlined. She was suddenly aware that she wouldn't see Paul again after this day. She touched his shoulder and gazed into his face. The light that filtered through the clouds reminded her of a moment on a day in Leningrad when she had looked at Volodya in just this way.

Something flashed. "Give me hope," he had said. A thought struggled to be born. It came slowly, gathering momentum, then raged through her with terrifying speed. It electrified her. Paul felt the jolt through her arm. His eyes widened. "What?"

"Don't tell anyone about leaving."

He held her gaze questioningly.

The idea was so thrilling, so disturbing, but suddenly she knew it was meant to be. It would account for everything: Paul's departure, Volodya's hopes, her future.

"We don't have much time. Don't tell anyone what you're doing." She pulled him behind the ugly statue. "Look, is there some way you could stay with Vera and maybe arrange some papers and identification for yourself? Not tell anyone you're Canadian? Just blend in. Pretend to be Soviet?"

"This morning you were warning me not to leave. Now you're telling me to blend in. What's with you?"

"Well, is there?" She was growing impatient.

"You mean by—how? Buying papers or bribing someone? I've heard it's done here, but I don't know if we could arrange it. Why?"

"I want your passport." Paul was listening hard, but before he could answer she went on.

"You said this morning that if I loved Volodya the same way I would do the same thing. Well, I do love him—but I can't stay here. And he doesn't want to stay here either. He can't get out. He's not going to be given an exit visa no matter how hard he tries. But if we had your passport..."

"Whaat! That would never work. Just walk out pretending to be me!"

"Yes. Yes, he looks like you. About the same height, same eyes, everything. He could leave the country with me...that's in just three days' time. You know, he could pretend to be you for the last days of our trip, then he could stay being you even in Canada. He would have your identity, everything. You could get another identity here. Oh, God, what an idea!"

Paul shook his head and glanced up at the statue's grim face. "It's illegal to use a false passport."

Jennifer didn't believe she had heard the words correctly. "You're talking to me about illegal! You've done lots of illegal things lately—jump ship, stay in non-permit areas…you don't know how many Soviet laws you're violating."

"But, Jen, I'm the only one that gets in trouble for my actions—and I'm prepared to take that chance. You're wanting me—and others—to take part in a conspiracy. Defrauding border guards, smuggling illegal aliens. And if he replaced me for the rest of the trip, then all the students would be involved. Is that fair to them?" He glanced over at Ted and Maria who returned his look anxiously.

"So that makes it worse than what you're doing?" Jennifer found that her breath was coming in gasps. "You're putting us all in jeopardy by leaving. They'll ask us who knew and we'll have to admit that we could have stopped you…or we have to lie about it."

"No, you couldn't have stopped me."

"Keep your voice down. I understand now that nothing we say can stop you. I'm prepared to take that chance, too. Will you help us? Will you talk to Vera? I couldn't in all conscience walk off with your passport if I thought it would get you in worse trouble."

"As crazy as that seems, you may have come up with something. At least I wouldn't be interrogated. If I can get a Soviet passport no one will ever know." Jennifer could feel herself relaxing a little; this scheme was so right for everyone.

"I'll talk to Vera," he went on. "She's supposed to meet me here—somewhere. She said she'd find me." He glanced about nervously.

"Thank you, Paul, thank you. This could change my life." As Jennifer said it, she knew it was true. She had cast her lot now—with the man who up until two weeks ago was a total stranger. Of course, there was still her marriage to Michael back home in Canada. The divorce would be inevitable. She resolved not to think too much about that until she returned.

"You can't tell Natasha anything," she said. "Just come on the tour today. Act normal. And we'll have to huddle with the others who know you're leaving. I'll need their help."

"Whoa…this is happening way too fast." Paul staggered a little, then found his footing.

Jennifer turned to him. "I can't believe you'd think that. You set the pace—when you decided to live with someone you've known for two days."

"I disagree. You started it, Jen, when you met Volodya."

★

Eventually, the hapless bus driver was located having a nap in the harbour shed, and he was ushered back to the bus by a grim-faced Natasha and smiling Chopyk. Jennifer also returned to the bus with a strange, light-headed feeling.

"Go on, ask her about the free time," prodded Hank. Jennifer jumped. For a moment she couldn't think what he was talking about.

"The free time…instead of going to the museum," he prompted.

Dutifully she turned to do battle with their security guard over what now seemed such a trivial issue.

★

Vera caught up to their tour at the Lenin home. She was on foot.

"All the tour buses come here sooner or later," she said simply. "It was not difficult to find you."

Jennifer kept Natasha and Chopyk busy in the modest garden where the Ulyanovs had once planted potatoes, by fostering a debate about class struggle—a subject that was usually good for a lengthy discussion—while Paul, back at the bus, hugged Maria and shook hands with Ted and David.

"Tell Jennifer I've got to talk to Vera today about something important," he told David, "and that Jen should meet us at the civic park this afternoon. There's a hedge there with the word 'Lenin' carved in it. It's easy to find. Jen knows what it's about."

The couple set off down the street together, Vera casting adoring glances up at Paul, he swinging his pack jauntily.

When the time came to load the bus once more and Natasha began her usual head count, Jennifer stepped forward.

"Paul's already on the bus," she said casually, surprised at how easily the lie unfolded. "Oh, and the twins have just gone off to take a photo down the street." As she had suspected, Natasha would regard the latter problem as more serious, and she trotted off on her sensible heels to round up the strays. When all were aboard, the bus went to Lenin's schoolhouse, after which they had been granted the requested free time in downtown Ulyanovsk. The bus pulled up outside a yellow-tiled department store with the stark title of "Clothing," and Natasha released the group only after copious street directions and strict admonishments to return to the boat two hours before departure time.

"Lock-up time, you mean," snorted David. "The boat's not moving on tonight, according to Ivan Nikolaevich. We leave in the morning."

"Good," said Jennifer, "because we may need all the time at our disposal. I've got to meet up with Paul and Vera at a park—the one he described to you—and I'd like it if you were to come with me. I want to tell you about my idea."

"Sure. It beats a day with Natasha and the boys. And I've got to see this hedge called Lenin for myself…."

They went on foot in the wrong direction at first, stopping to ask the way of bemused citizens happy to speak to the foreigners who knew their language. One of them pulled out a chocolate bar from his pocket and offered it to them; another one turned around on the spot and walked them to a crossroads. After some delays and backtracking in which they passed the same department store twice, they spotted a landmark fountain in front of the park gates.

"So give. You still haven't told me," David reminded her.

Jennifer hastily summarized her plan for Paul's passport and Volodya's departure. David whistled.

"I thought it was something like that. Tell me, do you really love this Volodya guy?"

"Why?" she answered sharply.

"Just wonder how much trouble you'd get into for him?"

"Apparently a lot."

"I don't think this is actually illegal until you go to leave the country," David said thoughtfully. "So you still have a few days to change your mind."

"Thanks, but you're optimistic. If Vera and Paul really go for it, I'll be in possession of someone else's passport."

"That's nothing. He could have lost it and you were just about to turn it in." He smiled.

Entering the civic park, they admired the hedge clipped into the shape of the letters of the Soviet leader, then caught sight of Vera and Paul on a park bench engrossed in one another.

"So, changed your mind yet?" David asked of Paul.

David laughed, but Paul regarded the question seriously. "Not me. Have you?" he said to Vera.

"No, not at all. This is the best thing in my life." Jennifer felt a brief sadness for a time when she met Michael.... They had known this feeling, too.

Paul turned to Jennifer. "I've got something for you," he said, and he handed her the passport.

"How will you do without it?" She must know or she wasn't going to take it.

Vera answered. "We have a plan—a good plan. He won't need it again."

"I'd feel better if I knew the plan." She made it a statement, not a question. There was only one chance to find this out.

"It's better if you don't know." Vera was also firm.

The two women locked eyes. "Maybe you're right," Jennifer considered. "But Paul, you've got to lie low at least until we leave the country. Don't try anything right away, please."

"We leave—that is, you leave Moscow on the 22nd, right? Maybe we should have a signal to say that everything's okay. You could send Vera's father a telegram from Paris or Montreal. I'll write the address."

Jennifer thought of the signal she had worked out with Volodya. "Jazz with Ella" she said. "Okay, it's a signal that we all know, including Volodya."

"Got it," Paul replied. "There is something else you need to do for me, Jennifer. Here are all my cheques. I want you to take them back to Vancouver and use them to get at my inheritance in the bank." He pulled out his pen again to sign them. "If you have any problems, you should go to my estate solicitor—I'll write his name here—and tell him everything. He'll keep it confidential and he can get access to the funds. Then you'll have to figure out some way to get the money to me..."

"In US dollars, please," Vera spoke up. "The best way is to send the money as cash with somebody who's travelling here. The mail is not reliable. Money is stolen."

"Okay, I think I've got all that."

Paul extended his hand to Jennifer. "I wish you all the best, my good friend." Then he reached over and hugged her tightly.

"You too," she said sincerely. "We'll miss you." She smiled at Vera who nodded. "There's something I'd like to give you." She reached into her purse and removed her wedding ring from where she had tucked it. "You might need this. Please take it. It brought me happiness for a while." Paul nodded. Vera took the ring wordlessly. Her eyes filled with tears.

"Uh, aren't you forgetting something else?" asked David.

"The leather jacket? It's in my cabin—for you." They all laughed.

"Hey, thanks. But I was actually thinking about what we should say to people back in Canada. Do you have any family at all, Paul?"

He shook his head.

"Any friends who might report you missing?"

"Not any who'd really care. Jen's been my best friend. Oh, but you can tell Dr. Sommer at the Russian department what happened and tell her that she's an excellent teacher. I couldn't have done this without her. But otherwise, no, there is no one. My mother's been dead a long time now, and so has my grandmother who was my guardian. My dad disappeared—probably because of gambling debts."

By now Vera was crying openly. "You have family now," she told him, and Jennifer was overjoyed to see how eagerly he hugged her.

★

Just three blocks away, their tour guide, Natasha Alexeyevna Kuchkov, was sitting on the warm cement buttress of a public fountain. Two other women dressed in *sarafani,* light cotton dresses, were dipping their bare feet in the fountain's pool and giggling. Such behaviour was not for her. In any case, the telegram recently received from her director had induced a cooling effect right to the bone. Phone me directly you reach Ulyanovsk, it had ordered. *They don't know what it's like in the field any more,* she thought. *When we arrive, I have visits to organize, vouchers to fill in, local staff to supervise. How much time do they think I have?*

Thus she had been almost relieved when the rebellious students asked for some afternoon time off, though she wouldn't admit as much to them. It had given her an opportunity to find the nearest postal and telegraph office where the long distance phone booths were located. She dialled her director on his personal private line and after some buzzing, whining, and several hang-up clicks, she was finally put through.

"We have a little worry," he had grunted to her.

"We." That always meant that someone from above, the KGB or the Politburo, was riding him on some sensitive issue. "Yes, Natasha Alexeyevna, naturally you've done an excellent job to date. But we have a little worry."

She could imagine him sitting in the cool bowels of the Intourist building in Moscow at his leather-topped desk, his fat stomach spilling over the blotter pad, his glass of tea in front of him, eyes on the clock.

"Please, director, tell me how I can be of service." It was as well to be polite with this man; he took offence easily.

The director launched into the problem. It seemed that someone on high had recently determined that this particular Volga cruise would be going into uncharted territory. It was the first time there would be American and Canadian tourists journeying into areas of great sensitivity—industrial complexes, military bases and so forth. Moreover, some of these tourists could speak Russian, the director went on when Natasha tried to interrupt. They would be asking awkward questions, taking forbidden photos, possibly bringing contraband items to upstanding Soviet citizens and corrupting them. It was an ill-advised tour. They should have stayed in the centres: Moscow, Leningrad—maybe even Kiev if they wanted some Kazak history—but never be allowed to wander up and down the Volga among the proletariat.

Natasha listened to this amazing speech from her director. At least she knew that she had done nothing wrong. The trip had been approved long ago; if the mandarins at the Politburo were only now figuring out what had been asked of them, then only St. Nicholas, the miracle worker, could help them now—as her old grandmother used to say. She declined to tell him so. One didn't know who was listening to the phone conversation.

"Yes, Comrade Director," she replied. "No such harm has been done yet. I have seen to that—along with Ivan Nikolaevich, the cruise director, of course."

There was a brief silence. "Ah yes, Ivan Nikolaevich." The director repeated the name as if he were only just registering the thought.

Uh-oh, what's Ivan done? She knew that the director usually had no patience for hearing about surveillance agents. Natasha was silent.

The director went on. "I don't think you quite understand, Comrade Kuchkov. We want *you* to report on the problems you will inevitably find there. Should you find any disturbing incidents, for example, the corruption of Soviet citizens, or other evidence that the trip was ill-conceived, then you would have to report it to me. Naturally, I would have to feature it in my report to the Buro. Our worst fears would be confirmed and we would be perceived as knowledgeable. They would *not* have heard it from Ivan Nikolaevich. They would have heard it first from us, here at the agency." He paused to clear his throat. "Do you understand me? I hoped I wouldn't have to make this quite so transparent to you."

"Understood, Comrade Director. Say no more."

After she hung up the phone, she considered the astonishing conversation. It was typical. The director had once been an advocate of having a tour group of foreigners on the Volga. Now—while he hastily re-aligned his position on the matter to suit the political winds of the day—he wanted her to dig up the dirt preferably before Ivan Nikolaevich did so. She sighed. It was the usual switch about. One day the authorities wanted everyone to work harder, the next day they were to stop work for a state visit. Life in Mother Russia.

Natasha had thought about her next step. Luckily she knew she could find a "disturbing incident." The Canadian students were in a rebellious, shifty mood and had begged the afternoon off to go on their own adventures. She decided to follow them on their independent routes to see who would pose a problem. A simple announcement of a few peccadilloes should do the job. But she couldn't trail after all of them. Who would be the likeliest to offend? The answer didn't present easily. The bold blonde, perhaps? But Natasha had already spotted her shopping at the department store and there was no problem with that. The director hadn't exactly ordered her to generate an incident—and frankly she didn't want to do so. Only whatever was necessary to keep her job. She thought hard. The twins now, they were always trying to take photos of unsuitable places: factories, railyards. Well, they would do for a start.

But just as Natasha crossed the street in search of them, she spotted Jennifer and David hurrying off down the block. Yes, that would be a far better idea. Jennifer was given to liaisons with Soviets—as evidenced in her affair with that anti-Soviet fellow Volodya in Leningrad—and it would be just like David to accompany her on her adventures.

She followed them, observed how they chatted easily with strangers, but lost them again at the fountain where she sat down heavily to rest.

If they had gone into the park then…pshaw. Hundreds of Soviet people walked there, too. They could hardly get up to much trouble by viewing the ten or so edifying statues.

Rather than tramp the Ulyanovsk streets, it was far better to sit here and use her brain to solve her problem, Natasha reflected, and she gave in to the impulse. She removed her battered, sensible shoes and swung her bare feet into the fountain just as the other women were doing. The water oozed between her toes and she sat pondering in this way. This dalliance was refreshing—she almost forgot what she had set out to do. It was gorgeous and green here in the provinces in July. As a Leningrad girl herself, Natasha had never become accustomed to the lack of views in Moscow or the hot city streets. Then, as always, thoughts of her career with Intourist rose again to the surface. The idea came to her in a flash. Maybe, while all the students were occupied, her time would be better served checking out their cabins for seditious literature. She had overheard Hank and Marty talking on deck one day about Lona's mysterious assignations and the puzzling conversation had stuck with her. Definitely, Lona's cabin was the place to start. Hastily she shoved her damp, bare feet into her shoes and hurried down the hill toward the riverboat.

★

As soon as Jennifer returned to the boat, she went to her cabin and locked the door behind her. She flopped down on her berth and examined what she had been given that day. She held a Canadian passport in the name of Paul Mercier, and it said that he had been born in Montreal on May 26, 1947. That made him nearly 18 months younger than Volodya. She leafed through the pages. At the space for next-of-kin he had written "Yvonne Lavalle," and for relationship "grandparent," then that had been scratched out. He had also tucked in his university student card, a library card and the signed cheques.

She also withdrew a single sheet of thin, folded paper. Just a few words but it was thoughtful. "Use this passport to realize your dreams. We'll be okay. Good luck! P and V."

14.

ILLEGAL INTENT

ULYANOVSK, JULY 18, 1974

Maria's eyes were dreamy and romantic as she twisted her own "first promise" ring. "They were such a cute couple," she sighed. "Did you see how he looked at her—with so much love?"

"I only hope she feels the same way," Jennifer said.

"I can't believe he just walked out of that park without a backward glance," said David. "I couldn't do it. Leave my life behind, my family back in Canada..."

Jennifer, Ted, Maria and David had gathered at a dinner table aboard ship where they were reasonably sure there was no bugging device. They had determined this the day before by the simple expedient of dousing the table "accidentally" with a pitcher of water. A waiter had immediately stripped the table and replaced the cloth while they watched.

"We have to be cautious," said David, indicating the room at large. Only a few other diners were present and the dinner had been delayed once again. "Our first item of business..."

"Excuse me. Have we elected you leader?" Ted asked.

"Could you at least listen to me? Our first item of business is how much we tell the others—here's Hank now and he looks as if he wants to sit here. And then there's Lona, who some of us mistrust, and we should decide that before she arrives."

"Everyone's got to know," pointed out Maria, "except Natasha, of course. Don't you think people are going to miss Paul? Though maybe not everyone needs to know about the second part of the plan, about Volodya..."

"Agreed," replied Ted. "But there will have to be a few of us who know about the second part so that we can help." Jennifer thanked him wordlessly with a smile. "I suggest we talk to Hank right now and he can talk to Marty."

"Can he keep a secret?" asked Ted.

"We're going to have to trust him." David waved at Hank and he happily slid into a seat at their table. Quickly, David outlined the facts.

He's got a good organizing streak, Jennifer thought and was comforted. The group voted three to two, Hank and Jennifer opposed, to tell Lona about Paul's departure and about the subsequent plan for Volodya.

"She's a smart cookie—the sort of person who would figure it out—so it's better to have her on our side." David seemed relieved. "Call her over as soon as she comes in."

But it was Chopyk who entered the dining room first. He marched solemnly toward the group's table. Jennifer drew in her breath. David's mouth hung open. Maria looked guilty. *God, we're never going to make it out of the country if one glance from Chopyk throws us into such a tailspin.* But when Chopyk arrived, he addressed only her as if the others were not present.

"Finally coming into your territory then, Mrs. White?" he said. They were the first words he had spoken to her since the telegram incident and she didn't have a clue what he was talking about.

"Uh…you're referring to…?"

"Kazan. The Gorky museum, of course."

"Oh, of course." *The place where Maxim Gorky worked and lived. The very foundation of my thesis. Remember? This was supposed to be the highlight of my trip.* "Sure..." she continued, "I'm really looking forward to it." She hadn't thought about it in a week.

"We only have about four hours in Kazan before the museum closes, and we catch our plane to Moscow the next morning. Perhaps I can help you spend your time there fruitfully. I could take charge of the students while you're at the museum."

"Why, thank you—that would be great, oh…." She was aware that the faces around the table were stunned as if they had only just remembered that Chopyk was still in charge of the trip. She glimpsed David shaking his head, his eyes wide.

"Uh, but no…that's okay, Professor Chopyk." They hadn't yet had time to formulate a plan. "I imagine we'll all be going there together… that is, some of them may want to spend some free time in Kazan and so…" She stumbled on.

But, distracted by the plates of food arriving on the buffet table, he nodded vaguely as if he had understood every word. "Fine, just let me know if you need help."

When Lona finally entered the dining room, they were already eating. Despite her misgivings, Jennifer called her over and David jumped up and pulled out a chair for her.

"Thank you kindly," Lona said, looking surprised at the royal treatment. She placed her plate of sausage and vegetables on the table carefully.

"We'd like to talk to you," David said. She nodded. "And let's be honest," he went on, "some of the folks at this table have had some problems in talking with you in the past." Hank glared at her and she smiled back. "But let that rest here. There's something more important to discuss."

"I'm okay with that. Tell me what's on your minds."

David described Paul's situation briefly and she listened with interest. "Oh, that's so romantic…I won't breathe a word. But why are you all looking so worried?" When no one spoke, she said,"There's more, isn't there?"

David nodded. He described the passport and Jennifer's plan. At this, Lona was shocked. Her fork landed on the plate with a clatter and Jennifer could see the blood rising.

Lona repeated, "You're trying to get Volodya, Jennifer's friend, out of the country?"

A chill passed through Jennifer. She cut in, "You sound like you know him. Do you?"

Lona gave her a long look, then picked up her fork again. "Why would you say that?"

"Geez, Jennifer, you're really nervous," said Hank. "None of us have met him—though I admit we talked about him a lot." They all laughed. "Oh, yeah, we knew where you were on those white nights." The crude snicker broke the tension and even though she was the butt of the joke, she relaxed. She turned back to Lona. "We're asking you—and everyone at this table—to be part of a highly illegal act. Are you in?"

They were surprised when Lona gave an uncharacteristic wide grin and said, "Illegal is my middle name."

"I just bet," muttered Hank.

David went on, "Okay, that's settled. We each should tell one other student about Paul's departure only, please note, so that they can help with the head count problem until the end of the trip."

"I've been thinking about that," Jennifer said. "I'm going to ask that American from Tennessee if he will wear Paul's jacket in sight of Natasha and Chopyk. He's about the right height and if he were seen from the back, they might think it was Paul."

"That should work for tomorrow," Ted chipped in, "but I'm not sure when we part company with the Americans. Does anyone know when they fly back?"

"Then that's the next order of business. Find out as much as we can about the next leg of their trip."

"I've been thinking about the head count problem," said Hank. "I like Jennifer's suggestion about the guy who wears Paul's jacket. We could also use the oldest trick in the book."

"And what's that?"

Hank turned to Jennifer and said, "Smile. Have some coffee. You're looking terminally serious tonight. The best thing we can do right now is lighten up. Watch." *Always the show-off,* Jennifer thought. He looked around for the waiter who had given up on their table and was busy cadging a cigarette from one of the Americans. Hank caught the eye of the fuzzy-headed blonde waitress who Jennifer had liked; she had given some of the women authentic recipes for *pelmeny* and semolina cakes.

"Last day, my good friend," Hank spoke to her charmingly. She smiled, pouring coffee all around and slopping some on the table. "Will you come on deck and wave us all goodbye tomorrow?" Hank continued. She giggled. "Please come on deck and say 'till we meet again' to me. Bring all the staff." He smiled winningly.

"I am through dinner service at 10 p.m." she said pointedly. "Come to my cabin and I have a souvenir for you."

When the waitress left, rolling her hips, the reaction at the table was full of suppressed laughter. The speed and intensity of the complete sexual manoeuvre astounded Jennifer. Had she ever fallen for something like this? Of course she had.

"I presume that this display of libido is part of the plan?"

"Sort of…I didn't really intend to start a last minute affair. What I want is for all the staff to be up on deck as we leave. Have you ever heard of the old Chinese fire drill?"

David nodded, but Jennifer shook her head. "Apart from its racist overtones...no, tell me."

"High school days, right? Bunch of guys all pull up at the stop light, jump out of the car, run around, jump back in again in different seats." Jennifer continued to shake her head. She felt as if it was frozen in the position. Lona stared as if she were seeing Hank for the first time. "We do the same..." finished Hank, as if the point was obvious.

"The same what...?" Maria and Jennifer asked simultaneously.

"Get off the boat, mill around, come back in again, confusing the count. Chinese fire drill. Make crowds of people milling around, so that no one can take roll call."

The ensuing silence was probably one of Jennifer's lowest moments. *So this was the adolescent prank on which two lives depended.* Not only would it have to do the job, but she realized that she was grateful for any plan at all.

MORNING JULY 20, 1974

Sergey Ivanovich, the machinist from Novizavod, had sat in the Kazan airport all morning. You never knew how long you might wait for a flight, or even if there was any point in waiting, he thought. And even after you were allowed on the plane, they might bump you so that your seat could go to some senior bureaucrat who had only just wheeled up in a sleek black car.

He badly wanted to visit his sister in Moscow. That's all. But they didn't give much respect to people like him with their simple needs. In fact, he had already been told that the flight was fully booked, but he had not given up because, long ago, he had acquired those most valuable aids to survival in the modern Soviet Union: friends who did favours. This particular friend was part of the airport administration. That the friend had first listened to Sergey's tale and then had produced an extensive shopping list for the Moscow stores was not unusual. Sergey had simply tucked the list away, along with the five other shopping lists from neighbours and family, and had promised to do his best. The friend had also slipped him some crumpled bills in a foreign currency, acquired from international visitors at Kazan Airport. This was fine, too. Sergey was not even sure what type of currency it was, but he had tucked it away in an inside pocket. If he could locate a buyer—a friendly tourist—to go to the deluxe *Beriyozhka*, the foreign currency store in Moscow, and purchase some of the rarer commodities, he would be a winner.

On the basis of Sergey's sincere promise, the friend had ushered him into the Intourist Lounge at the airport. Strictly speaking, you were supposed to be a foreigner to sit there. But there was no one watching the door, and even the foreigners came and went as they pleased. He knew he really couldn't pass for a foreign tourist under scrutiny. His haircut was good; he was rather proud of it. His friend Masha had clipped it for him, after a style from a French magazine. He considered it very dapper and modern. But one glance at the shabby, plastic shoulder bag hoisted over his worn work jacket would reveal the truth. Waiting patiently in the lounge, Sergey tucked his bag under the chair, sat back, and attempted to look western.

"Wait until after the big tour group is given their boarding passes," his friend had said. "There'll be room." The big tour group were English speakers—at least they spoke mostly English and sometimes rather bad Russian. They were students, perhaps. Sergey wished he had learned English in school; it would be convenient in Moscow. Leaning over casually, he attempted to read the luggage label on a foreigner's flight bag. *Sanaba*, *Sanada*, something like that. Oh, now he knew: Kanada. Home of the Toronto Miple Lefs or was it Mapple Lifs. He saw a red maple leaf embossed on the luggage—definitely the hockey player country. Well, if he got bored waiting, there were always a few things to discuss about hockey that surmounted linguistic barriers.

Sergey Ivanovich drew his attention back to the matter at hand. He had some knowledge of the Aeroflot plane that already stood on the tarmac outside the window. He knew how many passengers it could hold. After the large tour group, which would get first priority in boarding, and after the five official-looking functionaries who also used the foreigner's lounge but appeared to be Soviets, and after the handful of soldiers he could see waiting outside of the lounge, it was dubious that Sergey Ivanovich would find a seat. He began to count, and as he did so, he did some thinking.

A worker such as he should have priority, but that was rarely the case particularly when you came from an outlying republic. The Tatar Autonomous Republic was actually part of the greater Russian republic; it was like the worm living within the swine. After raw materials had been extracted from the Tatar earth—crude oil on which the state depended—they might as well have been part of Siberia for all that Moscow was concerned. He didn't dislike Russians, in fact Sergey was the product of a Moscow-born father and a Tatar mother. His parents had met and fallen in love just before the war when his father was sent on a work assignment to Kazan. He had died in the trenches defending Moscow from the fascists.

Though Sergey had grown up in Kazan and loved the city, his sister had fought to live in Moscow, even going to the extent of marrying a Muscovite, then divorcing him, simply to get her Moscow housing permit. It was to Nadya's shared apartment that he was going now. The letter had arrived last week. She was pregnant and would not abort this time. The father was a scurrilous dog, Sergey decided, after meeting him on a previous visit. A heavy drinker, not the type for Nadya. It was his duty to go to Moscow at this time and dissuade her from this vicious pattern. Maybe she could come back to Kazan with him. Keep the baby, even. She had pulled enough strings to get to Moscow in the first place. Why couldn't strings be pulled to move her back home?

These thoughts buzzed through his mind as he sat and waited and counted and watched the flight desk where the boarding passes were neatly stacked.

After some time, he noticed a very curious thing. He was having great difficulty in counting the foreigners. The group from Canada would not stand still. They were always moving about. Every so often, one would sit for a moment, look around, get up and begin to walk again. He would never have obtained an accurate count but for overhearing the severe-looking one, the tour guide with the glasses and black hair, talk to the airline official. She reminded him of his local Party member and political officer. The Party member look-alike had given the figure of 18, counting herself presumably, though how she had counted the group when they remained in perpetual motion, he wasn't sure.

This group's activity was making him buzz. Perhaps it was the sugar they used in capitalist countries—apparently they ate a lot more of it than Russians did. He still placed a sugar cube between his teeth and strained tea through it, like his father had done before him. He couldn't imagine any other type of sugar except maybe the sweet gassy water everyone drank. Did capitalists drink vodka? He could go one right now. There was probably none available and with his limited funds it would have to be a warm beer from the refreshment stand. Leaving the lounge was a risk but there was only so long he could sit here with a thirst. Stowing his bag under the chair thus giving him an excuse to return to the lounge, he slouched off to the refreshment stand on the lower level.

Miraculously it was open, and there appeared to be a supply of beer. He found himself standing behind one of the frenetic Canadians.

"Good day," he said politely in Russian directly into Jennifer's ear. She jumped.

"I beg your forgiveness," he added hastily, at the same time seizing this opportunity to wedge one foot closer to the drink counter, before a particularly rotund grandmother stepped in his way. The girl from Canada understood Russian, he knew that. He had been listening to them in the waiting room, and he had noticed this one particularly. He handed his token to the attendant.

"You have 18 in your group," he said to the still startled Jennifer. It was better to know for sure. She might say that there's another group on their way and they are all ahead of you in line for the plane to Moscow. But, instead, she seemed astounded. Perhaps she had never been spoken to by a live Tatar before. Perhaps she thought we were all aliens out here in the republics. "You have 18 in your group. Is that correct?" he asked again.

Finally, Jennifer found her tongue.

"Yes… uh, no. What do you mean? My Russian is not so good, please." She seemed covered in confusion. She was not holding a drink coupon but continued to stand at the counter blocking the way.

"You must pay the cashier first," said Sergey helpfully, pointing at his bottle of beer that had been unceremoniously thrust at him. Perhaps she didn't understand.

"Oh yes, thank you," she answered, looking at his drink and moving away rapidly. Then she stopped and appeared to reconsider. She turned to him and said in impeccable Russian: "Why do you ask how many is in our group?"

When the call for loading finally came, Sergey Ivanovich, the machinist from Novizavod, walked out on the tarmac with the group from Canada, though in the rear. The severe lady walked right up front, having relied on an airline representative to do a count. But she might turn around and take stock of her brood at any minute. His English was not good enough to understand what was going on here, but he rather thought that even if he had elected the English language in school, he would be no more enlightened. One thing he had always been able to do well was count. There were 18 here all right—including him.

Just recently he had read an article in *Krokodil* that exhorted him to seize opportunities wherever they might be found to further the socialist struggle. Was he not getting on this very plane to Moscow looking like one of the foreign tourists and wearing a handsome leather jacket? On the other hand, what if they had tricked him into doing something illegal? The authorities could revoke all his travel privileges. Normally, he wouldn't have any qualms about sidestepping the authorities but it was just so important that he go to Moscow right now.

All these thoughts and more passed through Sergei Ivanovich's brain as the group from Canada traipsed slowly across the tarmac.

★

"The first thing I'm doing when we reach the hotel is to find a telegraph office and send a message to Volodya," said Jennifer, seated behind David and Maria on the tour bus, her chin hanging over the headrest. The teacher-student wall had completely crumbled; they were her friends. She was grateful for their help.

"I thought you'd already done that," answered David. Maria's head was nodding, more concerned with sleep than planning. "You mean you didn't wire him from Kazan?"

"No. You saw how Chopyk dogged us the whole time, plus I couldn't confirm anything. What if, all of a sudden, they'd decided to take us out of the country through Kiev instead of Moscow? You know there's no logic to the itinerary."

"It's always Moscow. I told you that," David said. "We're here for less than two days. That's not long enough to get Volodya from Leningrad and up to speed."

"There's the rest of today..."

"Oh, no, not at all," interrupted Maria suddenly, her eyes still closed. "According to Natasha we have an action-packed evening ahead." She looked around quickly as if expecting their tour guide to hear her name. But while the group had been given a late lunch in the airport dining room, Natasha had gone on ahead to make arrangements and would meet them at the hotel. "After check-in, we're to squeeze in dinner and some of us have tickets for the ballet. And remember when we were in Moscow last time you said that the juniors would be having a last lesson here and maybe taking a guided tour of St. Basil's Cathedral?"

David's grin waned. Jennifer sighed.There was another thought nagging at her. She had promised to call her cousins as soon as the group arrived and Misha and Marta knew she would be back in Moscow by now. She dearly wanted to see them again, but how would that work with Volodya?

"Most immediate threats first," she muttered. She pictured both Natasha and Professor Chopyk standing in the lobby of the hotel, handing passports to the registrar, counting...searching for Paul. Her stomach lurched. Once again, she must remind herself that she was not yet committed. If she did not summon Volodya then she had done nothing wrong. What Paul had done he would have done anyway—that was his problem. It would be at the moment that she asked Volodya to act that she would set the ball rolling. And that moment was galloping towards her.

She leaned forward once more, oblivious to Maria's irritation. "Everyone exits from Sheremetev airport, right?"

David nodded.

"I don't know whether to tell him to meet us at the airport given our tight time frame... Do you see what I mean? He might not be able to drop everything and leave Leningrad right away. If he can't leave until tomorrow, he should just meet us at the airport." Her voice had taken on a wheedling sound. She realized she needed reassurance like a child.

"I don't know whether Soviet citizens are allowed anywhere near an international airport because there's a lot of security," David pointed out. "Better he come to the hotel, then you have time to prepare him."

"Are you serious? And have Natasha see him?" *What was wrong with everybody? Couldn't they take this seriously?*

"It's a big hotel," he snapped. Then as if reading her thoughts, he turned to face her more fully. "Look, we'll help you with the Paul stuff. But you know, you've really got to make some decisions about Volodya for yourself. I don't want to know more about how you're going to do it. Do you understand?"

"*Da, ponyatno,*" she answered curtly. "I understand."

Maria's face wrinkled during this exchange but she kept her eyes closed. Jennifer leaned back in her seat.

Her thoughts were troubled. *Natasha is not the only problem. It's all the other border guards and officials who hang around and check up on us. Volodya's going for his life here. And we have Paul's future in our hands.*

The bus rolled along the wide boulevards and tree-lined streets, past the giant GUM department store. As it neared the Hotel Rossiya, the group shifted in their seats. Dozers woke up and began to reach for their hand baggage. But on the edge of Red Square the bus picked up speed and shot past the mammoth hotel, heading instead for a bridge over the Moscow River. Chopyk sat up and scrambled out of his seat, confused. They could hear his voice above the rumble of the engine but could not hear what the driver was saying in reply. Once over the bridge, the bus entered an older, shabbier part of town. There were not so many gargantuan buildings here although the open cobble stoned squares still dwarfed the vehicles. On the corner, a shop sign announced bakery and pastry. Crowds of shoppers were exiting, smiling and chatting, with bulky bags packed with loaves of bread. A stout elderly woman in a cloth coat—though the day was warm—ran out onto the street by Jennifer's window apparently on a suicidal collision course with the bus. At the last moment, the bus swerved as if the driver had seen her all along even though he was engaged in earnest conversation with Chopyk. The driver slowed, appeared to answer Chopyk, sometimes lifting his hands off the wheel perilously to make a point.

Tension was paralyzing her, she knew. Just two weeks ago she would have been the first one to run to the front of the bus if something had gone awry or just for the excitement of it. Now she didn't trust herself, and for once Chopyk appeared to have stepped up to the plate. Finally she gave in to curiosity and went up to the front.

Just at that moment, to everyone's surprise, the driver pulled up in front of an ornate grimy square building that looked as if it had seen duty under the czars. He jammed on the brake and began to gather his belongings as if this was the end of his trip. To Jennifer's surprise, they were back at the river again, actually still within sight of the Kremlin and the very bridge they had crossed earlier. They had done an elaborate block circling, snaking their way through endless one-way streets to arrive at the front door of...of what? "Hotel Bucharest" a sign proudly proclaimed.

"Well, that takes the cake," fumed Chopyk, turning to speak to the group. "It appears that we will not be staying at the Hotel Rossiya tonight."

There was a chorus of sighs but some giggles, too.

"I have just recently, very recently, been informed that we have been booked into this hotel—the Bucharest, which, as we all know, is the capital of Romania. You won't find the establishment in your Michelin Guides, but no doubt our Romanian comrades find it very comfortable."

This sarcasm was wasted on the driver who had already exited the bus and was lighting a cigarette. "I presume it has dining facilities and private bathrooms, but if not, I ask you all to be flexible. These are our last nights in Moscow and I, for one, don't plan to let this setback ruin it."

As this last was said through clenched teeth, most of the group doubted its sincerity.

Chopyk trod firmly off the bus, luggage in hand, looked briefly up and down the quiet back street, took in the worn matting at the doorway and a withered plant in a pot, and entered. The others followed. Inside, it was a monument to pre-revolutionary architecture. An ornately patterned Persian carpet, so threadbare their heels tapped on it, wound through the hallway to a high front desk draped in ornamental gilt moulding. Many niches and nooks had been fashioned into the walls of cool grey marble; within the niches stood chipped statuary, their colours dull from years of restaurant grease and traffic fumes. At least there was no doubt that there was a dining room because everything smelled of sour rye bread and fish. At the core of the curved marble staircase a large, gilded cage heaved and groaned. This proved to be the elevator. Chopyk stared at it, curiosity vying with irritation. It took a few moments of distraction by this cultural marvel of a hotel for Jennifer to realize that there was no Natasha there to meet them.

The desk clerk could not have been less interested in the leadership of the tour group. Chopyk engaged in an eloquent but losing battle with a ramrod straight, unsmiling concierge regarding unforeseen scheduling changes, dining arrangements and the possibility of sending a message to the Hotel Rossiya where the unfortunate Natasha must even now be waiting for them. Rudderless, while his captain was engrossed in this exchange, the clerk merely collected their passports listlessly and handed out room keys seemingly at random. He gestured toward the heaving gilded cage. *Davai, davai*, he waved them away.

"Looks like you got a single room, Jennifer," Hank said. "Going to be doing some entertaining? Nudge, wink." She reeled at his loud voice. And when had he started calling her by her first name? It was symptomatic of the changing relationships within the group.

"Let's not hang around here," Lona whispered. "Let's get up to our rooms before Chopyk learns which rooms we've been assigned to." They heaved their suitcases in the direction of the elevator. As if in camouflage, a wrinkled crone materialized out of the marble statuary, slipping off a stool lightly for one of her advanced years, and beckoned them. She opened the cage door, then the elevator door, and ushered them in. She waited patiently while Jen, Lona and Maria assembled their baggage. Three persons plus operator appeared to be the elevator's capacity. Then she closed the doors carefully and pulled a brass lever. Grunting with effort, the box lifted. "Three into seventeen," Maria calculated as the box jerked upward. "How many trips will this thing make, do you suppose, before we're all upstairs?"

Ordinarily, I would find this hotel an intriguing anecdote, thought Jennifer, *something to tell the folks back home. Right now, I just find it all an intolerable delay.* She was becoming quite adept at all the procedures. As she exited at the fifth floor, she went immediately to the dezhurnaya's desk and rapped smartly on the table. The clerk, another septagenarian, was nodding off in an easy chair. "Key to room 503," she said briskly in Russian, and proffered her card. This woman could be someone's grandmother, she thought, and though it's difficult to view her as the enemy, a nosy floor clerk who noticed that Volodya was Soviet, not Canadian, would be a nuisance or even fatal.

Jennifer opened the door to her room. It was dark and close but not what she would have picked for a briefing session. There was a private bathroom, she discovered with relief, and opened the door thankfully. It held a square, chipped, pedestal basin, a small bath, and gigantic toilet that sat lordly on a dais. Its tank was secured onto the wall above the bowl and there was a chain to pull that worked the flush. Either the last guest had pulled too enthusiastically or the fixture's age had rendered it incontinent. It had overflowed onto the floor.

"I'd better start working on getting this cleaned up right away," she muttered. "I don't want staff in the room while Volodya's here—that is, if I could even get staff to clean it up." Once again she was talking to herself—problems, delays. And underneath it all—fear.

Consequently, it was nearly six o'clock by the time Jennifer finally left the hotel, walked briskly along the riverbank, and turned onto the same bridge they had driven across on her way to Red Square. Possibly there was another telegraph office than the one she had already discovered near the east wing of the Hotel Rossiya, but it would save time to head directly toward the familiar one. As she walked, she thought how to word the telegram: "Returned to Moscow. Hotel Bucharest." That part was easy. Then what? "Jazz with Ella" and maybe she'd better add something about coming to see her off. Would that get him in trouble? No, he had asked her to write that—let's go out together or something like that. She hadn't remembered very well because she had been sure at the time that she would never need to use the code words. It had all seemed melodramatic.

She was well into Red Square, her mind replaying their last meeting, before she remembered something else he asked on the last day in Leningrad.

"Where do all the jazz singers live?"

"I don't know," she replied. "New York, maybe New Orleans," and she had shown him on the map.

Now, why did he ask that? Did he think that's where she was going? Well, Vancouver would have to do, though it wasn't considered a hotbed of black gospel and jazz music. Not for the first time the thought brought home to her forcibly what great change she was about to render in his life. She had the power to pluck him from his homeland, get him set up in her own, with a foreign language, culture, job—all done illegally. Then what? What did it mean for their relationship? In Leningrad, she thought she loved him, but now she wasn't so sure. Was she doing this as a charity or did she truly want him for herself? Or had he become the drowning child in the lake who she must save?

Her face grim, she hurried into the telegram office, stood at the same tall counter as two weeks ago and began to make notes on the provided slips of paper. She had just printed the first words, concentrating so there would be no errors in transmission, when she glanced across the room for a moment. A cold prickle started somewhere around her belly and rushed up her spine. It was all over. They knew. She was being followed. She could not take her gaze from the man standing at the far counter. It was him, the man from the Kazan airport. The one they had coaxed into standing in for Paul, wearing his leather jacket, which they had taken back from him on the plane, right under Chopyk's nose.

He was loitering, looking for someone. Her? Willing her eyes to go down to the scrap of paper, she tried to think. *I never did think well under pressure...responsible for bad performance during mental arithmetic in Grade 4...traumatized for life.* Her brain rattled on. She simply couldn't think what to do. Gingerly raising her head again, she snuck another look. It was him all right, same clothes, same tilt of the head, a nice smile. He was quite clearly following their group and had been since

Kazan. She was crazy to have involved him in the head count. They must have known right away. Why didn't they question her?

The horrible answer rushed in. Maybe they had already picked up Paul and he had confessed. Paul knew the plan, but he didn't know, hadn't really met Volodya so they would have to follow her to lead them to him. That was it. If she turned this telegram in at the counter, the man from Kazan would wait until she left and then stop the transmission. She imagined him flashing some sort of badge in front of the sour ladies, noting down Volodya's address, them wondering what was the problem, what had the foreigner done, but not daring to ask.

She must leave. Right away. Not reveal Volodya's address. It was off. She took the piece of paper, folded it and put it in her purse. She must leave quietly, pretend she had come in only to ask directions or something. She turned to a security guard by the door, the one farthest away from the suspect. "Can you tell me the way to the Beryozka store, please?"

Exiting from the door nearest the hotel, she walked rapidly into the vast portico of the Hotel Rossiya. A wave of relief washed over her. It was a stupid plan from the beginning. She had smuggled a few beers across the Canada-US border in her time, but to smuggle people! If Paul wanted to succumb to the passions of youth, fine. But playing with people's lives like God, well, she could get her adrenalin kicks by driving a fast car on the freeway and.... A headache screamed up her neck and her legs shook. In one of the massive vinyl chairs in the lobby of the Hotel Russia she sat down and wept.

★

"I can't believe you chickened out," Maria repeated. She had shown up quite soon after Jennifer's collapse, gliding across the vast football field of a lobby and up to her friend.

"Look, I came to find you because I'm sorry about what happened on the bus. You know, what David said. Of course we'll help you."

Jennifer blew her nose and struggled with her dignity. "You know, Maria, I don't think you've got it. This is not a fun elopement and I'm not a bride that has suddenly got cold feet. This is a serious business and that's what I was trying to get support for on the bus."

Maria lowered her gaze.

"Maybe he's right not to be involved too much," Jennifer went on. "I can't drag everybody into this. You could be caught, maybe jailed. I don't even know what the penalty might be."

"I'm not being silly," Maria returned. "I know it's not an elopement. But it's the most romantic thing I've ever heard of. And it's good, Jen. It's a good thing, not a bad thing. I want to be involved. I know it's risky."

"Please, let's not keep talking about it. Not here." Jennifer pointed at the metal grill halfway up the column. She felt sick and couldn't bear the thought of going back to the stuffy room at the Bucharest alone.

"Let's go then," said Maria, exasperated. "Come on. I'll take you to the restaurant and we'll have some of that strong Georgian wine."

★

Sergey Ivanovich, the machinist from Novizavod, was delighted. Luck was with him, and he was alert enough to take advantage of it. Good fortune had placed him on that Aeroflot plane in the first place, somehow as part of a group of foreign tourists. Not only that, but luck had seated him next to a green-eyed, laughing woman whom he had fallen in love with immediately. She had offered to shop for him at the Beryozka in Moscow. He could enter it, of course, but Soviets didn't shop there. It would only call attention to him if he began to flash around foreign currency. This plan of hers not only suited him well but gave him an opportunity to see her again. Lona, she said, was her Russian name. Her last name was Jewish, he felt sure. Lona was a magnificent name, an excellent one. Throwing caution to the winds, Sergey had eschewed the primitive airport bus in favour of a taxi and rode in from the airport using some of his neighbour's shopping funds—an unnecessary extravagance but he had loved every minute of it. Besides, it would get him to the Hotel Rossiya before Lona, so that he could meet her at the Beryozka that very evening before she changed her mind.

But after rushing into the city, he had been forced to wait for the Canadian's tour bus anyway. He couldn't stand in the lobby of the hotel too long; it would arouse comment and he didn't want to press his luck, so he had waited first in the telegraph office then on a street corner, somewhat conspicuously, he thought, but the latter gave him the best vantage point. The tour busses generally turned at this corner, whichever of the four entrances they used. He waited and watched every one. Dirty, creaking ones belching black soot. Shiny new ones from Germany and Japanese ones with colourful markings. He began to wonder if he had the wrong hotel.

Just when he considered giving up, maybe returning tomorrow, he saw her coming. She was a long way off, walking, not from the direction of the Hotel Rossiya, but from the direction of Red Square. As she got closer, he could see that she was laughing and happy. His heart gave a little lurch and she approached him quickly, still smiling. Wonder of wonders, she was apologizing to him:

"Sorry I'm late. We're not staying at this hotel after all. We were taken to the Hotel Bucharest, way over there. I walked across a bridge..."

"Da, da, da," was all he could think of to say, nodding and smiling in return. This was superb! Recovering slightly from his daze, Sergey linked arms with her like a sweetheart and they walked around the block, while Sergey ran through his various shopping lists. She interrupted several times to tell him that she hadn't seen such an item or there was a good supply of the other. Eventually he gave her all the foreign money, which turned out to be $45 American dollars, a few pounds sterling and some West German marks, and she disappeared into the store.

"Ech, you dope," Sergey muttered. "You could have offered her a drink or an ice cream from the stand..."

Once more he waited, this time choosing a different street corner, next to the GUM department store. He could shop at GUM himself later. The way he calculated it, shopping for goods like vodka and brandy at the foreign currency store would save him money because everyone knew items for tourists were at least four times cheaper than in their Russian stores—that is if you could find them in the Russian stores. Also, it would give him lots of time to procure out of stock goods elsewhere. The difference would probably pay for his wanton taxi ride plus maybe an evening at the restaurant...with Lona. Guiltily, he realized that he had been in Moscow for three hours and hadn't thought once of Nadya, his sister. He should telephone her; she had a phone installed recently and he had the new number. There was a pay phone across the way, but the receiver hung uselessly. Some one had placed a sign "Not Working" and it looked as if the sign had been there for months. There would be public telephone booths at the telegraph office in back of the hotel and they would be in good working order. He slipped over there to make his call.

15.
INTIMATE ASSIGNATION

MOSCOW, JULY 20, 1974

"You were right," Maria reported. "There is someone following us, but I don't think it's that guy from Kazan airport." She picked up speed and tugged on Jennifer's arm. She was walking Jennifer from the big hotel on Red Square back to their modest one to check out the hotel bar. Just before the bridge, they hastily scooted down stone steps to the river's embankment to see if their pursuer would follow. Crouching in the shelter of a ragged shrub, they turned to look.

"Kick me if I'm wrong, but that man looks like Paul!" Maria peered through two branches in the bush. The man was now standing at the bridge's entrance, looking around.

"What?" Jennifer cried and also peered through. "*Bozhe moy*! It isn't Paul. It's Volodya." She stood up, rooted to the spot. Her legs didn't want to move any further, it seemed.

"Volodya! Wow, he does look like Paul. So what are you standing there for? Go to him," Maria demanded.

"Of course, I…We should be careful. That's not who I saw in the telegraph office."

"Oh, flipping hell….I'd be running into his arms…Call him over then. There's no one else around." She scanned the embankment; two senior men sat on a bench some way off but Jennifer reckoned she could safely call out and have the words drowned in the traffic noises.

Volodya spied them and darted down the embankment, a huge grin across his face, and he dropped a bulky knapsack to the ground. He took her hands modestly, ignoring Maria. "I have been waiting at the Hotel Rossiya all day—but I didn't know which entrance. Then I see you leaving the lobby with this lady. Oh, my *sladki*, it's so good to see you."

"But how did you get here? Why were you at the hotel? Our group is across the bridge at another hotel. How did you...?" The questions tumbled out. "I was just going to telegraph you."

"This was written in the telegram. Go to Hotel Rossiya."

"What telegram?"

"Let's not talk here," he said, his glance falling on the two elderly men who appeared to be dozing off. "Let's talk out of sight of Red Square. You lead the way and walk across the bridge. I will follow."

They walked across the bridge—apart from one another. Jennifer was conscious that she was now walking like a Soviet, head down, no eye contact, from fear of being stopped and questioned. Once across, she and Maria ducked down an alley, Volodya joined them and all three started talking at once. Maria was introduced formally with much hand shaking and grinning, then after mentioning that three was a crowd, she offered to let the two go back to the hotel while she watched to ensure they weren't followed.

"Keep an eye out for the other man from Kazan, please Maria," Jennifer asked her, and she nodded assent. "I know I didn't imagine him."

Jennifer and Volodya slipped into the hotel room unseen by the dozing *dezhurnaya*, and their first action was to embrace. Kiss first, questions later, she thought. But the kiss meant she had to press her body against his and she could feel the hard bulge in his pants pressing back. The heat rushed up to her face; suddenly she wanted no questions. She wanted only to stand naked with him, his erection on her belly, his tongue licking her neck, every cell stretched lazily in sensuous pleasure. Slowly they both began to shed garments. No words were spoken. Finally, after what seemed a long, long time, he pushed her gently back towards the wall, seized her under the arms and pressed her against the peeling wallpaper. He entered her quickly, his arm muscles working hard to keep her on tiptoes; she perched on his cock as he rocked to and fro. She groaned with the exertion as well as the joy of feeling him move within her. Before the spasm hit, he relaxed his grip and they tottered toward the bed. There she rode him, staring straight into his eyes, her breasts grazing his chest, coming again and again in waves of sensation.

By the time they got around to asking questions the evening had faded into darkness and she was satisfyingly relaxed, muscles loose, tension forgotten.

"Now, tell me about the telegram," she asked.

It was from Kazan, he told her. It was unsigned and did not use the words "jazz with Ella" but it gave the date of their arrival at the Hotel Rossiya. He looked uncomfortable.

"But I don't understand. I didn't send a telegram," Jennifer told him.

His face crumpled. "So there is no hope for me. I will not leave the country?" he asked.

"No…yes, there is hope," she responded breathlessly. "So you know nothing of the plan…I wonder who sent the telegram. David? No, because he asked me…and it couldn't have been Maria because she…"

"Forget telegram. What plan? Tell me quick."

"I'll do better. I'll show you." She produced Paul's passport from its hiding place in her money belt and held it in front of his face. "You are now Paul Mercier, my dear. Here's a picture of you. Saturday, you will fly out of the country under this name."

She watched mixed emotions: awe, anxiety, and maybe some hint of calculation in his expression. He took the passport from her fingers and gazed at it. A minute passed.

Finally, he spoke. "For such a long time, I have waited for this. I thank you from the bottom of my heart." His speech was curiously formal considering that the two of them had been rolling in intimate embrace not 20 minutes earlier.

"Well, thank Paul, too." She thought it odd he hadn't asked her how she had acquired the passport or what Paul was going to do. But perhaps the full impact hadn't sunk in yet. "Now, Mr. Mercier, I have to trim your hair and find you some new clothes. Maybe even some Hush Puppies, like you wanted."

It was past midnight before she dressed again, kissed Volodya on the lips, and darted down the hall to David's room. She knocked softly and he opened the door immediately.

"Come in. Just writing in my notebook. It's hard, you know," he told her. "I can't write anything about you-know-who in case someone reads the journal…" He looked at Jennifer.

"You're glowing. I take it your reunion with your beloved was satisfactory."

Jennifer blushed. "It sounds as if Maria spread the word. I'm sorry to bother you so late…I'm looking for clothes." David moved to turn the radio on to drown out their conversation in case anyone was listening. "I need the leather jacket again and any shoes that you can spare.

But David, there's another thing and it's a real mystery." She described the telegram that had been sent from Kazan. "That was a dreadful day trying to avoid Chopyk's sheep herding efforts, trying to see the Gorky Museum and not think about Paul, all at the same time. Did you…?" But David was shaking his head.

Jennifer felt a wave of fear again. "You were one of the few who broke away from the group so I thought it must have been you trying to surprise me. Please tell me it's not someone else trying to pull a fast one. "

"I didn't send any telegram. If you think about it, it would have to be someone who knew Volodya's address—and knew the code words."

"No, it didn't have the code words in it. He thought I'd forgotten them and came anyway."

"Natasha? She would have quick access to telegrams…she knew his address from the telegram he sent you…"

"Natasha—it has to be her." Jennifer was stunned. "But why? I don't get it. You know I suspected her back when the other telegram came in. She's from Leningrad, you know, and they might have known one another while he worked for Intourist."

"I've thought there's more to her than what we're seeing. That's gotta be it, but you won't get a chance to ask her because we're trying to avoid her like the plague right now." David began to sort through the closet for the jacket and shoes. "Do you know if she caught up to us here at the hotel?"

"Oh, for sure, but I don't think she knows what rooms we're in. If you hadn't told me your room number, I'm sure I couldn't have got it from the desk clerk. They seemed terminally uninterested."

"Listen, why don't you ask Volodya if he knows Natasha? Let's sleep on this matter," he yawned politely, "and get you-know-who fixed up with clothes in the morning."

But when she returned to her room, Volodya had fallen into a deep sleep sprawled across the utilitarian single bed. His pack was open, contents spilled onto the floor, with his clothes hanging neatly on the racks. Coaching would have to wait.

★

The next morning Jennifer slipped from the room again, promising to return with breakfast for Volodya-Paul. She found Chopyk at the buffet table and approached him right away before she lost her nerve. "Professor Chopyk…" She tried to keep the pleading out of her voice. *Be relaxed, natural.* "I would very much like to see my cousins again before I leave the country." He looked blank. "You remember, Mikhail and Marta and their daughter Nadya—they came to visit when I arrived in Moscow. It was quite a surprise to me to find that I had any family here…" she rattled on nervously. "Anyway, they live in Tula, you know, the samovar city. I'm proposing to take a quick trip there by taxi—yes, I know it's expensive—(she forestalled that argument before it could get going)—and return tomorrow, before we leave for the airport. In fact, I could join you at the airport. Would you mind rounding up the students and getting them out to the airport by yourself?"

Chopyk lingered before loading scrambled eggs onto his plate. He appeared to be considering this request with all the earnestness of a barn owl, his lips frozen in a pucker.

"Well…I guess that would be satisfactory." His face belied his words. "It seems that classes have gone by the board anyway. But please get to the airport in plenty of time. I don't want to be waiting for you with Natasha hopping about."

"Oh, I would be absolutely sure to arrive in lots of time. Thank you for stepping in." She turned to go. "And there's one less for you to worry about—Paul is going with me to Tula, so don't look for him with the other students. Okay?" She waved across the room cheerfully as if Paul were sitting at a breakfast table.

"But what about your luggage?" Chopyk asked.

"Oh, we'll take it with us to Tula. Don't worry. I'm sure this will work."

He frowned but turned back to the buffet as if there were more important issues to be considered among the bacon and sausage.

She ate hurriedly, sliding three rashers of streaky bacon and cheese into a roll wrapped in a paper napkin and quit the dining room before anyone spoke to her. No Natasha in sight. This was the answer to a prayer: visit her cousins again just as she had wanted, and hide "Paul" away in Tula until just before they would board the plane. It had two advantages. Not only would Chopyk and presumably Natasha not worry about the two of them, but it would keep the others from becoming too involved in what was really her own dangerous escapade.

Now, there were just a few details to take care of: phone her cousins and let them know about her impending visit, get Maria or someone from the junior class to make good on her promise to arrange a trip to St. Basil's while she was gone, find clothes and shoes for Volodya-Paul… oh, and a suitcase. Really there were a lot of things to do. She fought the rising panic.

16.

LUCKY LONA

HOTEL BUCHAREST, MOSCOW, JULY 20, 1974

Lona Rabinovitch returned alone in a good mood to her hotel room after her outing with Sergey Ivanovich, the guy from Kazan. It had all been a rush job—zip around the Beryozka store for cartons of cigarettes, French cheeses, brandy, then have the acquiescent Sergey—he really was sweet—take her by taxi to the apartment of her Moscow accomplice to pick up a number of items, as previously arranged, for transit.

Sergey proved a loyal and tenacious bodyguard—it was a stroke of her typically wonderful luck that he had been available as an escort because she hadn't wanted to visit Krov's apartment without protection. On the previous occasion in Moscow when she had to do her business with him in the street, he had grabbed her arm savagely and had not been intimidated by the many spectators or the street police. *Really, he knows I would never expose his black market scam*, she thought. *So he's got me over a barrel.*

"Comrade Krov, you scare me," she said aloud before realizing that even in this dingy hotel room infrequently used by western visitors, there might be microphones. She shushed herself but continued to hum.

Her list, written in a kind of shorthand in her black book had been drawn up by the consortium in New York. The men that ran this profitable importing scheme had also provided her with a list of contacts, hired hands who would find objects fast, or who already had them for easy sale, though how any one of those friendly, entrepreneurial guys had ever got connected with a creep like Krov, she couldn't understand.

As it was, she had taken on smuggling an additional item out of the Soviet Union, purely because she had fallen in love with it. Now she pulled it out of her purse. It was a small icon, St. John Chrysostom, a very popular fellow for centuries, though not of her own faith. However, something about its crackled surface, the pale face of the saint, the gilding around the border and in his halo, and the very worn appearance of the icon touched her. It had been used by worshippers for centuries, loved, handled carefully. Even if it was essentially an Orthodox Church image, it spoke of devotion, the same kind of devotion that her people afforded to religious items and objects.

Staring at the gilt image again, she was reminded that there was purpose to her endeavour: to track down items of great religious or artistic significance before they were lost or defaced forever in this country. The Soviet political will toward their own ancient relics was appalling. Right around the Hotel Rossiya she had noticed a ring of decrepit small churches that no one cared about. The group had heard tales of centuries-old churches being used to store grain or left to tumble down. Why, in some cases, she reasoned, she was merely the instrument that provided a return of possessions lost decades ago by their rightful owners who had been forced to flee the country because of war or persecution. They would have to buy them back now from the consortium, of course, but that was a small price to pay. Of course, hoodlums like Krov upped the purchasing price and there were costs associated with running the business including the tidy chunk of change that was going into her own pocket for taking the risk.

Lona did not always understand the reverence that Jewish people paid to their history. It seemed to her as if they were always grabbing the long lost past and while she acknowledged the past, she preferred to look to the future. *I'm sure if I had been alive during the pogroms, I would feel differently,* she thought. As in all ventures like this, however idealistic in motive, there was always a lot of money at stake. The solid silver menorah would fetch many dollars so it was definitely worth hiding the bulky thing. It had not come from Krov, but from another kinder, gentler man who said it had belonged to his grandmother. He had provenance, unusual for these under-the-counter deals: a photo of his granny in Poland with the menorah. In the black and white photo the grandmother stood regal and proud, and the surrounding room appeared to be rich with *objet d'art* and other treasures. When asked, the man had told her that most of the art works had been buried in the garden when the family thought the Nazis would soon be at the door. But his grandmother had died in a concentration camp, and since that time, the home had been razed, the site transformed into a factory with thick, concrete floors and the family's riches lost forever. A sad story, Lona thought. She wondered how many other homes had buried treasure—perhaps the owners didn't even know it. Back in New York the buyers would be interested in stories like this one.

When she got home should she find a buyer for the icon, too? No, she wanted the icon for herself. She would not be turning it over to the businessmen on her return, but somehow, she would have to account for the cash—it had cost $50 U.S. dollars—that she had been given to purchase these items. She would cross that bridge when she came to it. She considered its size, weighing it in her hand like tomatoes at the grocery store. She checked once more that the door was locked, then she carefully unwrapped the distinctive Beryozka wrapping paper from a newly purchased balalaika, a musical instrument with a long narrow neck and a triangular body. There was no mistaking its shape even in wrapping paper. Once the paper was removed from the balalaika she wrapped the icon in her kerchief, then squeezed it into the space between the strings and the body of the instrument. It just fit. She re-wrapped the Beryozka paper around the balalaika, being careful to tape it in exactly the same spots as before, then held it up for inspection. You could hardly tell a thing—just the merest suspicion of something rectangular. She placed the wrapped balalaika into a mesh shopping bag such as the Soviets seemed to carry everywhere. This one she would be taking on the plane with her and stowing in the overhead baggage compartment. That done, she pulled out a kit from her suitcase that contained some acrylic paint such as children use and bottles of powder and Vaseline.

The jewellery, a pendant of solid gold and very old, was easy to doctor up; it was not of religious significance, although Krov had tried to tell her otherwise. It would find a buyer who was simply looking for something pretty and special. She considered if she had time to invent a provenance for it—a story about some czar giving it to his mistress, perhaps? The consortium had rapped her knuckles once before for inventing but she couldn't resist. Who's to say that it was not true? What Russian peasant before the revolution would own such a rich thing?

She removed the elaborate gold chain and put it with her own modern jewellery, then re-hung the locket on a leather strip. She put the locket into a tiny, leather, filigreed sack. She would wear it around her neck.

The prayer scrolls were also easy. They would be placed among the pencil sketches of St. Isaac's Cathedral that she had completed while at the Hotel Astoria in Leningrad. She took two sheets of artist's paper and sealed them along three edges using a small bottle of Lepage's glue. She carefully unrolled the first scroll and placed it between the sheets, then put the seemingly blank sheet in among the other sketches in her knapsack. She repeated this process with the others. None of this would stand up to a vigorous border guard grilling, she realized, but she would take that chance. With any luck, and perhaps a diversion of her own making, she would slip through.

The ceramic ewer was ancient and covered in symbols. What purpose it had served in ritual, she was not sure, but the buyers would know. Over the years of recovering lost art and religious items for the consortium, she had developed an intuitive sense of what would sell and what would not be worth the trip. She dipped her tiny artist's brush into the paints and with great attention to detail, she painted the ewer a hideous, bright green. It would scrape off later. She would have to wait for it to dry before she painted the words "Souvenir of Rostov" on the side. The ewer was bulky and would have to be packed between the wool socks that she had brought with that purpose in mind.

It was the pictures that would be the most difficult to pack. She set the ewer aside to dry and picked up one of the paintings. "The Mushroom Gatherers" she said aloud. The oil painting had been the easiest score of all—it had just been dropped off at her hotel room, courtesy of Volodya. More luck. No one could say she wasn't co-operating with the others; she had been helpful in finding a way for Jennifer White's handsome Russian man to have a grubstake in the new land. She examined the painting again. Beautifully done. She had told Volodya she believed the artist to be of minor importance, a guess based on a drunken conversation with one of the American art professors, Dr. Henry Smith, on the riverboat. But her instincts were kicking in again and she would place a bet that it would sell for three times what she had paid Volodya for it. Now that he was leaving the country with the group, perhaps he could be persuaded to carry it in his own luggage. No, that wouldn't work. It was not a good idea to call attention to him. Maybe Linda's big suitcase would be better. The menorah could go in Hank's luggage and the figurine into Chopyk's.

There was one more item to pack in her own bag: a small painting of the Romanovs—she wasn't sure of the age or artist but was quite sure of its high interest to a collector—and she had yet to make a new cardboard backing sheet for it. Using nail scissors she cut a piece of very modern looking waxed brown paper removed from the hotel room's wastepaper basket lining and pasted it onto the back of the original painting, covering all traces of the previous backing sheet. She signed it with a calligraphic pen and dated it 1970, then packed it among her clothing.

She still had to ensure that the other pieces were safely scattered in other people's luggage before they finished packing but that would have to wait until morning. It was good that she could always find help when she needed it. She was lucky that way.

17.

FAMILY REUNION

TULA, JULY 21, 1974

"You must eat more," Marta admonished Jennifer. "Look, here are pickles, cheese, sausage. You have not tried my eggs."

Marta and Mikhail (or Misha as she thought of him after the fond salutation in her mother's letter) had greeted her warmly when she and Volodya had arrived, after a hectic taxi ride from Moscow to Tula during which they had been stopped on the highway by a patrol car. She and Volodya were terrified by the interruption which was conducted in rapid-fire Russian, but as soon as they drove off again, the taxi driver sloughed it off with a grunt and a few expletives on the subject of police force.

"But why did they stop us?" asked Jennifer, while Volodya shook his head at her for bothering to inquire.

"Today it is gasoline," replied the driver. "Where did I get my gas? Tomorrow it is something else. Who knows?" was the most coherent comment they could glean from him. They realized they needed to negotiate a better price for the ride. She wished she had brought more American dollars as an enticement rather than the already converted roubles that she had in her pocket. With the delay, the two did not arrive in Tula until the afternoon. She had tried to phone, but got only a crackle on the phone line from the hotel lobby. She could barely hear a woman's voice under the whirring noise and had hoped the voice was Marta inviting her to visit.

It seemed that the family had indeed been expecting her, judging by the prodigious food supply.

"Well, of course, I'll try an egg," Jennifer replied and she bit into the creamy stuffed egg dusted with fresh dill. *Mmm—yogurt, green onion, salt.* It was delicious and she washed it down with a sip from a tumbler full of what appeared to be neat spirit. She was sitting in the family's combination living and dining room where the ornate, antique table was laden with small plates of food. Wise in the ways of Russian dining from having partied with Ukrainians and Polish, she knew that these were only the *zakuski*, the appetizers, and that a more substantial meal would follow. "No, really, now I'm full up." *At least the food is dampening the effects of the vodka*, she thought. "How about you, Paul?"

The man referred to as Paul looked up from a plate of bread and sausage and smiled shyly. "Thank you. You are good hosts," he murmured.

"Your Russian is so good. Did you study long in university?" asked Marta of Paul while Misha seemed distracted and regarded Jennifer solemnly. Paul-Volodya did not reply right away and Marta was interrupted by the sound of something bubbling on the stove. The afternoon so far had been wonderful, full of affectionate hugs and cheerful toasts toward Jennifer, friendship in which she reciprocated and in which Paul had been generously included. Their daughter, Nadya, was at school but the couple promised that she would return home very soon.

After refreshment, the cousins had spoken of their own hopes to leave the Soviet Union and live in Canada. The nervousness with which they raised the topic and the intensity with which they spoke made Jennifer realize how important this move was to them. They would need help and support in Canada. She didn't know much about Canadian immigration laws, but wouldn't they need a sponsor? Someone from within the country—a relative who would vouch for them, promise to provide for them? She thought at first of her mother as the closest relative but had an uneasy feeling these two were grooming their newfound cousin for the role.

Yet nagging questions persisted. Were they truly related to her? She wondered at their eagerness. They seemed to have everything here: a private apartment of their own, not too big but with a balcony that gave a view of the playground opposite. Their daughter enjoyed school and Young Pioneers, they said, and they were both working, he as a technician and she as a bus driver. This last gave Jennifer pause as she tried to envision the dainty, polite Marta in the driver's seat of a soot-black, fume-spewing bus, but she knew that the Soviet Union was ahead of the west in ensuring women joined the work force in many non-traditional jobs. Marta worked shifts so was off-duty right now, and Misha had taken time off work to visit with his cousin. She was humbled by how wholly they were honouring her but felt she had to have an answer to the questions.

"Why do you want to leave the Soviet Union?" she asked finally. "Don't you have everything here?" She glanced around the apartment.

Misha squirmed in what was obviously his place, a well-worn stuffed armchair—while Jennifer and Paul-Volodya sat on a lumpy, uncomfortable sofa—and he looked around for Marta before replying. She came back from the kitchen and stood by his chair.

"We are fortunate in having this apartment, it's true," Misha said, "and Nadya is happy in school…"

I hear a big "but" coming along, Jennifer thought. Volodya looked up expectantly.

"But…we want to start a new life in Canada." Misha gazed at her. It was the first she had noticed his large and expressive eyes. "Here," —he gestured around him—"we have wealth by the standards of our country: furniture, hot water, full pantry. But would this be a wealthy person's apartment in Canada?"

Jennifer shook her head. It would be about the equivalent of one of those ugly apartment blocks in Toronto somewhere along Spadina Avenue, she thought, modest and low rent. So it was economic advancement that would send them to Canada—not a desire to see Lila and renew the family relationship. Jennifer felt her doubts grow. Misha spoke again.

"But it's not only riches," he went on, dropping his voice from habit even though he surely could not be overheard by a neighbour. "We can only go so far in our careers in the Soviet Union before we pay the price. You understand, there are important people to please, favours to be given if we expect favours in return. We must never put a foot wrong."

It was all adding up now, the uneasiness, the determined stance of Marta, the desire to see their Canadian cousin again. Jennifer hastened to forestall the inevitable.

"So you would go first to Israel?" she asked.

"Yes, yes." He seemed impatient. "That is what's expected. After that, we want to go to Canada, see your mother, meet your father, get a decent job…We hoped you would help us."

"I want to have a car," said Marta abruptly. "That will never happen here or in Israel, do you understand?"

"Yes, I truly understand," said Volodya-Paul sliding to the edge of his seat. "I feel that way too," he went on, oblivious to the puzzled look from Misha. "We are cramped, confined here. There is no freedom to do the things closest to our hearts. I play piano—I love jazz music but if I play in public I must play patriotic tunes or folk songs."

After this announcement, the couple turned to stare at Volodya. Jennifer also stared—in horror. He appeared seized by a moment of mercurial passion—the same passion she had come to love—that would jeopardize his own escape.

"Sorry for startling you," Paul-Volodya said. "Let me introduce myself again. I'm not Paul Mercier. I'm Volodya Mikhailovich and I come from Leningrad. This beautiful, amazing woman is helping me leave the country by finding me a Canadian passport."

"God…Volodya, what are you doing?" The room swirled around Jennifer. She darted a glance at Misha who was registering amazement. As Volodya continued to tell his story in some detail, both Marta and Misha appeared frozen, the same questioning expression on their faces. Just as Jennifer thought she must jump in, say something, anything, to explain this madness, the front door opened noisily and little Nadya ran into the room, dropping her schoolbooks on the floor.

"Auntie Zhen, Auntie Zhen!" she cried in pleasure, throwing herself at Jennifer and hugging her. The tension eased.

Marta hugged Nadya next. "Pick up your books and wash your hands for dinner," she told the girl. Volodya halted in his story and everyone smiled. "Go on now!" Marta called out.

But when she turned back to Jennifer and Volodya, side by side on the sofa, the bantering in her voice changed. "This is a very serious risk," she intoned. "You'll certainly be discovered. You might be thrown in jail, both of you. The KGB will investigate you, your friends, your family; they might even investigate us." She glanced at Misha whose expression had become increasingly distraught.

He nodded agreement. "You've brought us into danger as well," he told Jennifer. "If you are caught, this might hinder our chances of getting out of the country legally." There was a slight emphasis on the word legally.

It was Jennifer's turn for stunned silence. "I'm sorry," she faltered. "I didn't know…"

Misha turned to Volodya: "But you knew, didn't you? How dangerous it is?" He leaned forward. The two men glared eye to eye.

"Yes, God forgive me, I knew—but so what?" He gestured angrily. "I'm not trying to do anything different than you. I want the same things and I am prepared to take a risk—and yes, risk other lives if I must." Misha reared back suddenly as if Volodya had slapped him. "I was not born a Jew, that's all," Volodya continued. "If you're so free to leave, why don't you go on and leave and not bother your cousin with talk of help?"

"We are her family," Misha retorted. "We have a right to ask. Who are you?"

"Stop," Jennifer interjected. "Please stop…" She put out her arm between the two men as if they would back down on this feeble gesture. She had noticed Nadya peeking around the doorway, horrified by this interchange. "I think we'd better go." Truth was she didn't really want to go at that moment because she knew that she would only cry all the way back to Moscow. This was her chance for having a family who she liked and she had blown it. Actually, it was Volodya's fault, she thought angrily. Why couldn't he keep his mouth shut?

"No, no," Marta said hastily. "You must not go right now. It is not right to fight like this." She turned to Misha in appeal. "Please everyone, please not to say anything for one minute. Then we will talk." Jennifer almost laughed. It was so like the kind of advice any mother anywhere in the world might say to a child who was fretting with a sibling. She stifled a sob and drew a deep breath. So many emotions: love, anger, fear.

Volodya eased back into the sofa and Misha turned his face to the window. They kept this frozen pose for almost twenty seconds during which time Nadya melted away from the doorway.

Jennifer was first to break the silence. "I'm very sorry," she began quietly. "I didn't mean to bring this on you. I've fallen in love with Volodya and he asked for my help. I didn't want to leave him here. When I saw a chance to get him out of the country, I took it. I didn't think about anyone else." There didn't seem too much more to say, so she stopped. There was another silence.

Finally, Misha shook his head then raised his glass solemnly. "Then may the Holy Torah help you on your journey without being discovered."

"I'll drink to that," offered Volodya, all resentment vanishing.

But Marta stalked away to finish preparing dinner. Jennifer followed her into the kitchen wanting to atone somehow for the troubles she had brought with her and determined that her last night with this family would at least be cordial. The galley kitchen was utilitarian and old-fashioned with a two-burner gas stove, a scarred countertop and a tiny porcelain sink. Marta peeled cucumber and kept her back to Jennifer, her posture erect.

"May I help you?" Jennifer asked. There was no answer. Suddenly Jennifer knew exactly what to say. "Is that cabbage rolls I smell?" she asked. "Mom used to make those—were they ever good." The shoulders relaxed slightly and Marta turned, wiped her hands on a dishcloth and said with a wan smile, "Yes, they are Misha's favourite, too."

The conversation was polite but not warm over the dinner table although Nadya recovered some of her childish energy and rattled on to Jennifer about her school work and her friends. As soon as the dishes were cleared away, Marta directed Volodya and Jennifer to Nadya's room, hastily vacated for the night in order to accommodate the travellers. The single bed had been made up with clean sheets for one person and a series of cushions had been placed on the floor with a quilt on top.

"I'm sorry we don't have more beds and another room for you," Marta said coolly. "But I think you will be comfortable in here." Marta closed the door behind her, leaving Jennifer and Volodya staring at each other wordlessly. She turned away, wanting only to sleep and too exhausted to challenge his behaviour. He began undressing with no further comment. But as they prepared for bed, a knock on the door startled them. Misha's head appeared around the door.

"Can I see you, Zhen? I'll be in the living room." Wrapping her robe around her, she glanced at Volodya and left the room.

Misha was sitting on the uncomfortable sofa. "This is where we should have started—right when you arrived, Zhen." He patted a worn, leather-bound album. "Forgive me that I did not show you this sooner."

Family photos, thought Jennifer. *How will this help?* Misha opened the album lovingly, smoothing the pages. She sat beside him. Most of the pictures had been taken in the last few years and they showed the couple at their wedding, traditional photos posed in front of the war memorial, some scenes from their trip to Sochi and many of Nadya's childhood. Flipping through the book quickly, Misha opened it at a page of older, grainier photos. He pointed at one dog-eared print. Jennifer gasped. The picture depicted two teenagers standing together solemnly, kerchiefs around their heads, their faces forming weak smiles, their arms linked.

They looked fragile. There was no doubt that the teen on the left was Jennifer's mother, Lila, and the other was her aunt, Eva.

"My father kept this photo with him during the war," Misha said. "His women, he called them, and he let the others think they were his girlfriends, not his sisters." He paused to let her take it in. A welcome feeling of warmth and comfort washed over Jennifer and she hugged Misha. He laughed and hugged her back.

"There are very few photos of the town they grew up in," he went on. "But this one here"—he pointed at a blurry scene of a village street that looked as if it had been taken from a newspaper clipping—"this one was taken shortly after the war as an example of the devastation that some of the villages suffered, so close to the enemy lines." Jennifer stared at the desolate street and the few emaciated people in the photo. She had trouble finding her voice but finally said, "You know, I doubted that you were truly my cousins. I thought you were simply trying to use me to leave the country."

Misha did not answer but she noticed that tears had filled his eyes.

"Thank you for showing me this," Jennifer told him. "It means the world to me—and to my mother as well. I can't wait to tell her. You've probably brought new life to our family."

For the first time in a week she slept peacefully.

★

The next morning in the taxi back to Moscow, after ascertaining that their driver spoke no English, she grilled Volodya about his behaviour. Why had he done it? Or more importantly, would he be able to keep his mouth shut now, not only until they reached Canada but for the rest of his life? "That's what it's going to take," she warned him. "You can't put Paul in jeopardy by talking about how you got out of the Soviet Union—or about the lack of freedom or shortages or anything else that you couldn't have found out by being a Canadian student traveller. You must *be* Paul now."

"Yes, yes, I know." He was impatient with her and turned to the window to stare at the passing fields and occasional rustic cottage. "You don't understand," he said finally after a long awkward silence. "This is not a game; this is my life."

Jennifer gave an exasperated snort.

"No, really, you do not understand how deeply those people, your family, care about their dream of a new life. I could feel it from them. It touched me and I wanted to show that I understood, that I care."

"I care, too." Jennifer was irritated. The air in the taxi had suddenly become stale, close, and she opened a window.

"You sit like a wet fish, nodding, when they tell you they want to leave."

"What—?

"Yes, yes, I have seen this nodding before. When I asked you to help me leave the country that day—'I'll do what I can.'" He parodied her voice on that Leningrad street at what seemed like light years ago. "You nod then you return to your pleasant group and laugh together, while I must go on with my life," he finished dramatically.

"You selfish…I'm the one that's getting you out of the country! Remember?"

"Only because your friend Paul suggested it. And when were you going to contact me to tell me to be in Moscow? Do you not think I need time to make plans, say goodbye? If I had not received the telegram from Lona, I would not be here today."

There were so many accusations in that statement that Jennifer didn't know how to begin to answer him but one thing jumped out. "You got a telegram from Lona?"

He waved his hand dismissively. "At first I thought it was from you, but it did not say 'jazz with Ella' so I knew it must be from Lona. She wanted to make arrangements for the painting, that is all. I sell it to her."

"The painting… The painting from your room, the one of the women picking mushrooms? How did she know about it?" Jennifer was aware that she had put the bigger issues aside in her rush to pin the blame somehow on Lona for what was going wrong between her and Volodya. Inevitably she would have to confront the more fundamental problems.

"Simple," Volodya replied irritably. "I meet her in the park while I wait for you one day. She is looking at a book about art. I ask her if she likes art. Does she want to see my old and valuable painting? We introduce ourselves; I realize that she is one of your group. All friends together, right? I offer to take her to my flat…"

A blinding wave of jealousy overcame Jennifer. That experience, so golden in her memory, was suddenly ruined. She had been special, the only woman visitor to his apartment, or so she thought, not just one of many. Surely Lona had not used the same table for their petty business transactions, the table where Volodya had first called her "sweet." Surely the two of them did not sit on the single bed where she and Volodya had made love?

Volodya appeared oblivious to these sentiments and he continued, "She offered to buy it but first she wanted to research the artist. I explained that I could find no artist's name but she smiled. She's a clever one!" He grinned and Jennifer felt like smacking him. "She asked for a tool, what do you call it? A screwdriver, and she prised off the bottom frame. There on the picture under the frame was a signature. It was difficult to read, but she noted it and said she would check the name at the library. Then, from Volga somewhere, she sent me a telegram saying that she would buy it."

Well, that cleared up that mystery. "Then you sent her one back," Jennifer said flatly, "care of Natasha, thanking her and saying that she gave you hope?"

"Yes, how did you know that? Does not matter. Anyway, I received another telegram—the unsigned one—from Lona in Kazan telling me to come to Moscow with the painting. So I am here. End of story."

The jealousy was like a balloon, swelling in size and suffocating her; she would have to get a grip on it, deflate it. It would be no help in the next few days. Another long silence passed and the taxi rattled on to Moscow.

18.

DOSVIDANYA

SHEREMETEV AIRPORT, JULY 22, 1974

When the two arrived at the airport in the taxi, later than expected and breathless, Hank rushed up to Jennifer with the words that made her blood freeze.

"Jen, Chopyk knows and he's furious." Hank noted the look of horror and the way Volodya grabbed her hand.

"How did he find out?" She didn't have to ask again; she could see the answer in Hank's eyes.

"What was I supposed to do? He cornered me. He thought I'd done something to Paul."

"But I told him that Paul was going with me to Tula." Her exasperation was turning into a bubble of fear that she could physically feel in her gut.

"Well, geez, you could have told me that…I didn't know what to answer so I told him the truth—that Paul was staying in the Soviet Union." He backed away from Jennifer's anger. "He was going to find out today anyway. How were you going to hide his disappearance on the plane?"

"The same way we did before! It worked—remember, you idiot?" Her voice rose above a shout but then she realized they were still standing in the airport doorway, and she forced herself to stop.

But Hank continued, talking over her. "Listen, I think you should talk to him right now, get on the offensive because I didn't tell him everything and I can't figure out how much he knows."

This rapid fire exchange in English left Volodya behind, but he was picking it up quickly.

"Let's go meet your Professor Chopyk," he said to Jennifer. "We tell him everything and get his blessing."

She looked at him as if he was crazy. "He's not the bloody pope," she replied. "We don't need his blessing. We need him to keep quiet about it." Leaving Volodya to pick up her suitcase she stomped into the terminal to find their gate number and locate Chopyk, trying all the while to control her ragged breathing. The building was quiet, only a handful of travellers around the ticket desk and several heaps of baggage—she was reminded of the day they had arrived, that wonderful day of promise only a few weeks ago when she had looked forward to achieving the dream of a lifetime—a visit to the Soviet Union. She felt a bit sorry for herself that what was essentially a study tour had turned into such a drama and she realized that she even felt a bit sorry for Chopyk who had surely not asked for this kind of trouble to cast a shadow on his academic career.

The tour group was not difficult to locate—there was only one counter that listed Montreal as a destination and the line-up was fairly short. The students were clumped together, some attempting to be comfortable on the rigid vinyl seats, others sitting on their baggage dolefully. There was no Natasha in sight. Maria was pacing a few yards away from the group and she rushed up to Jennifer.

"Hank has already told me," Jennifer forestalled Maria's torrent of words. "But where's Natasha. Does *she* know?"

"That's the beauty," Maria whispered. "She's already said goodbye. We thought she would see us through customs inspection but she shook hands with some of us very quickly, dashed into that office over there, that grim looking place with all the dark curtains, then disappeared. Don't ask me what that was all about..."

Jennifer spied Chopyk fiddling with the lock on his suitcase, clearly irritated, and she strode up to him purposefully. He turned anguished eyes on her. "There you are, finally."

"Professor Chopyk, I'm sorry it turned out this way," she said. Better to take the offensive as Hank says.

"I simply want to know...what you were thinking—trying to hide this from me?" His face appeared open and candid; it had lost its fussy expression. Several of the students sidled away from what threatened to become a major argument, but a few, Maria and Lona included, actually eased closer to listen.

"Sir, (she had never called him that before, but she felt this might be the time) no one could have got Paul to change his mind. You've got to understand, he's in love with this woman."

"Mrs. White, you lied to me," he hissed. "You hid the truth and you made me believe that Paul was going with you today to see your family. How can I ever trust you?" His eyes were glittering: tears or rage? "And you could have thought about me. How am I supposed to explain a missing student? I should have forbidden your trip to Tula, but I was too soft-hearted. I didn't like to prevent you from seeing family members. But we would have got to the bottom of this yesterday in time to go to the Canadian Embassy in Moscow."

"Again, I'm humbly sorry that I tricked you…"

"No, we tricked you," interjected Maria loyally. "We knew too."

Chopyk whirled to look at her with sad eyes. "I'm disappointed in you, Maria. Not you Lona. I know you didn't know about it." Lona opened her mouth as if to speak but closed it again, clearly baffled.

At risk of starting a new outburst, Jennifer had to ask another question. "What could the Canadian Embassy have done?" She was puzzled.

"What could they have done?" his voice soared into the higher registers and he almost squeaked. "They could have stopped him, persuaded him—they know the territory here—maybe taken his passport away from him. He's probably not the first young Canadian to be taken in by a Soviet under some ruse of marrying in order to leave the country."

But Jennifer had stopped listening at the word passport—it was clear he did not know about the second half of the plan, the part in which the "missing" student would be smuggled out of the country. She could see Maria squirming on the vinyl seat and she knew that within minutes, seconds even, Hank and Volodya would appear beside them. Should she tell Chopyk or not? She hesitated, experiencing a strong sense of falling over the brink. Things couldn't get much worse.

Taking a deep breath, she placed her hand on the man's arm. It was the closest they had ever been. "Professor Chopyk, there's something more I want to tell you," she said. Over his shoulder, she could see the man she loved moving toward them and she knew she must speak quickly.

Tour guide Natasha Kuchkov was fuming. She had entered the airport security office at 1400 hours precisely (she knew because she checked her watch before being allowed to step through the secured door and her watch was always accurate), and then she had been kept waiting for 28 minutes while a junior functionary in a uniform noted her particulars on an excessively complicated yellow form. The questions revolved around Natasha's registration as an Intourist agent. Her name, address and identity number? How many years had she been in the profession? What was the nature of her complaint?

Finally she rapped her knuckles on the desk to capture the pimply-faced youth's attention with a sharp rebuke. "While you sit here filling in your forms," she began in a steely voice, "a foreign tourist is committing an offence against the Soviet Union." She made sure to speak clearly and simply. Perhaps the man was retarded. "Will you kindly put this matter in front of your supervisor in the next ten minutes before the tourist is allowed to leave the country with property belonging to the state."

"Of course, comrade," he replied. But the man made no move toward the closed cubicle door that presumably housed his superior. "If you could simply tell me one more time—for the purposes of the document, you understand—would you consider your complaint to be one of the following: a personal offence involving life or property, a political offence involving life or property, a violation of ....

"Stop! That one, the second one, an offence involving property..."

"Involving state property, you mean?"

"Yes, yes. That's what I've been telling you. The tourist is leaving the country with art treasures that belong to the state. Please check her baggage. I can show you which tourist if you'd only come to the window." The curtained window had one way glass in it. She could see out but those in the airport would see only their reflection in a hazy mirror. The functionary stared at her, slack-jawed, but did not rise from the desk. "And have you proof of this?"

"Not exactly...but if you examine her baggage..." Here she was on shaky ground since most of her allegation had been deduced from searching Lona's cabin and from overheard mutterings from Hank and Marty. But she would stake her reputation that it was true.

The man leaned back in his chair. "Then there is nothing we can do."

Natasha's frustration reached new heights. "If you won't contact your superior, then let me contact mine," she said huffily. "Get me Director Bogovich of the Intourist Bureau on your phone." She had already informed the director about her suspicions of Lona in a phone call from the Volga district. He had thanked her, but typically he was not so interested in the nature of the transgression as he was in the fact that she had told him first before he heard it through other channels such as

Ivan Nikolaevich, the second rate agent. Still, she wanted the director to know that she had been correct in her suspicions.

"*Da, da*, yes, of course," nodded the functionary, pawing through his desk drawer searching for something. *The man's an idiot*, she thought. *This is the quality of worker who stands guard over the country! Saints preserve us, as my old grandmother used to say.* Finally, the man produced another form, this one on blue paper. "In order to use the official phone line, you must fill in this form."

"Phone him now!" Natasha raised her voice in hopes that the supervisor would hear her and look out his door. "I'm not filling in one more form!"

The man's expression did not change but this time he abandoned the new form, picked up the receiver and asked her for the number. After some dialling, waiting and dialling again, he announced that he could not get through. He replaced the receiver quietly. "The supervisor will attend to your complaint tomorrow," he told her.

Natasha struggled to control her breathing. "Tomorrow WILL BE TOO LATE. She's passing through the line now; I can see her from here." Indeed, Lona had already slipped through the passport control while they had been on the phone. The young man's face creased in a troubled frown. "Very well, comrade. I will take the name of the tourist and her flight number and pass it on to the customs officials myself."

Now we're getting somewhere, Natasha thought. "I'll go with you," she said aloud. She took a certain perverse pleasure in being in on the moment of discovery. Of course the poor fool Chopyk would be angry with her...

"I'm sorry, comrade, that will not be possible," the guard replied. "It is not permitted to pass through that door into the airport again. You must leave by the fire exit." He gestured at a door on the far side of the room. "It is a regulation. Thank you and good day."

Natasha drew herself up to her full five feet, four inches, cast one more withering glare at the man, and stalked toward the fire exit and out of the lives of the tour group from Canada.

"Documents, please." Jennifer watched as Lona, standing in front of her, tensed at the command. She could feel her own apprehensiveness growing as she waited, her toes behind the yellow line. This first barrier marked Passport Control was a preview to the inspection room.

At least he's relaxed, she thought, turning to look at Volodya standing behind her. He was expressionless, even calm. A lock of hair flopped on his forehead and she had to look closely to see the beads of sweat underneath it. He was walking in shoes two sizes too big for him but managing very well. Summoned forward, Jennifer handed her passport to the guard at the barrier. He didn't look at her photo. Just as well. He did glance at her particulars, then quickly flipped to the back of the book. She eased out her breath. This control guard required only the typewritten visa that had been stapled into their passports on arrival. He removed the form, stamped it, nodded. She stepped through the barrier and half-turned to watch Volodya pass through the control. The guard did not even glance up but simply removed the visa, just as he had done for Jennifer. Volodya tucked the returned passport away in his jacket pocket. David had told her that the next search would be more thorough.

There were only two doors in the next room. One, wide and swinging, that funnelled all the airline passengers into the inspection area and the other at the far end, small and forbidding, through which they hoped to walk on to a waiting plane and home.

This examination area was illuminated with harsh, brilliant fluorescent lighting that shone on the battleship grey walls and ceiling. The only adornment was a poster, high up on the wall, of Vladimir Ilyich Lenin, and above it the slogan: Glory to the Communist Party. Glory to the Motherland. *Why that particular slogan here?* Jennifer wondered. *You'd think they'd at least wish us* dosvidanya, *Farewell, or even Safe Journey.* A windowed cubicle stood on either side, marking the start of the two passenger line-ups. Jennifer joined the longer of the queues, still behind Lona, and both lines crawled past the officials. The man with the shuffling shoes followed so closely that at times he grazed her shoulder.

Standing quietly was the first moment of inaction that she had experienced all day—make that the past three days. The events were catching up with her: the terrified moment at the telegraph office when she was convinced the jig was up, the arrival of Volodya and their passionate reunion, the different type of reunion with her family in Tula and the subsequent argument. The final stressor had been the sight of Chopyk's face.

As the two columns inched forward, each tourist was asked to hoist all belongings up onto plain wooden desks for examination, but it seemed that they were not checking every bag. There was nothing in Jennifer's bag that would attract their attention. An inspector conferred first with the passenger, then with two uniformed attendants who remained a few steps behind the desks, but whose eyes roamed everywhere. Jennifer tried to avoid staring at the watchers. Every time she did she could feel the sound of swallowing in her throat, her heart pounding. Instead, she turned to smile at Volodya. He smiled back pleasantly but didn't say anything. She watched Chopyk go through the process with the official giving a perfunctory glance at his luggage, then David following right behind. She and Volodya were almost the last ones in their line. It was difficult to discern exactly what these inspectors were searching for. Drugs? Guns? Manuscripts for publication in the west? If they were looking for anti-Soviet propaganda, you'd think they would conduct that search when the group arrived, not when they were departing. Yet she noticed one guard riffling through what looked to be Maria's classroom notes, pausing to read a few words out loud.

"The Hermitage, or old Winter Palace, contains over 40,000 treasures…."

She glanced over at Hank in the other queue, with Marty behind him as usual, who was just now closing his suitcase and was about to head outside to the airport tarmac. Before he went through the far door, he glanced back at her, reassured her with his eyes. *Go on, Hank,* she thought. *Don't call attention to us.* He passed through whistling.

Now it was Lona's turn to lift her bag on to the desk, which she did cheerfully, along with a string bag that carried the wrapped shape of a balalaika. Lona reached into her cavernous handbag to produce a passport but seemed to be fumbling a lot. Her suitcase still bore a sticker from the New York bus terminal, Jennifer noticed irrelevantly. When the gigantic suitcase was opened, the inspector sighed briefly, then thrust his hand among the clothing at random, his eyes averted from Lona's most charming smile. He withdrew a small flat object wrapped in gift paper and opened it carefully as if expecting to find a bomb. No longer smiling, Lona's face appeared impassive. Jennifer had a good view of the item: a miniature painting, a portrait of a family set in an elegant gilt frame. The guard examined Lona's passport once more, looked her in the eyes, then handed the passport to one of the attendants who glided forward effortlessly. They conferred together in mumbles, while Lona continued to stand frozen. Jennifer dared not look at her. The two moved back to Lona, setting the painting aside, and the uniformed one told her in stilted English. "You are not permitted to take art objects out of the Soviet Union."

"I'm so sorry," gushed Lona, turning on her charm once more. "It was a gift—I had no idea that it wasn't allowed..." He stared at her unnervingly. "I'm very sorry," she repeated. "It was a gift from a friend. Her father painted it a few years ago. It's not antique or precious or anything. If you look, it gives the date on the back, just on the backing sheet."

The two guards turned their heads away from the queue and one spoke urgently to the other. Jennifer distinctly heard the name Natasha Kuchkov. *Oh boy, I bet I know why Natasha disappeared so quickly. She's blown the whistle on Lona!*

The two scrutinized the small painting, flipped the screws in the frame's backing cardboard, peered in and touched the art paper. They relaxed slightly. Wordlessly, the inspector reached for a pad of forms and handed Lona a pen. Two other watchers gathered around him, staring at her, at the forms, the painting, in turn. They seemed to forget about the suitcase and one of them motioned to her to close it up which she did with some speed.

This delay might work well for us, thought Jennifer, who could feel Volodya's chest almost at her back.

"You may remove this item from the Soviet Union without penalty," said the guard solemnly, "but only with a permit." She nodded. "You must fill in this application for a permit and sign it." Reaching for the pen, Lona turned to Jennifer and said casually, "Would you like to go ahead? This could take some time." And she stepped aside to give them both a wide berth.

Jennifer and Volodya hoisted their suitcases on to the desks simultaneously, proffered their passports, and the inspector, still watching Lona as if she was going to vanish, waved them on right away. Hardly daring to look up, Jennifer latched the suitcase, grabbed it and walked through the exit door with Volodya right behind her. Outside on the tarmac, David was waiting for them, a small smile of triumph on his face. The three walked to the plane together.

19.

CONVERSATIONS IN THE SKY

SOMEWHERE OVER THE SOVIET UNION

The atmosphere on the airplane was like the aftermath of a party gone wrong—at which the host had done something embarrassing or insulted esteemed guests. He or she is mortified but defiant, and secretly the other guests have enjoyed the spectacle while publicly shaking their heads and frowning.

As the victim of a wrong, Professor Chopyk refused to meet Jennifer's gaze as she and Volodya shuffled down the aisle to their seats, a few rows removed from the others. It was just as well because she could barely contain her sense of relief at the moment. She was as mortified as the embarrassed host for having drawn so many people into this conspiracy, but she couldn't help feeling jubilant that it had turned out so well. Just Canada Customs left to hurdle—and that would be far easier.

Lona arrived next and settled by the window with a magazine on her lap, looking smug and ignoring them. David was grinning from ear to ear, visibly relieved. Ted appeared nervous and uncomfortable. Hank winked. The twins were oblivious as usual. Maria, just one row over in an aisle seat, gave Jennifer and Volodya the thumbs up.

No matter, they had done it—left the Soviet Union. Volodya would be free. She pictured him in Canada listening to live gospel music for the first time—an expression of awe and gratitude on his face. In Vancouver, she would take him to the Hot Jazz Club, an after-hours dive off Broadway, or they would dance together on the sprung floor of the Commodore on a Saturday night. Somehow they would find work—she didn't expect to be given much gainful employment in the Russian Department after this escapade was over. Maybe she would work in a nightclub—or write a novel and forget about Russia.

Volodya would live his music and she would be part of it. She wanted to discuss it with him, to babble, to enjoy the moment, but he was unnaturally quiet.

Volodya had settled into his seat on the aisle with a mixture of excitement and triumph. He reached over, took her hand and brought it slowly to his lips. He did not say a word as the call for seat belts flashed (an international flight this time—all the belts were in working order), and as the plane lifted from the runway, he closed his eyes and the tension drained from his shoulders.

The stewardess passed out hard candy on a silver tray and promised to return with drinks. The plane banked and circled Sheremetev—the next stop would be Paris, briefly. Only when all the passengers eased back in their seats, Maria had stopped grinning at them, and a drink was firmly settled on his tray, did he speak again. This time, it was so softly she could hardly hear him.

"You know, my sweet," Volodya began gently, "you are my light. But there's something I must say. You understand, of course, that it will not work between us." At first she didn't think she was hearing him correctly. The smile stayed frozen to her lips as the plane soared up to cruising level. "You know that. I know that. You have been wonderful, amazing; I owe you my life."

The aircraft hummed, occasionally giving a vibrating *thuck thuck*. Her drink, a fizzy orange pop in a thick, worn glass, sloshed onto her tray. She could feel her smile fading, a lump welling in her chest. Afterwards, she thought about how quickly she had grasped what he was telling her. How instantly she had understood that this would be the inevitable outcome. But at the time, she could only stare at him, hoping she wasn't going mad. The question that really bothered her: had he intended this all along? How long ago was this planned? Before they met, or was it when he first asked for her help on that Leningrad street? Or was it in Tula when he berated her for not responding to her family?

"When we stop in Montreal, I'll slip away," Volodya continued. "They say it is a big city, a good city. There will be work for a musician, no? Or I will go to New York. I think it is not so far. I will be happy, very happy, and will always thank you for giving this to me."

Her first reaction was not exactly sadness. It was a sense of irony—they were behaving like a Russian novel, the characters always trying so hard to live within the power of right but always failing and being overtaken by a grim fate. She was like a tortured Anna Karenina in love with the wrong man. *How melodramatic.* Volodya was startled when she suddenly snickered. The betrayal was only beginning to sink in.

Just as her humour was giving way to anger, an extraordinary thing happened. A garbled voice boomed over the intercom—"What did he say?" asked Jennifer aloud—and the stewardesses moved through the plane with more speed than they had hitherto shown, speaking quietly to passengers as they went.

"We're making an unscheduled landing," Maria said, leaning over, looking frightened. "I'm sure I heard the words 'prepare for landing.'"

After conferring with a stewardess, Chopyk stood up to pass the message on to the others. "No need to panic, everyone. They assure me it's not an emergency." He made a soothing gesture. "There's nothing wrong with the plane. We're putting down at a minor airport for a security check, the stewardess says."

After 21 days in the Soviet Union, during which time the group had heard many contradictory claims of safety given by many so-called authorities, the passengers seemed disinclined to believe him. Even Hank and Marty were terrified and Lona fidgeted nervously.

"Where will we land?" asked Volodya loudly. No one answered him.

"Hey, it's got to be Sweden," Hank called out. "We've already passed over the Gulf of Finland."

"I'm not so sure about that," Jennifer muttered, turning to stare out of the window. The ground was moving to meet them very quickly and the terrain appeared to be solid forest. No towns, no bodies of water. "Could be Sweden or Finland, or…the Soviet Union." She saw that Volodya's face had turned ashen. Lona looked around anxiously, rose from her seat to exchange a few words with Chopyk.

"Seatbelts, please," intoned a stewardess. "Return to your seat, *devushka*. This stop will delay the flight by 20 minutes only."

"But where are we landing? The Soviet Union again?" Lona asked the woman. The attendant only shrugged as if it were of no consequence to her. The passengers fell utterly silent for the next few minutes.

"It's probably Sweden," Jennifer whispered to Volodya. "Don't worry." But she had to admit that a small part of her was taking a vengeful enjoyment from the timing of this crisis, as if some mighty ear had heard Volodya's betrayal speech.

In so far as she could tell, there was, indeed, nothing wrong with the aircraft. It circled over an airport that suddenly appeared, concrete runways carved out of a dark evergreen forest. As the landing gear dropped, she searched the surroundings for clues as to its location. It was unmarked, deserted, except for a few small fighter planes. *This is eerie*, she thought.

Volodya closed his eyes, then opened them again to stare at her pleadingly. "If anything happens..." he started to say. At that moment the plane thumped to the ground and coasted toward a frame building. When the aircraft came to a halt, the same garbled voice buzzed and whirred over the intercom.

"Well, what are we supposed to do now?" Lona asked aloud. "Just sit here?"

After a few moments, the tour group became aware that the front passengers were exiting slowly taking their hand luggage with them, although no directions had been issued. Impatiently, Lona pushed her way through. Jennifer and Volodya stood up more slowly then followed Maria and Hank down the steps and onto the tarmac. But as soon as they stood in the fresh summer breeze on the open runway, Hank ran ahead and caught up to Lona to talk hurriedly in her ear. David limped up behind Jennifer, flexing his arms.

"Good to have a stretch. What do you think this is all about? Hey... steady, guy," he said to Volodya who looked as if he were close to fainting.

"Beats me," replied Jennifer. She was almost beyond caring what happened to Volodya or her. Let them put her in a Soviet prison. Let them beat her with a cat-o'-nine-tails like a Russian peasant. She didn't care. All the effort that she had made on Volodya's behalf had ended in this sad moment. It was a terrible justice.

A line-up stretched ahead into a plain, institutional building, also unmarked, and a uniformed guard moved down the queue stopping to share a joke with some passengers.

"There's your first clue that we're in Sweden," pointed out David. "Have you ever seen a Soviet guard smile like that?"

"I don't believe it," said Volodya gloomily. "It is a Soviet trick. They know about us."

"We are going to be searched," Jennifer replied. "I'm sure of that." She turned to Volodya and his gaze met hers.

"Here, I will give you the passport," he murmured. "No, don't say anything...Just hold it in your hand. If I decide to run, I will not need the passport and you will hide it to save the secret of your friend Paul."

He looked at her fondly. For a moment, there might have been no airport runway, no guard, only that moment over the kitchen table in Leningrad. "I am a bad man for wanting to leave, but I am not so bad that I want you to suffer. If I run, then you must act like you don't know me. Do you understand?"

"Yes, I understand," she relented. Again the irony. In that moment that she was supposed to be denying his existence, she discovered that she knew him only too well, better than ever before. "I'm convinced they're not looking for you," she told him. "Stay in line. Don't run. Please."

The line had ground to a halt and she could see the twins and Ted sitting on their flight bags as if they were in for a long wait. "What's happening, Ted?" she called out.

He joined them. "The guy in the uniform says that we might as well make ourselves comfortable. Our suitcases are not on this flight—they're on another one that's arriving soon—make that 'soon' in Soviet time, so who knows when? Then we're supposed to grab our own bags and go through a security check."

"What are they looking for?" David and Maria crowded around, encircling Volodya protectively. *They want him to be safe*, Jennifer thought. *It's touching.* "Weren't we just checked pretty well when we left Moscow?"

"Who knows what they're looking for? I can tell you one thing, both Hank and Lona are pretty upset. It seems Hank is carrying some of Lona's things in his luggage and he's not too happy about them poking through his bags again."

"Did the uniform tell you where we were?" She asked the question that she knew was on Volodya's mind.

"He wouldn't answer," Ted replied. The last of the colour drained from Volodya's face, and his eyes cast about wildly sizing up the airport fence and the chain link gate.

"But surely we're in Sweden or Finland?" David went on, putting one hand on Volodya's arm, sensing his fear. "They're entirely too casual here for the Soviet Union. Look—no armed guards or slogans on the wall."

"Hang in there, Vlad...uh, Paul." Maria said.

"Yeah, I think you're right," Ted replied. "Probably because it's a military airport, he's not supposed to tell us much about it."

"Hey, here comes a plane. Can you beat that? It arrived 'soon'—just like they said."

A Scandinavian Airlines jet circled the site, landed at the far end of the field, then taxied to a halt nearby. The rolling steps were moved from their plane to the new one and the first passengers to emerge, blinking and bewildered, looked familiar.

"My God, it's the Americans from the Volga cruise," Maria cried. "No end of surprises today."

To Jennifer this seemed more sinister. It was as if the Americans were following them. And what about this Professor Henry Smith that Lona had consulted? Would he be among the group? And what if he were? There was no harm in Volodya selling his painting. She was panicking unreasonably. She slipped her arm through Volodya's to keep him close to her. *Fear does strange things,* she thought. *I feel sorry for him even if he's being a jerk who wants to leave me the moment he gets to Canada.* It would be a good thing if he got to Montreal. It would be less messy than having him run and what?—be shot trying to escape the airport? No one here was brandishing weapons. They would simply pull him in for questioning and he would be returned to his homeland.

"Hey, remember me? Jim from Texas," said one of the Americans loping towards them, hand outstretched. "This sure ain't Copenhagen. Did you guys have a bomb threat, too?"

"Is that what they told you?" Ted asked. "They haven't given us a clue as to why we're here."

"Sure thing. They're calling out the old bomb squad. And you guys have your luggage on our plane—it's a real screw up."

Other Americans came crowding over to surround the Canadians and the tension eased while the tour group were reacquainted with their Volga cruise mates.

"It was a bomb threat," Jennifer whispered to Volodya. "I told you. Relax. They're just doing good security."

Some of the colour returned to Volodya's cheeks and he mumbled, "They're only saying that to fool us." But he surreptitiously reached for the passport in Jennifer's hand, his eyes still scanning the fence and gate.

As the bags were unloaded, passengers claimed their own and moved towards the check point. "Lona is sure acting strangely," David said. "Look."

The blonde had snatched her bag, totally ignored one of the Americans who looked delighted to see her and raced for the building. "She's got contraband stuff in her suitcase," David reported with the air of a detective. "I heard something about it from Hank."

"Hank doesn't know when to keep his mouth shut," Maria pointed out. "I think he told Natasha about it. That's why Natasha went into that little secret office just before the plane left. At least that's what I figured out."

"That doesn't make sense. If she has stuff to hide, why would she rush into the lion's den?"

"I don't think she knows it's a bomb scare. Probably wants to get the search over with."

"No," replied the American. "I think she's in real trouble 'cause I heard them call her name out like they were looking for her. Hope she wasn't the one who planted a bomb!"

"Who? Lona? She would never do something like that," Jennifer told him. She couldn't help but defend the woman until she remembered that she was still jealous of her.

Lona Rabinovitch sat in a folding chair in front of four uniformed inspectors trying not to think about her suitcase. It was like trying not to think about the elephant in the corner. *Shit, shit, shit. Just not Hank's bag*, she thought. *Not Chopyk's bag. Not Linda's.* In the end, there was very little to worry about in her own bag: the scrolls, well hidden, and the ugly ewer. She didn't think they would search the little locket at her neck. When she was called to the front of the line she hoped it would be good news; she would slide through the line first using her dazzling smile, then distract the inspectors as much as possible as they searched the other suitcases. But all had not gone according to plan. She had been told peremptorily to lift her suitcase onto the counter, and to sit down. She placed her cavernous purse and the wrapped balalaika at her feet.

Her bags were searched by three men and one woman, all of them dressed in navy blue uniforms and standing shoulder to shoulder like surgeons surrounding a patient. Carefully and patiently, they probed, opened each zipper and felt in each pocket. Many items were removed and placed on the desk: her shoes, toiletry bag, books. The taller surgeon reached in with both hands as if after the heart and other organs; several wrapped items were pulled out and set aside and her clothes returned to the case.

A few other passengers crowding around the door looked on in trepidation that this level of scrutiny might soon be for them. Then the tall man carefully removed the wrappings from Lona's packages while one of the others made notes like a medical student during an operation. Lona could feel herself shrinking in her seat. The ugly pitcher that said Souvenir of Rostov was the first to emerge from its wrappers, and she willed herself to remain cool. When the tall surgeon scratched the paint gently with one fingernail, Lona knew. *Busted.* She pressed her brain to think quickly—how to get out of the situation with the least amount of damage. But before she could come up with a strategy, she was ordered to go to a curtained cubicle for a full body check.

"Hoo, I don't like this situation." David, who had taken a quick jog to the front of the line, returned to report to the others. "Lona's been hauled away and she looks frightened."

Soon, Professor Chopyk cut through the waiting line and moved toward the cubicle presumably to assist Lona in any confrontation that might occur. He was ordered back by a pleasant but firm attendant and was asked to lift up his baggage for a search, too. He complied reluctantly, his face in a grimace. The other passengers shuffled through the line up, raising their baggage to the table and being dismissed rapidly, while Chopyk continued to stand to one side as two of the surgeons examined each item carefully.

Finally it was Jennifer's turn to walk toward the inspection. The younger of the surgeons looked up, smiled at her and waved her through. She was stunned. Her eye caught Professor Chopyk's for a fraction of a second and she saw sadness there. Trying not to turn around or call attention to Volodya somewhere behind her, she passed through the stuffy building and out in to the fresh breeze of the tarmac. *I may have the world's worst luck with men, but I sure am the darling of border guards,* she thought.

Maria, with her innocent face, was led away for a strip search but she emerged less than five minutes later with a harassed look. "If this is a bomb search, why are they examining my inner cavities?" she asked. "And why are they just lifting things out of the bags without checking first as to whether they're ticking?"

There were no answers. Jennifer watched Hank emerge; he seemed calm. Then Linda and Hank chatted together as if they were back on campus on an ordinary day. No one had searched either of their suitcases. Volodya hung back to the end of the line. Jennifer knew now that he would not flee; he would brazen it out. Besides, he had the passport. Soon David was there beside her, as always, to support her.

"Pull yourself together," he urged her, glancing at her worried frown. "You haven't been implicated in anything."

"They'll ship him back to the Soviet Union."

"No, I think it's Lona that's going down today."

She was just beginning to calm down when one of the Americans approached her with a shout. "Hey, Jen. Why are they beating up on your guy?"

She could feel the blood rush away dizzyingly. "What do you mean?" Her voice had faded to a whisper.

"They've got him by that desk as if he's gonna be there for life." The man laughed crudely. "He doesn't look like a terrorist with that little pointy beard." With a huge sense of relief, Jennifer realized he was talking about Chopyk as "her guy." Not Volodya. David let out a long breath. *He was thinking the same thing.*

The time crawled by. The line snaked through the shabby building with most of the passengers being released to mill about on the apron in front of Jennifer.

As Jennifer remained at her post, Volodya finally appeared from the building walking carefully, nervously, but his eyes held that same light of triumph as they had just a few brief hours ago. He joined her, wordless. David shook his hand.

The very last people to exit the building were Chopyk and Lona who had linked arms. Her face was crumpled like that of a pouty child. Chopyk stared straight ahead and explained nothing as he passed the group. They were ushered to their plane. Volodya resumed his seat beside Jennifer. The plane took off.

Once again, someone had spoiled the party and the tension filled the stuffy cabin. A swarthy young man—Kazak or Uzbek, maybe—walked down the aisle, stared at Lona with interest and finally addressed her in thickly accented English. Jennifer could not hear the exact words but soon the man had insinuated himself into the vacant seat beside the blonde who still looked dazed. *He's either security keeping an eye on her, or she's found yet another admirer.* At least, this time, the trouble was not about her, Jennifer thought with relief.

As the plane levelled out, she relaxed a little, pushed her seat back and prepared to resume her conversation with Volodya that had been interrupted so abruptly. He turned to her with apparently the same thought. They began simultaneously, then both broke the conversation off and simply held hands. There was no more to say. She knew that now.

"Excuse me," she said finally, placing his hand back on his knee and struggling up and into the aisle. They would be landing in Paris soon and there was someone else she needed to talk to urgently.

While the stewardess served vodka from the bar cart, considerably cheering up the passengers, Jennifer slid in beside Chopyk with a confidence that she did not yet feel. Her gut told her that this was the right thing to do.

"Professor Chopyk, we must talk." He turned to her. *He's ashamed*, she knew right away. Well, she felt a little ashamed, too, so it put them on an equal footing. This was the right time to negotiate for her academic career.

"I have nothing to say to you," he told her dolefully, "except that I'm sorry that you could not have trusted me with your secret."

"And you could not trust me with yours," she returned more snappily than she intended. "What did they find in *your* suitcase?" He winced. She had landed a cheap blow but the stakes were important. "It's easy to want to help someone like Lona, isn't it?" Jennifer went on. "She gains your sympathy, asks you for a favour. That pretty face and smile... Before you know it you're smuggling stuff out of the country. Well, I wanted to help Volodya leave the country. He deserved it. And before I knew it I was smuggling, too."

"It's not the same thing at all. If you had only sent Paul to me..."

"No." She shook her head. "That was impossible. He was determined. I tried to talk him out of it."

Chopyk's shoulders slumped and he turned away from her. There was a brief silence.

"Look," Jennifer went on in what she hoped was a friendly, conciliatory tone, "could we work together, please?" She waited to see if he would respond.

Finally he turned to her with curiosity. "What do you mean?"

"I won't mention to anyone—from the department or otherwise—your problem back there. No, before you get defensive...I know they opened your suitcase. Who knows what they found." She held up her hand in what she fervently hoped was a scouts' honour pose. He stared at the hand, fascinated. “I promise not to say anything. The only thing I ask is that you keep quiet about my activities, too.”

“But,” he spluttered, “they’re hardly on the same level. I was duped into doing a favour. What you did was outright illegal.”

“Nonetheless, I’m asking you…I’m begging you.” This was no time to be clever; honesty was best. “They may be two different problems but neither of us wants to suffer for them. What I’m suggesting is sensible. You don’t tell and I don’t tell.”

Chopyk wrinkled his nose as if she were a bad odor. “But how are you ever going to explain a young Russian man at your elbow when we get home? Have you even thought about that?”

“There’s an easy answer to that one. He’s not coming home with me. He’ll probably leave us at Montreal.”

“Whaat? All this for someone you don’t even want to be with?”

“He doesn’t want to be with me. Do you understand?”

For the first time she thought she saw a flicker of humanity in the man’s eyes, and she was comforted. Then he quickly disabused her of that idea: “Aha! So I was right all along,” he retorted. “He only wanted to marry you to leave the country. Admit it!” She nodded and he leaned back in his seat, mollified. “Very well, Mrs. White. As distasteful as this bargaining is to me—we have a deal.”

★

About 21 hours later and a stopover in Montreal, Jennifer White, fatigued beyond belief, trailed the others into Vancouver Airport, to begin the last steps of the journey to the baggage claim area. Even though they were contained in a modern glass airport building, they could smell the fresh summer air seeping into the passageways, savour the aroma of popcorn and cinnamon buns, enjoy the colourful murals and advertising displays. After the drab grey of the Soviet Union, it was an assault to the senses.

“It is so-o-o good to be home,” David exclaimed in joy.

“Amen,” replied Ted, hoisting his backpack in the air. “It was a great trip but I will be so happy to get back to a Big Mac and my girlfriend—in that order.”

“You guys! I want to see my boyfriend first of all,” said Maria, “and then after that maybe a Big Mac…and I’m never eating a cucumber again in my life. But you know we're all going to miss that great Georgian wine...and the music and the people...." She turned to look for Jennifer. "Come on, slowpoke. We need to make sure you're going to be okay."

Jennifer managed a wan smile. "I don't know if I'm ever going to be okay."

The oppressive black cloud that had followed her since Moscow—no, since that day in Tula—would be a steady companion. Worse, she was starting to become friends with it.

They waited impatiently for their baggage. The last leg of the trip had been on Air Canada rather than Aeroflot, and they had been forced to collect their bags in Montreal then submit them for yet another inspection, this time from Canada Customs. After this casual inspection was complete and they were walking towards their connecting flight, a surreptitious exchange of goods took place: a painting from Linda's suitcase and a menorah from Hank's were both transferred to Lona who thanked them with embarrassment.

She and Hank had huddled together intimately on a public bench in the Montreal airport, speaking in urgent whispers after which Hank reported back to the others. *He's matured on this trip*, Jennifer thought. *He's no longer the class clown*.

Lona had been caught, he told them, smuggling a very old jug from the country. The tall Customs officer that they had observed rooting through her suitcase at their unscheduled stop indicated his knowledge of her recent confrontation at Moscow's airport, and he had scrutinized once more the small family portrait that she had been allowed to keep. It had turned out to be older than it first appeared. Both items, the painting and the ewer, were confiscated and she was fined. She took full responsibility for the antique found in Chopyk's luggage and that item was confiscated, too. Clearly, they did not consider her a smuggler but only a misguided and naïve tourist. Her punishment could have been more severe, but Lona was not gloating; in fact, she appeared to be suffering an attack of conscience. She apologized to Hank for her behaviour and for using him in this way. Gratified, he immediately asked her for a date. That would be tricky, she told him, since she was not returning to Vancouver with the group but, as pre-arranged, she was taking the bus from Montreal back to her home in New York. Hank accompanied her to the exit, and later told the group with some pride that she had relented at the last moment, given him her address in New York and invited him to visit.

While the unlikely duo of Hank and Lona had been parting company, Jennifer and Volodya had also stood in the shadow of the exit sign once again making their goodbyes.

"Lona offered to take me to New York with her," Volodya told her, "but I refused..."

"Of course," Jennifer replied stiffly. "It would mean yet another border crossing and you don't want that, now do you?"

Volodya's face creased in a huge grin. "That's not the reason I refused, my amazing woman," he said.

He was teasing her, she realized. *He doesn't know what thin ice he's skating on.*

"She said she will contact me when my painting is sold. Ech, but I don't think she will—if the painting sells for more than she paid me, then why would she let me know? She's a business woman, right?"

He took Jennifer's hands in his, kissed them, hoisted his backpack onto his shoulders and walked backwards through the automatic doors still holding her gaze. Then he vanished into the humid Montreal evening.

In Vancouver, it was obvious that some of the baggage had been inspected yet again. Jennifer saw almost a full roll of sticky tape covering the top of Chopyk's suitcase as if the bag had not closed properly after the Customs had poked through it. She couldn't help but feel sorry for him. One student missing and three artworks smuggled. Whatever happened, it had been the trip of a lifetime—though just not a lifetime she would care to repeat.

"Whoever goes through first should look for our bus," called Chopyk. "Probably the driver will hold up a sign." It seemed like yesterday when she had been the first one through the gate at Sheremetev and the adventure had begun. This time, she lagged behind, reluctant to face the world. Carefully, she propped her things up on a baggage cart. When she finally passed through the sliding doors right behind Linda, she noticed someone waving, someone with black bristly eyebrows and an armful of flowers. The man was not waving at Linda. It had been so long since they had been together, and so much had happened to her in the last three weeks, that she almost did not recognize her estranged husband.

"Michael, what are you doing here?" Despite herself, a full, warm feeling dispelled the black cloud, if only for a moment.

"Picking you up." He smiled. "You don't want to go on a bus, now do you?"

She stopped her cart in front of him, oblivious to the crowds milling about and accepted the flowers. They were a mixture of daisies, baby's breath and scented freesia—friendly flowers, not romantic ones.

"We're through, you know," she told him. "I want to be clear about that." After all the lies, simple honesty felt good.

"Yeah, I know, I really do. But I'm still picking you up."

She caught Chopyk's eye as he glanced back into the crowd and for no particular reason smiled at him. She would press on, regardless, as her old Russian teacher used to say.

She turned to Michael. "Did you know that I have family in the Soviet Union?" she asked him. "I didn't know myself until the first night in Moscow."

"Really?" He took over pushing the luggage cart. "You are so lucky, Jennifer."

20.

FARMER PAVEL

VOLGA REGION, AUGUST, 1974

"I think we should mulch those gourds—or squash—or whatever they are," Paul told Vera.

"Spoken like a true farmer, but unfortunately you know nothing about squash," Vera replied. "They need to have air around them while they grow, no dampness, no bugs."

He smiled at her earnestness. "I'll learn. I never thought I would enjoy gardening so much." Paul—who now went by the name of Pavel—and Vera were busy settling in at her father's farm. She was obliged to continue work at the factory in Toglyatti for now, but she had made application to live on Fyodor Shukshin's farm on the grounds that her aging father was finding it difficult to cope by himself with the farm work.

"After we finish here, let's go into the pine forest for a while." He smiled at her. "Maybe there's a mushroom or two to pick." She smiled slyly at him as she remembered their last mushroom hunting adventure. After they had returned to the farm from Ulyanovsk on that memorable day, he had taken her hand in his and asked her formally to marry him. She accepted quickly—perhaps too quickly, but he was so right for her, and she was filled with confidence in their love and their ability to overcome any problems from his living in the Soviet Union.

The farm life was idyllic. Vera greatly preferred the work to labouring in the factory but she hadn't wanted to live at home with her father. It was good to get away from parents. Ever since her mother had died, her dad had been by turns melancholy and argumentative. His money-making schemes, which he seemed to think up at the rate of about one a week, had snapped him out of his gloom and he was always appreciative of her visits so he could explain the latest plan to her. However, he could be irritating, even when she loved him dearly.

After just two days of Vera and Pavel living together on the farm with her father, it became apparent that there would be a problem—they couldn't keep their hands off one another, but at the small farmhouse privacy was at a premium. As liberal as her aging father was, he still did not want to think of his daughter having sex in the family home right under his nose, and she was too embarrassed to talk about her love with her parent. After all, there was always the pine forest where many other lovers had gone in times of need. Better her father think that she was holding out for her wedding night. The truth was she did not want to wait that long. She couldn't wait to lie with Pavel. He often kissed her lovingly and he held her close in a passionate embrace, leaving no doubt that he wanted more. She also wanted more and her wedding night was in some dim, unforeseeable future.

Unwittingly, Pavel had suggested a while ago that they take a walk in the woods to hunt for mushrooms. She almost explained to him that it wasn't the right time of year—there had to be more rain to find mushrooms—but then she changed her mind and agreed to go with him. On the way there they held hands and talked about so many wonderful things: what kind of place they would live in, what beautiful children they would have, what career he would pursue. It was all she could do to keep from expressing over and over again how happy she was.

That day, under a trembling evergreen, on an old horse blanket, they had consummated their love. It was not as marvellous as she envisioned. In fact, the situation was uncomfortable, a tree root poked into her back and when a branch creaked they both started up for fear of being caught in the act. His weight on her was like a lump and he fumbled a lot in finding the right orifice. In all, it was amateur, awkward, and she loved him all the more for it. In that gentle moment right after the act, they gazed into one another's eyes and it was obvious they were thinking the same thought, though they had never admitted it before: they were both virgins. Instead of being embarrassed by it, Vera embraced the idea. Their love was for one another alone. Pavel seemed to have no male pretensions about his virgin status, he did not pretend that he had done it with many women. He was open and honest. She loved him deeply.

Since that day they had visited the forest many more times and each time the sessions improved. Today, if he wanted to go "mushroom hunting" again, she would try out a suggestion that a friend had whispered to her once to increase their enjoyment. It sounded like fun. But what would they do when winter arrived? Really, they needed their own place and that meant that Pavel needed papers—a passport, and a residence permit, at least. They would have to get busy.

★

It was a very different world for Pavel. Up with the rooster, check the chickens, water the market garden with buckets from the well. (Surely they had heard of garden hoses in the Soviet Union? He planned to do a little shopping in Toglyatti or Saratov one day.) Then, check the primitive irrigation system that watered the larger crop of barley. Estimate the height on the patch of sunflowers; as soon as they grew large enough, he had some great plans for intimate picnics with Vera among their stately stalks. She would look gorgeous, her sinuous shape naked in the fresh air. The pine forest was getting a bit old—he always returned with twigs and grit in his clothes. He hadn't yet thought about how they would find their privacy once winter arrived.

If it were market day, they would pick the early beets and new potatoes and Shukshin would drive the produce into the village using his antiquated motorcycle and attached cart, a vintage vehicle that had probably seen service in the last war. These visits usually entailed time spent in fixing the motorcycle when Shukshin returned. Pavel didn't know that much about mechanics either, but here he was learning faster. The way the parts fit together was engrossing; he found he could figure it out with some help from Shukshin, and he lamented all the years spent in studying academic subjects without getting a good grounding in what every adolescent learned while growing up: working on the family car.

The elder Shukshin thought he had died and gone to heaven; a good strong lad to do the farm work—at no expense to him other than some room and board. Granted, he wasn't trained, but then neither was the last lad that he had asked to help him. A dimwit—and he had been sent packing. Fortunately, there was no official record of his ever working for Shukshin. That was the good thing about living in the provinces—no one from Moscow was very interested in whether they stuck to the regulations.

Moreover, Vera was in love with this strong, bright lad. There was only one annoying problem—he was a foreigner. He would likely get fed up with working on the farm and want to take Vera away—back to Canada or America. He wasn't quite sure what had happened to Pavel's foreign papers—he only knew that it was better not to ask. Shukshin would have liked to secure Pavel's residency at the farmhouse for a long time but he knew that the couple would want to have their own home soon. It was inevitable. All that sneaking off to the woods. He knew what happened there among the trees; he had visited the forest himself in his younger years. They would marry and apply to move somewhere else… Perhaps he should marry again. But who? A widow would be best. Truth to tell, he was too old to break in a younger woman. He sighed. How to find a widow?

★

What a glorious day for a public official, thought Pyotr Vladimirovich as he pedalled his bicycle over the crude track through the field that led to Shukshin's house. His work was no more interesting than before but he was learning how to avoid it more cleverly. It was a new Pyotr in the making. His arrangement with Shukshin was starting to pay off for him, too. Amazing, he was finally learning to work the system. And there was the opportunity to drink Shukshin's rotgut liquor in the process. Shades of the old Pyotr surfaced: shouldn't he be confiscating such horrible and obviously homemade drink? No, the new Pyotr answered. You should be enjoying it when it's offered and not asking too many questions, like every other public official you know.

The new Pyotr was delighted that he was preoccupied a little less with his darling Tanya: the luscious dumpling with the round, smooth buttocks…the sexy fox that would shoot her plump tongue into his mouth…. She was always ready to open her legs for him, whether in the old boathouse or whenever he needed it. He could feel his bicycle slowing down as the heat of lust flashed over him. Well, it seemed he had not stopped thinking about Tanya entirely! But with the greatest of difficulty and a supreme concentration of will he could overcome these passions from time to time, at least long enough to get on with his business. It was better so–the relationship with the police chief's wife could only end in disaster. There was nothing like the sobering thought of Alexei Ivanovich's scowl to send a chill down Pyotr's spine.

Anyway, today was not a day for thinking about Tanya. He was on his way to Shukshin to cement their new alliance. He really could not say whether the idea had come from him or from Shukshin. It had been borne of a night of hoisting the jars in Shukshin's kitchen and the rest of that evening was hazy in the public official's memory. Shukshin would use a contact—which he had hastened to say was not his daughter—at the car factory in Toglyatti who would supply him with machine parts, coveted parts of automobiles that were often stolen or broken and not easy to acquire as replacements. Shukshin would sell them quite openly at the marketplace—that is, you would have to know who to ask for but after the initial word of mouth referral there would be no furtive transaction—a simple exchange of money or goods in the open marketplace completed quickly and quietly. Just an honest petty capitalist in a country of state socialism, trying to make a living, was how Shukshin explained it.

Pyotr's role was simple: he would turn a blind eye and divert the attention of other enquiring eyes. For this, he would receive a percentage of the profits, plus he would, in the course of time, acquire the appropriate parts for the broken-down government vehicle that he had once used. Eventually, it would be running again and he would not be forced to bicycle all over the district. Of course, the parts had to be stolen from the factory in Togliatti...but the new Pyotr wasn't going to think too deeply about that. Yes, it was a wonderful day.

Whistling, he pulled up in front of Shukshin's place and was surprised to see the new farm hand out front. The man, Pavel, was working with Shukshin now and he was obviously in love with the daughter. Pyotr chuckled. The first time he had visited he had thought Shukshin was trying to match him with Vera. She was nice but too skinny, not his type. Young love, he thought pleasantly, completely ignoring the fact that Vera was only a few years younger than he. Isn't it wonderful? His happiness knew no bounds later when, seated at the table, Vera served him an appetizer of shiny round mushrooms in sour cream baked in ceramic pots. It was one of his all time favourites and he told her so, while the father poured him another jar of his fabled liquor. The rest of the dinner was boring—fat old hen stewed with beet greens. Given the surrounding farm, he could almost have predicted the menu, though it was tasty enough. He noticed that Vera, Fyodor and the boy Pavel ate with great relish and the three of them seemed to be buzzing with some kind of inner glee—or perhaps that was just the effect of the vodka.

"Well, Fyodor Mikhailovich," he said, turning to the older man. "I think that we have business to discuss. Perhaps we should let the young lovers go while we talk privately."

"Not this time, Pyotr Vladimirovich," replied Shukshin. "These two need to hear what we'll talk about." He rose, looked out the window and closed the shutter. Pavel and Vera shuffled in their seats expectantly. Pyotr felt nervous for the first time. *Uh-oh, something about Tanya...No, it couldn't be that. It was only another of Shukshin's schemes.*

"You're scaring me, Shukshin. What's this all about? Why did you invite me here and ply me with fine food..." he nodded at Vera..."unless you want something? I know you."

Unexpectedly Pavel answered him. "This discussion is about me, Comrade Pyotr Vladimirovich Korpov."

He had not been addressed in this formal way for so long the public official had almost forgotten his whole name. The young man had an interesting accent—from the Baltics, perhaps? He sat up in his chair, reached for the bottle. "Please go on."

"As you have been told by Shukshin, I have been helping him on the farm for some time now and, as you've also astutely observed, I love Vera and have asked her to be my wife."

"Yes, yes, perfectly natural...to your health!" He tossed back a shot.

"There's only one problem. All my papers, identification and other documents have been lost."

"Lost? As in stolen? It should be reported to the police. I am acquainted with the chief of police. I could convey your complaint."

"No, not stolen," Pavel replied. "I don't need to involve the police." But Pyotr felt he was holding something back. "Just lost," he finished lamely.

"I understand," Pyotr answered. A silence fell over the room. "You're not from this region, are you? You're supposed to be working somewhere else and you abandoned a project to move here? Where is it? Latvia, Lithuania?" He thought Vera smothered a smile at this comment but Pavel seemed disturbed. "One of those countries, isn't it? I knew from your accent. You can't put anything past me," and at this he nodded at the older Shukshin to let him know that he was working with a sharp customer. "If you had papers for this area, I would know about them. After all, I am the public official for the Volga region."

"Indeed you are, Pyotr Vladimirovich," Shukshin stepped in ahead of Pavel who had stopped in mid-conversation. "Indeed, and you are the very one to prepare new papers for Pavel so that he can continue to be a contributing member of the region and so he can marry my daughter."

"Prepare new papers…Are you serious?" Pyotr felt a jolt of anxiety. *What were they trying to pull?* "You said you lost them all: your passport, your work book?"

Pavel nodded.

"Your residential permit? Your special permit?"

He continued to nod: "All of them."

Pyotr stared at him in disbelief. Surely no one could be that careless unless he deliberately lost them because he had something to hide. He glared at the three faces and they smiled back at him.

"I could write you out a special permit allowing you to be here. Yes, I could do that, as you know. But your registration, your work book? All those years of employment records? I couldn't give you those." He thought they would at least register disappointment. "In fact," he went on, aware that all three seemed confident that he would comply, "the only way you could get one of those now is to report it missing to the authorities and be issued a new one. I'm sure there's a fine."

"Or it could be forged," said Shukshin.

Pyotr stared at him in disbelief, then he leaned back in his chair, drink in hand. He was sure now that Shukshin was just testing him, having a joke at his expense. "Well, I couldn't forge one. I'm sure of that." He thought he'd play along with the little joke. "And the records of employment could easily be checked."

"Yes, you could forge it. You have access to the blank work books. It would be easy enough to steal a new one and fill in some new information. If anyone checks with past employment…well, previous records are often missing or are unintelligible. It happens all the time."

Pyotr was silent.

Shukshin continued: "You don't have access to the domestic passports, I know, but surely one could be found—perhaps a young man who has passed away and the widow has not turned in his passport—and we could use your stamp of office on it."

"Ech, you sly old man," Pyotr finally replied. "You're testing me. Now why would I do such a thing as steal a workbook? Or comb the black market looking for stolen passports? I could provide you with a *propiska* registration; it's close enough to my line of duty, if that's what you want. But tell me, why should I help you?"

"Because you don't want to face the consequences of not helping." Shukshin glowered at the public official.

"What do you mean?" Pyotr became agitated. "Are you threatening me? If this is a joke it's gone too far!"

"It's no joke." Pavel spoke again. "I need all of the documents: permits, *propiska*, passport, whatever is necessary, and I need them soon. As to why you should help me then I'm afraid it's like Shukshin says. You don't want others to know what we can tell them about you."

Pyotr froze to his chair. It was not a joke.

To his surprise, Vera chimed in. They were all in it together. "You were seen…at the boathouse. You understand me?" He remained silent so she continued. "With the police chief's wife—what's her name, Tanya?—and we all know that the police chief would not like your activities with his wife, would he?"

Pyotr was stunned. It was all collapsing in front of him—the careful secrecy, the hidden assignations. "We…simply meet to talk. There's nothing harmful…." He stopped. Vera was shaking her head. "We have photos," and she pointed to a large American-style camera on the bed. "We took photos of you and Tanya together. Believe me, you were not just talking."

"What! Devil take it! Give me those photos. You have no right…" He stood up, prepared to invoke some bureaucratic rule that would force them to comply—or what? Report them to the police? They sat politely while he worked through his tantrum, sputtered another oath or two and smacked the table with his fist. Finally he sat again and slumped in the chair.

"May I pour you another drink?" Vera inquired with a sweet smile as if he were a friendly visiting uncle. "I think it would be best to find the passport first, don't you? That way we can make the other documents match whatever the name on the passport."

"Yes, I suppose so," Pyotr agreed at last. "I know of just such a widow who would probably give up a passport for a sum of money. I hope you people have some cash to pay her."

"We'll find the money," said Pavel. "You find the goods."

"And some cash for me, for my trouble in locating the passport," the official continued. But Shukshin had only to glance at him quizzically and indicate the camera once more for Pyotr to understand that any cash benefit to him would not be forthcoming.

He admitted defeat. "All right. After I issue the appropriate permits,

I do have one condition and you cannot deny me this. You will give up the photos and their negatives. Is that understood? And you will not say a word about this to anyone."

"It's a deal then," said Shukshin. "Let's toast our fine public official for devotion to duty in this matter."

"To the devil," muttered Pyotr. "That's my toast."

They all lifted their glasses solemnly. Then Shukshin spoke again: "Maybe, Pyotr Vladimirovich, if you would be so kind, you'll tell me a little more about this widow? Is she attractive?"